ISBN: 978-1-955853-09-5

spindlefern.com

Love on Hold

Love on Paper

Love on Film

SARAH WRIGHT REED

MERRY LITTLE *Letters*

www.spindlefern.com

For Sandy
with a wish that you were
still here to read it

THE WEATHER INSIDE IS *Frightful*

"NOW YOU FLIP THE SWITCH, AND YOU GOT yourselves a genuine redneck air conditioner," the YouTube guy on my phone announces. "Simple physics, y'all."

Easy for him to say. I got a C-minus in Physics, and that was with significant curve assistance.

But I've followed every step. I've watched this video three times. I've got my cute fifties metal desk fan, my Styrofoam cooler tricked out with PVC pipes, my ten-pound bag of ice that cost four dollars I probably shouldn't have spent.

I flip the switch.

Cold air. Actual cold air. It hits my face and I almost cry with relief.

"Marry me!" I tell my beautiful creation, positioning myself directly in front of the blast. "I'm so sorry for all the names I called you while putting you together. You didn't deserve that."

For three glorious seconds, I am a genius. A survivor. A

woman who doesn't need a landlord or a man or a functioning AC unit—

Right on cue, the compressor of my old college mini-fridge kicks on.

Pop.

The fan dies. The lights die. The mini-fridge that caused the problem shudders into silence with what I swear is smugness.

Sweat is already prickling my skin.

"Okay. No problem. I built the swamp cooler once. I can fix the fuse and build it again."

I find the breaker box and flip the tripped switch. The lights come back. The fridge hums to life. The desk fan does not.

"No. No, no—please?" I toggle the power switch back and forth. Nothing. Apparently my apartment's ancient wiring zapped the motor on my cute vintage fan.

I look at my sad, broken swamp cooler, my sweltering apartment, my mostly evaporated life. And here's where I'm at: unemployed, single, and currently experiencing what I can only describe as a heat-induced existential crisis in my sports bra.

My phone buzzes for the fourteenth time in an hour. I know who it is without looking.

MOM

Potential job opportunity!

Your father says Uncle Bill's sister-in-law's nephew is hiring in timeshare sales if you're interested.

We can talk it over at Thanksgiving!
Love you!

I love my mother. I really do. But if she sends me one more LinkedIn article about *pivoting careers in your thirties,* I'm going to pivot myself directly into the Gulf of Mexico.

I'm twenty-nine. Not thirty. There is a difference.

I navigate back to Indeed and scroll through the same depressing listings I've been staring at all week. "Event Coordinator needed. Political experience required." "Wedding Planner. Must have impeccable references." "Senior Event Manager. Requires portfolio of successful high-profile events and proven track record."

Yeah. About that proven track record...

I close the laptop and reach for what remains of the pint of Cherry Garcia that's been my primary food group for the past three months. It's that special kind of melted where the ice cream is still a little cold but has achieved a soup-like consistency. I eat it anyway. This is what rock bottom tastes like: room temperature with a side of nausea.

My studio apartment is approximately the size of a box of Louboutins—specifically, the signature black slingbacks I wore to every event I planned, the ones I sold to help fund last month's rent. In this heat, it's a convection oven testing my will to live. The whole place smells like it's given up—the stale air, the garbage I should have dumped yesterday, and something vaguely synthetic from the carpet that only emerges when it's this hot. The ceiling fan is doing its best impression of a helicopter trying to land, making a rhythmic whump-whump-whump that I'm pretty sure is Morse code for *move to a place with central air, you fool.*

Should I put on pants? It is two p.m. on Wednesday.

Instead, I open Instagram, which is a mistake. The first thing I see is a photo from Britta, my former colleague. She's at a gorgeous rooftop fundraiser, cocktail in hand. The caption makes my stomach hurt: *Another successful gala for the books! #EventPlannerLife #LivingTheDream.*

I throw my phone across the room. Thankfully, its landing is cushioned by the pajamas I shed earlier in this sweltering day, since God knows I can't afford to replace it.

That should be me. That was me. Three months ago, I was a senior event coordinator at The Palms Resort, one of the top wedding and event venues in Miami. I had a title. I had velvety hand-pressed business cards. I had an espresso machine in my office.

And then: The Incident.

I don't like to think about The Incident. Which is too bad, because my brain, as usual, begins playing the lowlights reel without my permission.

The celebrity wedding. The bride who shall not be named (but whose reality show you've definitely seen). The custom ice sculpture that was supposed to be two majestic kissing swans but arrived looking more like two hysterical chickens. The bride's subsequent meltdown, which someone filmed and posted to TikTok, where it went viral. Four million views and counting.

Devon—my boss, my mentor, the woman who promoted me twice and told me I was the best coordinator she'd ever worked with—sitting across from me and listing what the bride had told her. That I kept making errors the bride had to catch herself. That I'd been difficult from the beginning. That she'd had problems with me for months.

Never mind that I had email receipts proving I'd ordered the right sculpture, or that I found out about the hysterical chickens at the exact same time as the bride, approximately thirty seconds before her viral freakout. Never mind the hundred late-night phone calls where I talked her off ledges.

The scores of last-minute emergency meetings. Apparently there were months of problems I'd never heard about. A whole list of errors.

A list I could have disproved if anyone had asked. But no one asked.

And the truth is, I did run three events that month. I don't think I missed anything—but I can't be sure. And that's the part that keeps me up at night. Not the lies I know she told, but the question of whether even a fraction of it was true. Was I difficult? Inflexible? Did I somehow drop the ball?

Seven years. Seven years of flawless performance reviews and glowing client feedback. Devon knew my track record better than anyone—she's the one who kept handing me the high-profile clients. But she's also the one who explained to the press that the mix-up was "an unfortunate error by a member of our event team who has since been let go."

Me. The member was me.

One day I had a career. The next day I had a cardboard box of desk supplies and a security guard escorting me to my car.

The ice cream has hit that point where it's no longer remotely solid. I'm basically drinking it now.

So it's a milkshake. Which is fine. Everything is fine.

My phone rings.

I lunge for it with the desperate hope of someone whose bank account currently shows eight hundred forty-seven dollars and whose rent is due in twelve days. Maybe it's a job offer. Maybe it's Publishers Clearing House, if that's still a thing. Maybe it's literally anyone with money who needs an event planner who definitely did not mess up that swan sculpture—

SIENNA, bookended by yellow hearts, flashes on the screen.

I answer immediately. "Please tell me you're calling with good news. Or money. I'll take either."

"Maddie!" Sienna's voice is audible sunshine. "How are you doing?"

"I'm eating ice cream soup for breakfast in my underwear at two p.m. How do you think I'm doing?"

"Still no luck with the job search?"

"Unless you count the timeshare sales position my dad's brother's obscure relative wants me to take, which I absolutely do not." I shift on the couch and immediately regret it as my thighs squelch against the leather. "Miami is freaking sweltering for November. I'm roasting like a turkey over here. If I die of heatstroke, make sure my obituary says I stayed classy to the end."

"Madison Lark, gone too soon. Last seen eating ice cream soup in her skivvies to combat freak Thanksgiving heatwave, still too fabulous for this world. More at eleven."

"Exactly the legacy I'm going for. Thanks, friend."

"Always," she says, and I feel a little bit of the tension in my chest ease. The best thing to come from freshman year at University of Tampa was Sienna and I bonding over a shared hatred of our misogynist Intro to Marketing professor. She's the friend who knows my cocktail order, my deepest fears, and exactly what to say when I'm spiraling.

Like now.

"So..." she says, and there's a particular tone to her voice. The one that means she's about to say something I'm either going to love or hate. "I might have a solution to your unemployment problem."

I sit up so fast the Cherry Garcia nearly tips over. "I'm listening."

"Okay, don't freak out—"

"That's a terrible way to start a sentence."

"—but a job just opened up here in Colorado."

"You mean at that Christmas village place that Tyler dragged you to?"

Sienna had followed perhaps the dopiest boyfriend ever to Colorado three years ago. Tyler was seeking purpose through woodworking or meditation or some other thing that people who've never had real problems do. Instead of finding himself through enlightenment, he found himself a cougar with a McMansion in Silicon Valley. But Sienna had stayed for the scenery.

"He didn't drag me. I had agency," Sienna says, though her tone suggests she knows how that sounds. "And yes. Winterbloom Market and Chalet. Our operations manager got fired today—like, threw-her-headset-at-the-owner fired—and we're desperate for someone to fill in."

"Sienna, I'm an event planner. I don't know anything about managing a Christmas village."

"Christmas market. And it's mostly coordinating details. Managing events and vendors. And it's temporary. Just for the season."

"The season?"

"The core holiday season. The lodge and restaurant are open year-round, but the market only operates Thanksgiving through New Year's. You'd be done in early January. It's only six weeks of work, but the pay is decent and housing is included. Not fancy housing, but your own room in the chalet."

A decent-paying job with free housing. I could ditch this apartment and find something better when I come back with a reference that hadn't fired me (God willing). Plus, there's no way it's ninety degrees in Colorado.

Still. Another failure is not on my bucket list.

"Sienna, I'm not a manager. I plan weddings and corporate events."

"Trust me, this is basically six weeks of non-stop events. Markets, dinners, Santa meet-and-greets, craft workshops, sleigh rides—"

"I don't know anything about sleighs."

"You don't say? Imagine you piloting a team of horses through the snow." She laughs her signature snort-giggle that means she's picturing exactly how badly that would go. "You don't have to drive the sleighs. You coordinate them. Which is exactly what you do."

"Did. What I did."

There's a pause. "Okay, real-talk time. What are your other options right now?"

I look around my sweltering apartment. At the stack of bills on my counter. At the unmade bed I can see from here because this place is that small. At the Indeed tab still open on my laptop, mocking me with its zero new opportunities.

"That's what I thought," Sienna says gently. "Look, I know this isn't your dream job. But it's a job. And you'd be doing me a massive favor because if we don't find someone, I'm going to have to absorb some of those duties and I'm already drowning in content creation and influencer partnerships."

"Influencers? I thought you were the concierge."

"I got promoted! I've just been too busy to tell you. The owner's kids want her to sell to a developer, but she's not ready to let it go. She asked me to revamp the marketing this season to see if it increases business. Check out our Instagram. We're very cute online. Very aesthetic. Lots of twinkly lights."

Despite everything, I smile. "Okay but seriously, why

would they hire me? Don't I need some sort of operations management experience?"

"I've already talked to Gloria—she's the owner—and I showed her your resume. She was impressed. Plus, I vouched for you, which counts for a lot here. It's a small operation. More like a family than a corporation."

Corporation. The word makes my stomach twist. The Palms was a corporation. My boss was corporate. The ice sculpture debacle was handled with corporate efficiency. Throw someone under the bus and move on.

"It would be a white Christmas," Sienna adds in a singsong voice. "You've always wanted to experience the holidays in a winter wonderland."

This is true. I grew up in Naples and have lived in Miami since college. The closest I've come to a winter wonderland is the fake snow they spray at the mall in December. And who am I kidding? I've watched enough Hallmark movies to have developed elaborate fantasies about ice skating and hot cocoa.

Hot cocoa could be a nice change from ice cream soup.

But I've also watched enough Lifetime movies to know that small mountain towns are where serial killers hide. Where your car breaks down during a blizzard in front of a haunted hotel.

"What's the catch?" I ask.

"No catch. I mean, it's a lot of work. The holiday season is intense. Gloria's grandson is stepping into operations this year, too, but he's not known for his work ethic."

"Great. So I'd be doing my job and his job."

"Probably. But Mads, you're a problem solver. Even without operations experience, you could do this in your sleep. And honestly? Getting out of Miami for a while might be exactly what you need. Fresh start. New scenery. No one here knows about the swans."

The swans. Even in this heat, I feel a chill.

"Plus," Sienna continues, "you'd be close to me. Living right down the hall! We could have girls' nights. I'd introduce you to all the cute local guys. The charmer who runs the brewery has a very nice—"

"Sienna. Get serious."

"What? I'm just saying, a rebound romance could be good for you."

"I'm not rebounding. You have to date to even have a rebound, whereas I was married to my job for the past seven years."

Saying this makes me realize that getting fired was my equivalent to getting divorced. No wonder this has been so hard.

"Anyway," I tell Sienna, swallowing the urge to cry. "I'm not interested in going out with some mountain man who's probably named his beard."

She unleashes that laugh again. "See, you're making jokes. That's progress."

I stand up and walk to my window, looking out at the heat shimmering off the parking lot below.

Six weeks. A paycheck. A respite from my malfunctioning AC. And most importantly: an escape from this apartment, this city, this increasingly desperate scrolling through job sites while my savings account slowly bleeds out.

What's the worst that could happen?

I shake my head. Is that where I am? Muttering literally *the most famous* last words?

"Okay," I hear myself say. "I'll do it."

Sienna shrieks so loud I have to hold the phone away from

my ear. "Really? Oh, Maddie, this is going to be amazing! You're going to love it here. The mountains are gorgeous and the town is so charming and—"

"When do they need me?"

"Well, Gloria was hoping...tomorrow."

"Tomorrow? Thanksgiving Day?!"

"I know, I know, but the season starts the day after Thanksgiving and we're really in a bind. Can you swing it?"

I look around my sparse apartment. Turns out being roommates with your boss is a bad idea; I'd moved into this awful place the weekend after she fired me. My lease is month-to-month, since I'd fully expected to move again, thinking I'd bounce back within weeks.

Narrator: She did not bounce back.

"Yeah," I say. "I can swing it."

We spend the next twenty minutes going over details—salary (decent), responsibilities (extensive), and the fact that Gloria apparently runs the place "like a benevolent dictator, emphasis on dictator."

When we finally hang up, I stand in my underwear in my sweltering apartment and feel something I haven't felt in three months:

Hope.

It's quickly followed by terror, but I'll take it.

I grab my laptop and open a new Google tab. Time to research.

what to wear in colorado winter
how cold is too cold to survive
do people really die in blizzards
snowdrop colorado

The search results show a small mountain town, population eighty-two hundred, elevation seventy-four hundred feet. The photos are absurdly picturesque: snow-covered peaks, quaint downtown, Victorian-era buildings with Christmas lights.

I click on Winterbloom Market's Instagram.

Oh.

Oh wow.

It's beautiful.

Like, aggressively beautiful. Bavarian-style architecture, wooden vendor stalls covered in twinkling lights, a massive ornament-studded tree in the center of a cobblestone plaza. There's a photo of a whole row of polished sleighs. Another of an old-world style Santa suit that looks like it was hand-stitched by elves. Couples kissing. Kids drinking hot chocolate, their upper lips fluffy with whipped cream. Everyone is smiling and rosy-cheeked. They look like they've never experienced the particular despair of eating ice cream soup in their underwear.

This is either going to be the best decision I've ever made or the worst.

I take a shower and start packing my suitcase, then realize I have to text my mom.

> Good news! Sienna helped me get a temporary job in Colorado. Leaving tomorrow. So sorry I'll have to miss Turkey Day.

Her response is immediate.

> Oh, sweet Sienna. But Colorado?! That's so far! And you'll miss Thanksgiving?

I know, it stinks, but I really need this job. I promise I'll be back for Christmas.

I realize after sending it that's a lie. I'll be in Colorado for Christmas. Working. At a Christmas village.

I think about my nieces—little stairsteps, ages six, five, and four, that my older brother jokes are planned pandemonium. Every year since Suzette, the eldest, was old enough to toddle across sand, we've had our thing. Christmas Eve at my brother's place in Naples, hot chocolate on the beach at sunset, building what the girls call *beach snowmen* out of sand and shells. Suzette always weaves seagrass crowns. Harper decorates with seaweed scarves. Rosie insists on finding the perfect spiral shell for the nose.

And then on Christmas night, I take them to the botanical garden lights—just me and the girls, holding hands through tunnels of color. They're the most magical two hours of my year.

I haven't missed it once in six years. But this year I will.

I'm typing that message to my mom when her next text pops up.

Your father is googling Colorado right now. Do you know how much snow it gets?! Do you even own a winter coat?

I'll buy one.

With what money, sweetie?

Ouch. Accurate, but ouch. I know she's about to offer to Zelle me some money—she recently learned how and finds it quite thrilling—but my retired parents are on a fixed income. They've already helped me enough.

No worries, it's a business expense. See you in January. Love you.

I silence my phone so I don't have to respond to more questions I can't answer. Then I open a new tab and search for winter coats under fifty dollars. Because if I'm going to move to a frozen mountain town to coordinate sleigh rides at a Christmas village, I'm at least going to have a coat.

The search results are depressing. Everything is either extremely flimsy or extremely ugly or extremely four hundred dollars.

Whatever. I'll find something tomorrow morning before I leave. I can splurge on one little coat.

Oh. Except my closet is filled with sundresses and sandals. Not exactly appropriate for winter weather.

I start packing by tossing my champagne-colored sequined skirt into my suitcase on a whim. It's Christmassy, even if it's not weather appropriate. I add a couple pairs of jeans, my two too-thin cardigans, and two long-sleeved tees for layering. A few sets of the flannel pajamas my mom gives me every Christmas Eve. But that's pretty much all I've got.

"Okay, Madison," I say out loud to my empty apartment. "Time to figure out what people wear when they can't live in tank tops year-round."

I grab my phone and start googling again.

snow boots
can you wear regular boots in snow
how to drive in snow
wait do I have to DRIVE in snow

By the time I finish my research spiral, it's dark outside, and I'm fairly certain I'm making a huge mistake.

You know what? Forget it. I'll pick up a coat on the way to the airport, pack my ankle boots and my best *professional event planner* suits, and buy a couple of souvenir sweaters at the Christmas market. Problem solved.

Because maybe it is a mistake. I'm going anyway. Staying here—in this apartment, in this heat, with my melted ice cream and my zero prospects and that video of the swan sculpture disaster haunting the internet and my dreams—isn't an option anymore.

At least in Colorado, if I fail again, I'll fail somewhere new.

THE FIRST THING I LEARN ABOUT COLORADO IS THAT its definition of *winter coat* is drastically different from mine.

I'm wearing what I genuinely believed was a coat—a cute navy one I found on a discount rack that the tag claimed was weather resistant. After fighting my way through the Thanksgiving airport crowd, I step outside into the pickup area and—

Nope. Nope nope nope.

It's like someone opened a freezer and I walked inside. Except the freezer is the entire outdoors. The air physically hurts my face. My lungs seize up. My eyes start watering immediately.

And this is just Denver. Sienna said Snowdrop is colder.

A car horn honks and I turn to see a Subaru Outback pulling up to the curb. The window rolls down and Sienna's grinning face appears.

"Maddie!"

She's out of the car and hugging me. I wrap my arms around her puffy coat, which looks like it could survive an

Arctic expedition. She's also wearing boots that come up to her knees and a knit hat with a pom-pom.

Yes, my Florida-native bestie is wearing a pom-pom on her head.

"You're here! Winterbloom is saved!" She pulls back and looks at me, her smile faltering slightly. "Is that...what is that you're wearing?"

"It's weather resistant," I say through chattering teeth.

"Maddie. Sweetie. That's a windbreaker."

"The tag said winter coat."

"Florida lied to you." She pops the trunk and grabs my suitcase. "Come on, get in the car before you get frostbite."

We catch up without pausing for two full hours before Sienna merges onto a different highway. About twenty minutes later, we leave the highway behind and take a winding two-lane road.

"This is the tricky part about Snowdrop," Sienna says as we climb. "We're not on the main highway like Vail or Breckenridge."

"Is that a problem?"

"It's why the town struggles in the off-season. Less drive-by traffic. But it also means Snowdrop has stayed...I don't know, authentic? It's not overrun by chain restaurants and luxury condos. Yet."

I watch as the landscape starts to change—more trees, more elevation, more snow. The setting sun is turning the Rockies pink when she finally says, "Okay, I need to prepare you."

"Prepare me for what?"

"Everything. Let me give you the download on Winterbloom before we get there."

"Please do. I've been googling but I still don't really understand what I'm walking into."

"Okay, so the owner is Gloria Bennett. She and her late husband Ford built Winterbloom almost sixty years ago. It started as a small Christmas tree farm with a little shop, but over the years they expanded. Now we have the main chalet, which is a gorgeous lodge with a restaurant and event spaces, plus the outdoor market with Santa's Workshop and all the vendor stalls."

"How many vendors?"

"About thirty. Artisans, food vendors, a bakery, ornament shops, that kind of thing. Winterbloom is situated on a gorgeous alpine lake—"

"Naturally."

"Naturally. We're in a Hallmark movie, after all," she says with a laugh. "Anyway, we offer ice skating with a Victorian-style warming hut. And of course there are the horse-drawn sleigh rides, available with different packages—from s'mores and a fire pit to private dining in a glass yurt. It's all very Instagram-worthy. We're starting to attract a lot of influencers."

"Thanks to their new marketing coordinator. You!"

Sienna grins winningly, then adds, "Oh, I almost forgot about our hothouse. It's attached to the chalet. Gloria's husband built it for her. So super romantic. It's full of winter-blooming flowers. You'll love it."

"A hothouse?"

"Like a greenhouse but fancy. It's really warm." She glances at me. "Miami warm."

My frozen soul perks up slightly. "That I can work with."

"I figured. Anyway, the core holiday season runs from the day after Thanksgiving through New Year's, although they used to stay open Halloween through Easter. The restaurant and grounds are open year-round for locals, and we get the occasional wedding or corporate event, but..." She pauses.

"Honestly? As Ford and Gloria got older, things started slipping. The property needs some work. Paint, repairs, some updating. They haven't had the revenue to do it. Or the heart. Ford died last year and it hit Gloria hard."

"That's tough. So it's struggling?"

"It's *charming,*" Sienna says firmly. "It just needs some love. And better marketing, which they're getting now that I'm on the job. Thankfully I was posting photos of Winterbloom to my own Instagram the whole time I was running guest services. I did it because I genuinely love the place, but guests started finding us through my posts. Gloria noticed and made me Winterbloom's first-ever marketing coordinator. We're trying to make a real push this year."

"Because of the developer?"

She sighs and turns my way, focusing her troubled eyes on me for so long that I get nervous and motion for her to look at the road. She makes an exaggerated show of locking her eyes straight ahead and placing her hands on the wheel at exactly ten and two.

"You're a wimp, Miami. But yeah, because of the developer. Gloria's kids have been pushing her to sell. And her son has been talking with this developer who's been buying up property in the valley. Her son really thinks selling to the developer is the way to go."

"What's the developer's plan?"

"He for sure wants Winterbloom. The lodge and the property are huge. But he'd be stupid to overlook the ski lodge. If he snagged them both, he'd practically own the valley."

"Winterbloom has a ski lodge?"

"No, it's the property next door. The Alpenglow Lodge. It closed a few years ago. The original owners died and the grandkids inherited it. But they live out of state. The whole place is just sitting there, fading. Both businesses need some TLC, but if a developer gets them..." She wrinkles her nose. "Condos. Hotels. It would completely change the vibe of the town."

"And Gloria doesn't want to sell."

"Gloria would rather die than give up Winterbloom. It meant everything to Ford. But she's eighty-three. She had a cardiac thing six months ago, and her kids think she can't handle it anymore. Ford wanted their grandson to take over, but he's kind of...I'm not sure if the right word is shiftless or inept. Gloria's giving him a chance, but she doesn't seem hopeful. That's why this season is so important. We're trying to prove that Winterbloom still has a future."

"No pressure then."

"You'll do better than Phoebe, the last operations manager. She was terrible with details, and she and Gloria clashed a lot. Like I said, their last big blowup led to her getting fired two days ago."

"What was the fight about?"

"I think she double-booked one of the event spaces, maybe? I don't know the full story. Anyway, Gloria's desperate. You're basically a gift from heaven right now."

"I'm really not."

"You are. Trust me." She reaches over and squeezes my hand. "Forget about the chicken-swans. You're going to be great, Mads. I can feel it."

I want to believe her. Part of me almost does. But as we climb higher into the mountains and the snow gets thicker and my ears pop from the altitude change, all I can think is *what have I done?* Especially because Sienna drives like someone who's forgotten she's from Florida. She's zipping around like there's not a foot of snow lining the road.

"We're fine," Sienna says, fiddling with the radio and not even looking as she takes a curve. "I've got snow tires."

"Snow tires don't defy death!" I tell her, gripping my seat like it's the only thing keeping me from flying out of the car.

"So dramatic. This isn't even real snow. Wait until January."

"I won't be here in January."

"We'll see. You may love it and stay forever."

Not likely, I think, looking at a row of icicles hanging from a fence. But then we round another bend and—

"Oh," I breathe.

Snowdrop.

It looks exactly like the pictures, except somehow even more perfect. The town is nestled in a valley surrounded by mountains, and everything is covered in a quilt of snow. Victorian buildings line the main street, their roofs peaked and perfect, their windows glowing like amber in the evening light. There are Christmas decorations everywhere—wreaths on lampposts, garland stretched across the street, a massive tree in what looks like the town square.

"Pretty, right?" Sienna says.

"It looks like the Hallmark Channel threw up all over the valley." I turn to her and grin. "I love it."

"Wait until you see Winterbloom." She takes a right at the town library, and suddenly says, "Oh, look!"

She slows the car and points to a cherry-red mailbox on the corner, trimmed in white with a little sign I can't quite read from here.

"Letters to Santa. There are five boxes scattered through town and one at Winterbloom. It's this thing Snowdrop does. Kids write letters to Santa, drop them in one of the mailboxes, and volunteers write back. Every single letter gets a response."

She says it with the kind of pride that tells me she's fully adopted this place as her own. "Ford Bennett started it fifty years ago. Now the community center coordinates the whole thing."

I watch the red mailbox disappear in the side mirror. "That's...actually really sweet."

Sienna gives me that warm grin. "Fair warning: This place will make you feel things. I cried the first time I saw a little kid mail a letter. Like, actual tears. Don't judge me."

"I would never."

"You already are."

"Only a little," I say, and we laugh until she lets out that familiar snort, slapping a hand over her mouth like she's nineteen again.

We drive through the little downtown—past a brewery, a bookstore, a café with a line out the door—and then turn onto a winding road that takes us uphill. Through the trees, I catch a glimpse of ski lift towers standing still and silent against the darkening sky.

"Alpenglow," Sienna says, following my gaze. "Sad, right? It used to be really popular."

And then, around a final curve, there it is.

Winterbloom Market and Chalet.

Despite Sienna's best efforts, I'm not prepared.

The massive Bavarian lodge is classic European, all dark wood and white trim and steep roof lines. It's at least three stories tall, with huge windows and balconies and chimneys puffing smoke. Around it, spread out like a fairy tale village, are wooden stalls and small buildings, pathways lit with old-fashioned lampposts, trees wrapped in white lights.

And snow. So much snow.

It's beautiful. And cold. And terrifying.

But mostly beautiful.

The air here is nothing like Miami. It smells like woodsmoke and pine and something clean and sharp underneath—maybe the scent of cold itself, if cold has a smell.

Sienna was right. As we make our way from the parking lot to the chalet's entrance, I can see the wear. Paint peeling on several vendor stalls. A few lights out on the pathways. A shutter hanging slightly crooked on the chalet's second floor. It's the kind of shabbiness that comes from love without enough money, from a place that's been cherished but not quite maintained.

It makes me like it more, somehow. It feels real.

We walk through a massive wooden door into an entry hall that's basically a cathedral to Christmas. Twenty-foot ceilings with exposed beams. A stone fireplace that's legitimately big enough to stand in. A chandelier made entirely of deer antlers, which is creepy until Sienna reminds me that the antlers fall off naturally. And decorations. Everywhere. Garland, lights, ribbons, ornaments, a tree in the corner that's at least fifteen feet tall.

"Madison!"

A woman appears from a side hallway, and I know immediately that this is Gloria Bennett. She's on the tall side of average—around five-seven, like me—and she carries herself like a queen. Silver hair in an elegant bob, black cigarette pants and a matching cashmere sweater. Her sharp eyes assess me in three seconds flat.

I straighten my spine and try to look like someone who wasn't eating ice cream soup in her underwear yesterday.

"Mrs. Bennett, it's so nice to meet you."

"Gloria, please." Her skin is paper-thin, but her handshake

is firm. "Thank you for coming on such short notice. Sienna speaks very highly of you."

"I'm grateful for the opportunity," I say, which is mostly the truth. I think.

"Good. Because we have a situation." She gestures for us to follow her down the hallway, past a restaurant anchored by another two-story stone fireplace to a hallway of offices tucked in the back.

The little place she introduces as mine is chaos. Papers cover the wooden desk and nearly bury the desktop computer that looks to be circa 2010. A whiteboard that takes up one wall is covered in schedules and vendor names and notes in different colored markers.

Gloria pulls a binder off the shelf behind the desk. "Our season officially starts tomorrow. We're already behind on supplies, half the entertainment bookings need to be confirmed, and the schedule for Santa's workshop is a complete disaster."

She slides the binder across the desk to me.

It's worse than I thought. The supplier contracts are a mess—some signed, some not, some with conflicting dates. Events are scheduled on top of each other. There are scrawled notes everywhere with cryptic messages like *Call About Reindeer???* and *Derek says lights broken. CHECK!*

"The previous manager was..." Gloria pauses, choosing her words carefully. "Not detail-oriented."

"I can see that," I murmur, flipping pages.

"Can you fix it?"

I look up at her. There's something in her face—not quite desperation, but close. This place matters to her. This season matters.

And suddenly I'm back at The Palms, standing in front of

Devon, my former boss/roommate/friend, trying to explain that the swan sculpture wasn't my fault, that I had emails, that I'd put the order in right. And being told it didn't matter. That the client was insistent. That corporate agreed. That someone had to take the fall.

I am not going to be that person again.

"Yes." I lift my chin and look the owner of Winterbloom square in the face. "I can fix it."

Gloria's expression softens slightly. "Good. Your room is upstairs, third floor. Sienna can show you. Dinner is at six if you'd like to join us. We usually eat in the staff dining area, but this being Thanksgiving, we'll be using the Evergreen banquet room. Tomorrow morning we'll do a full walkthrough of the property, but tonight we give thanks and celebrate the start of Winterbloom's holiday season."

"Sounds perfect."

Gloria hesitates.

"One more thing." Her expression shifts. "My grandson will be working with you. He's been...more involved of late."

The pause is telling.

"He has a lot of ideas for Winterbloom," she continues carefully. "Good ideas. But executing them has been..." She stops, seems to reconsider. "He's trying. He was learning the business from his grandfather before Ford passed. But he's not experienced in operations, and I needed someone who could hit the ground running. Someone with your organizational skills."

I read between the lines: *I hired you instead of letting him do this, and he's not happy about it.*

"I understand," I say.

"Thank you. If he's prickly at first, don't take it personally. He'll come around."

"I'm sure we'll work together just fine."

Gloria's gaze lingers on me a moment longer. Something like satisfaction eventually settles into her expression.

"Yes. You're focused. I have a feeling you're exactly what this place needs." She closes the binder with a snap and hands it to me. "Welcome to Winterbloom, Madison. We're pleased to have you on as our new interim operations manager."

Interim operations manager. The title feels very big and very official. And even more intimidating, knowing someone else thinks it should be his.

Sienna leads me up two flights of stairs to the third floor, chattering the whole way about the staff ("Derek does lighting, he's quirky but sweet; Judy the baker is protective of her kitchen but makes the best cranberry-orange muffins you'll ever eat") and the vendors ("Mrs. Chen makes amazing dumplings; the soap lady is intense about essential oils; Hank who runs the brewery in town is very cute and very single, just saying") and Snowdrop's general vibe ("arty, a little hippie, small-town cozy, very sincere about the Christmas spirit").

My room is at the end of the hall—small but clean, with a queen bed, a tiny but private bathroom, and a window that looks out over the market below. The lights are already on, twinkling in the fading dusk.

I drop my suitcase and collapse onto the bed.

"So?" Sienna flops down next to me. "What do you think?"

"I think I'm in over my head."

"You always think that. And then you always pull it off."

"The swans—"

"Were not your fault. And also? No one here knows about

them. Fresh start, remember?" She bumps her shoulder against mine. "Come on. Dinner in twenty minutes. You should meet everyone."

"Can I at least change into something warmer? I can't feel my toes."

"Yes. Also, I've got a coat you can borrow. That windbreaker is not going to cut it."

After she leaves, I sit on the bed for a long moment, looking out at Winterbloom Market below. People are already walking around—families, couples, groups of friends—drinking hot chocolate, browsing the stalls, taking photos.

It's magical. Worn around the edges, maybe, but magical.

It's also a logistical nightmare waiting to happen based on that binder. But I can do this. I can organize chaos. That's what I do. Did. Whatever. It's what I'm going to do now.

I layer a tank top beneath my blouse for extra warmth. Can I get away with a sweater under my suit jacket? No, that's probably too desperate. I settle for smoothing my travel-worn hair into a bun before heading downstairs.

The Evergreen banquet room is warm and loud, filled with what I assume is the Winterbloom staff. Long wooden tables, family-style serving dishes, the smell of turkey and dressing and all things delicious that make my stomach growl.

Sienna waves me over and starts introducing me to people—names and faces that immediately blur together because there are so many and I'm exhausted and also mildly hypoxic from the altitude.

I'm chatting with Derek, Winterbloom's sound and lighting tech, about his intense love for playing classical guitar when the door opens and someone walks in.

Late.

Covered in snow.

Hair sticking up like he just rolled out of bed.

"There you are." Gloria's voice cuts through the chatter. "How nice of you to join us."

"Sorry, Gran. Lost track of time." His voice is deep and warm, with a hint of sheepishness he probably thinks is charming.

I watch as he shrugs off his coat and brushes snow from his hair, smiling apologetically at the room. He's tall with dark hair that's a smidge too long to be professional—come on, it curls over the top of his ears—and sage green eyes that scan the room.

He's also, annoyingly, quite attractive. The damp from the snow has made his hair wave perfectly—short, loose almost-curls that probably look best when messy. The kind of effortless that immediately makes me suspicious.

Those eyes land on me. My stomach does an unwelcome flip.

And: No.

He smiles at me.

My stomach does it again. *No,* I hiss at it silently.

Gloria stands. "Come meet Madison Lark, our new interim operations manager. Madison, this is my grandson, Ben Bennett."

Ben Bennett? I almost laugh. That's not a person, it's a cartoon rabbit in a children's book who learns a valuable lesson about sharing.

Good. This helps. He is twenty percent less attractive already.

He's crossing the room toward me, hand extended, smile frozen into place. "Hi. Buford Rudolph Bennett the Fourth." A pause. A self-deprecating grin that knows exactly how ridiculous that sounds. "Which naturally means I go by Ben."

I shake his hand. Strong grip, warm palm. I immediately drop it. "Ben Bennett?"

"Family curse. Four generations of questionable naming decisions."

"I see. It's nice to meet you, Ben."

"Welcome to Winterbloom." His smile stays in place, but there's something behind it. Something insolent. "I've heard a lot about you."

My spine stiffens. *What* had he heard? Had he googled me? Had he seen the viral video of my professional humiliation?

"All good things, I hope," I say, and I hate how brittle it sounds.

"Gran is excited to have you," he says easily. Which isn't an answer at all.

He smiles again, and recognition flares inside me. He's one of those guys who's never had to work for anything, who coasts on charm and good looks and family money. I've worked with a thousand Ben Bennetts—the owner's nephew, the client's son, the guy who shows up late to meetings and still somehow gets credit for other people's work.

"I'm looking forward to working with you," I say, and it's already a lie.

"Same," he says, and I'm confident from his forced politeness that he's lying, too. "Gran says you're going to fix all our problems."

There's an edge to the way he says it. Not quite resentment, but close.

"That's the goal," I say, matching his aggressively pleasant tone. "Though *all* might be a bit ambitious for a six-week contract."

Something flickers in his expression. Surprise, maybe, that the new girl has teeth. Then his smile widens. "Guess we'll see."

He holds my gaze a beat too long. I don't blink.

Gloria clears her throat. "Ben, you and Madison will be working closely together on the opening weekend preparations. I trust you'll give her your full cooperation."

His jaw tightens almost imperceptibly. "Of course. Whatever you need."

"Great," I say, forcing a brightness I don't feel into my voice. "Maybe we can start with a planning session tomorrow morning? Go over the projections then?"

"Sure. What time?"

"Eight?"

He winces. "How about nine?"

"Eight-thirty."

"Deal."

We shake on it, and I tell myself that the little spark of tension between us is only because I'm tired and this situation is awkward. And definitely not because I've already decided that Buford Rudolph Bennett the Fourth is going to be a problem.

FA LA LA LA *Augh*

By quarter to nine on Friday morning, I have solved three crises and averted two more, and I am currently standing in the freezing cold outside the chalet's staff entrance, waiting for Ben Bennett to show up to the meeting we scheduled less than twelve hours ago.

He is not here.

I can't believe it. He's really not here. I've been putting out fires since before dawn, and this guy is probably still in bed.

Allow me to back up so you get the full picture.

My alarm went off at five-thirty a.m., which felt illegal after three jobless months of sleeping in. Gloria's text arrived at six:

> Staff meeting in thirty minutes. Opening Day.

Thankfully, Sienna loaned me her spare coat—a fluffy faux fur concoction that likely hits her five-two frame right at the hip. At my five-seven, it's cropped right below my bottom rib.

Sienna no doubt looks like an adorable polar bear cub in it. I look like I wrangled my torso through a throw pillow. No matter. It's warmer than anything I brought, so I tossed it over my arm and ran downstairs to find controlled panic already in progress.

Gloria read us a report of the imminent issues: the lights in the east section of the outdoor market were flickering like a haunted house. The sound system kept cutting in and out. The pretzel vendor's generator was dead. And Irwin, the longtime Santa who has apparently never missed a day in fifteen years, had called in with a flu so severe that Gloria winced when describing it.

"The market opens in two hours," Gloria announced to the room. "And unfortunately, we have no Santa."

Silence. The particular silence of people hoping someone else will volunteer.

"What about Mike?" Sienna suggested. "He has a daughter. He'd be good with the kids."

Derek snorted. "You just want an excuse to talk to him."

Under the fluorescents in the staff room, Sienna's cheeks went pink. "I do not. I'm being practical. He's—he has good energy. Kids like him."

"Uh-huh."

"He's also a vendor, here to make money." Gloria's voice cut through. "Derek. Do you have a better suggestion?"

"Pete's got a beard." Derek shrugged. "Sort of."

We all looked at Pete, the maintenance man, nursing a coffee in the corner and clearly hoping to be invisible. He has a graying goatee that, with some creative cotton ball application, might pass for Santa-adjacent.

"Never mind that. We have a fine Santa beard that you can

wear," Gloria said. At Pete's lack of enthusiasm, she added, "If you'd be kind enough to fill in, of course."

"I'll do it," Pete muttered. "But I'm not doing the ho-ho-ho voice."

Crisis one: handled. Kind of.

I threw myself into the rest. The backup generator was in the maintenance shed; I found Derek and pointed him toward the pretzel stand while I handled the vendor herself, assuring her we'd have power restored within the hour. Meanwhile, I tracked down the sound system issue to the east section—crackling speakers, intermittent cuts—and radioed Derek once he had the generator running.

"Loose connection," he diagnosed after two minutes with the panel open. "Probably vibration from the cold. I can fix it, but I need ten minutes."

"Can you make do with seven? The carolers start at nine."

He grinned. "Yes, ma'am."

I stationed myself at the junction of the two problem areas, fielding vendor questions and redirecting foot traffic while Derek worked his magic. I moved on to dealing with three vendor placement disputes, two complaints about parking, and one passive-aggressive exchange with the woman running the holistic wellness stall who insisted her assigned spot had hostile energy.

By eight-fifteen, most of the fires were out, although I was still searching for an acceptable solution to the hostile energy. The market was humming to life around me—vendors setting up, the smell of cinnamon and roasting nuts beginning to drift through the cold air, early guests trickling in from the first shuttle.

By eight-thirty, I arrived at our agreed-upon meeting spot, tablet in hand, ready to go over the day's schedule with Ben.

By quarter to nine, I was still standing there. Alone. Mentally recapping this morning's drama and physically fuming at Ben.

It's now eight fifty-two, and I am giving up so I can tend to the thirty other micro-crises that popped up while I wasted my time on him.

An hour later, I find him near the hot cocoa stall. He's laughing with the vendor—a girl about my age whose entire aesthetic screams Instagram influencer. Her stall is a confection of powder blue and baby pink, with hand-lettered chalkboard signs and gold accents and a display of artfully arranged hand-cut marshmallows. She herself is wearing a powder blue ski jacket with a baby pink scarf, hat, and matching mittens, coordinated perfectly with her shop. Everything about her photographs well. And she knows it.

For a minute, I'm self-conscious about the shaggy sheepskin rug currently doubling as my shrunken coat. Then the girl reaches over to touch Ben's arm, lingering as she giggles at whatever he's said, and I decide his fun is over.

"Ben Bennett," I say, fighting hard to not scowl.

He has the audacity to smile at me. "Madison, hey. How's it going?"

"Fine. Considering I've been handling everything alone since six a.m."

"Right, yeah, sorry about that." He runs a hand through his hair, which looks like he rolled out of bed approximately twelve minutes ago. "Got caught up. You know how it is."

I do not, in fact, know how it is. Because I have been working. While he has been flirting with Hot Cocoa Girl.

"We were supposed to meet. An hour and a half ago."

"Were we?" He looks genuinely confused, which somehow

makes it worse. "Sorry, I forgot to write it down. Anyway, I'm here now. What do you need?"

What I need is for him to take something seriously. What I say: "I have to put out some other fires now. Can we meet tomorrow? Two o'clock. Staff conference room."

"Sure, yeah. I'll be there." I give him a look that says *will you?* but don't bother voicing it. "Until then, I guess...come find me if you need me?"

Yeah, sure. I'll get right on that.

The morning continues in a blur of small disasters and smaller victories. But amid the chaos, I remember that I'm good at this. Every crisis that comes my way I figure out how to solve. Every problem, I find a fix. I am a machine of spreadsheets and solutions and professional smiles that never crack.

And then, around noon, the wellness vendor situation explodes again.

She's been moved to a different stall—one I personally negotiated as a compromise—but now she's claiming the new spot is even worse than the original. Something about foot traffic patterns and "the energy of commerce flowing incorrectly."

I'm in the middle of talking her down, using every conflict resolution skill I've learned in seven years of event management, when Ben appears.

"Agnes!" He sweeps in with an easy charm. "What's going on? Talk to me."

And just like that, he has her attention. He listens—or pretends to—nods thoughtfully, makes some joke about Mercury being in retrograde, and within five minutes has her smiling and agreeing that yes, actually, this spot is fine, and thank you so much for understanding.

He turns to me with a satisfied grin. "See? Just needed to get the planets aligned."

Agnes is beaming at him like he's solved world hunger. And I hate that I notice the way he stands—easy, confident, taking up space like he belongs in it. Like charm is just something that happens to him.

I want to scream.

Instead I say, "Thanks. Glad that's sorted," and walk away before I say something I'll regret.

By six p.m., the market is glowing with Christmas lights and the daytime families are accompanied by couples and friend groups clutching mulled wine. Pete has survived his Santa debut with minimal trauma. The pretzel stand's generator is humming along. The lights have stopped flickering. By every measurable metric, Opening Day has been a success.

I should feel proud.

Instead, I feel invisible.

This is the job. I know that. In event management, success means everything runs smoothly and no one notices you. I used to love that, the quiet satisfaction of a perfect event. Knowing I was the reason it all came together even if no one else did.

I used to love a lot of things about this work.

I'm just tired, I tell myself. But standing here shivering in borrowed clothes, in a place I didn't choose, it's hard not to remember what I had. The team I built. The reputation I earned.

One mistake—not even mine—and suddenly that's all I am. Now I'm just the ice-chicken girl. Instead of organizing events for Miami's elite, I'm spreading small-town Christmas cheer on the side of a frozen mountain.

I walk back toward the chalet, Sienna's tiny coat pulled

tight around me. The market is beautiful in the evening light, all those twinkling bulbs and snow-dusted rooftops and families wandering between stalls with cups of hot cider. If I weren't so exhausted, I might appreciate it.

I'm passing the center of the market when I see it. The mailbox.

I've noticed it before, of course—cherry red with white trim, a little peaked roof dusted with snow, a brass slot worn smooth by decades of letters. The sign above it reads *Letters to Santa* in hand-painted script.

But I haven't really *seen* it until now.

A little girl, maybe five or six, is standing on her tiptoes to reach the slot. Her mother hovers behind her, phone out, ready to capture the moment. The girl clutches her envelope in her mittened hands, her face scrunched in concentration as she feeds it carefully through the slot.

The letter disappears. The girl turns to her mother, beaming.

"Santa will write back, right, Mommy?"

"Of course he will, sweetheart. He answers every single letter."

"Every letter?"

"Every one."

The girl's face lights up with the kind of hope I've forgotten existed. Pure. Uncomplicated. The belief that someone is listening, that her small voice matters, that magic is real and it will answer her.

Something in my chest loosens.

I stand there, watching them walk away hand-in-hand, and for a moment the exhaustion and the frustration and the invisibility all fade. There is only this: a red mailbox, a child's letter, and the quiet promise that someone will answer.

My walkie crackles to life.

"Madison? We've got a capacity issue at the skating rink. The fire marshal would not be pleased."

I sigh. Reach for the walkie. "On my way."

I start walking, then pause. I look back. The mailbox glows softly in the twilight.

Something about it makes my chest ache. I can't remember the last time I believed like that.

CHAPTER 4

THE MOST *Wonderful* TIME OF THE YEAR

GLORIA PROMISED ME A PROPER TOUR OF Winterbloom on Friday, but Friday had been consumed by generator failures and wellness vendor drama and whatever the opposite of a Christmas miracle is. So here we are, Saturday morning, playing catch-up.

Sienna is my guide. She hooks her arm through mine as we step out into the market, breath hanging white in the cold air.

"Ready to actually see this place?"

"Ready to see it without something being on fire."

"That's the spirit."

The market is bigger than I realized. Yesterday I'd been so focused on learning the ropes that I'd barely registered the scope of it. Now, in the crisp morning light, I can actually take it in.

Rows and rows of wooden stalls stretch across the cobblestone plaza, each one decorated with garland and lights and hand-painted signs. We pass Judy's café first—the scent of butter and sugar hits me before I even see the pastries—and then a candlemaker whose display looks like a cathedral made of wax, tapers and pillars in every shade of red and green and gold.

"There are thirty-two vendors total," Sienna explains as we walk. "Some rotate throughout the season, some are here every day. We've got eight different ornament vendors alone."

She points a few out as we pass: one specializing in handmade pieces from local artisans—delicate glass snowflakes and carved wooden Santas—another selling imported Czech glass that catches the light like frozen rainbows, and several with themed collections that range from sports teams to cats in Santa hats.

"The cat ornament lady is very serious about this," Sienna warns me. "Don't ask her why there are no dog ornaments unless you have twenty minutes."

Not having twenty minutes, I pledge that I won't.

We move past soap vendors and jewelry makers, woodworkers selling hand-carved nativity scenes, food stalls offering everything from roasted nuts to plank-smoked fish. The air here is filled with the fragrance of butter and cinnamon and something warm and vanilla-sweet that makes me want to track it down. Agnes waves as we pass, but whether it's with genuine warmth or a hex is still undetermined.

"Mike's place," Sienna says, and something in her voice changes. Just slightly. Just enough that I notice.

The man behind the counter is stretching dough with the focused intensity of someone whose work is both craft and livelihood. Mid-thirties, nice face, the kind of forearms you get from kneading dough professionally. A wood-fired pizza oven radiates heat behind him, and the scent is incredible—char and smoke and melting cheese.

An adorable little girl sits at a small table close enough to the oven to keep her warm but far enough away to keep her safe. She's bent over a coloring book with the concentration of a brain surgeon. Five, maybe six, with hot pink glasses and dark curls escaping from her ponytail. She catches sight of Sienna and her whole face lights up.

"Sienna!" She waves at us with both hands, nearly knocking over her crayons.

"Hey, Miss Evie!" Sienna's voice goes soft in a way I've never heard from her. "Evie is Mike's charming, brilliant, so-funny daughter," she says to me, loud enough that Evie can hear it. "Love the purple reindeer."

Evie beams. "Her name is Rita. She's Rudolph's sister."

"With that gorgeous glowing purple nose? It's clear they're family," Sienna says, like this is the most logical thing in the world. She turns her attention to Evie's dad. I watch her fidget with the zipper on her coat. Interesting. "Hey, Mike. This is Madison, the new ops manager."

Mike glances up from his dough. Offers us both a brief nod. "Hey."

We walk away, and I give her approximately three seconds before I pounce.

"So. Mike seems nice."

"He's...very dedicated to pizza."

"I could tell. He's cute, too."

"Hmm? Oh. Yeah." She's very focused on adjusting her scarf. "He's...yeah."

"Very articulate."

"Shut up."

I grin. She doesn't look at me, but her cheeks are pink again, and it's not from the cold. She speeds up. "Oh, look, there's Bree's stall. It's so adorable."

Smooth subject change. I file it away for later interrogation.

We approach the Instagram-perfect hot cocoa stall I noticed on Opening Day. The vendor lights up like someone just hit record.

"Sienna! And you must be Madison!" She clasps her pink-mittened hands together, her smile camera-ready even though no one's filming. At least, I don't think anyone's filming. With influencers—and I already know she is one—you never really know. "I'm Bree. I've heard so much about you. Welcome to Winterbloom! Let me know if you ever want a behind-the-scenes for your socials. I'd love to collab!"

I don't have socials. At least, none I've touched since the swan disaster.

"Bree's got fifty thousand followers," Sienna explains as we walk away. "Gloria loves her. Great for visibility."

Bree looks like she was born holding a ring light. No wonder Ben found his way to her stall instead of our eight-thirty meeting. Men are simple creatures.

We complete the circuit and I head back to the chaos office feeling slightly more oriented. The market makes sense now. It's a village unto itself, with its own rhythms and relationships and hierarchies. Most of which I know nothing about.

One step at a time, I remind myself.

By mid-morning, I'm knee-deep in logistics. The flower arrangements from Petal and Pine Florist are split across Monday and Thursday deliveries—great for freshness, but a nightmare for the service entrance. If we switch to greenery and winterberries, we can consolidate to one delivery a week. But since Ben coordinates all things green and growing at Winterbloom, I need his sign-off. I'd asked him to review it by nine so we could give the florist advance notice.

It's after eleven. His signature line is still blank.

I check his office, one door down from mine. Empty.

I try his radio. Static.

I find Derek near the main tree, adjusting a string of lights. "Have you seen Ben?"

He answers without looking up from his work. "Saw him heading toward the back lot about an hour ago. Probably in the hothouse."

"The hothouse."

"His cave." Derek grins. "He disappears in there a lot."

Of course he does, I think. While the rest of us handle actual work.

I head toward the back of the property, past the staff parking area. The hothouse is behind the chalet—Sienna pointed it out during the tour but we didn't go inside—and I'm almost there when I spot him at the picnic table near the maintenance shed.

He's got a notebook open in front of him, and he's writing something. Not typing on a laptop, not checking his phone—actually writing, with a pen, in what looks like unhurried, focused concentration. A cup of coffee sits beside him. Unlike the rest of the Winterbloom staff, he looks peaceful. Relaxed. Like a man without a care in the world.

Like a man who definitely doesn't have a delivery schedule that needed his sign-off two hours ago.

I'm about to interrupt his journaling session when someone else beats me to it.

She comes around the corner of the maintenance shed carrying a crate of winter greenery—tall and cute and Barbie-thin but dressed in practical work clothes. Sturdy boots, no-nonsense blonde ponytail. Her canvas jacket sports the Petal and Pine logo. I'm ten feet away but I can read the monogram below it: Lacey. She sets down the crate and says something I can't hear from this distance, and Ben looks up and laughs.

Not a polite laugh. A real one.

She punches his arm, and he grins at her. She reaches over and adjusts his scarf, her hand lingering a beat longer than it needs to when she smooths it down his chest.

I watch from behind a delivery truck, feeling like a spy and not particularly caring.

First Bree with the giggling, I think. Now this one getting cozy with his scarf. Busy guy.

I decide not to interrupt. I'll get him to sign off at our rescheduled meeting today at two, and if the florist gets annoyed, she can take it up with him. Anyway, I'm due at the main entrance in fifteen minutes to help today's Christmas carolers get situated. The Silverbell Singers go on at noon.

According to the schedule Gloria gave me, Winterbloom brings in a different caroling group each day of the season—local church choirs, school groups, a barbershop quartet from Breckenridge on Thursdays. Today's group is from the Methodist church in Pine Ridge, and they're supposed to perform near the big Christmas tree for ninety minutes. Ben confirmed them. It's on the schedule in his handwriting, his initials next to the date.

By quarter to noon, I'm stationed near the performers' entrance with a clipboard and a smile, ready to greet them and get them set up.

By ten past twelve, I'm still waiting.

The crowd near the Christmas tree is growing restless. Families with kids in puffy jackets, couples holding hot cocoa, a group of at least twenty older women in matching red scarves who've claimed the best bench and keep checking their watches. The schedule board by the welcome booth promises live caroling at noon. It's now quarter after twelve.

I try the contact number on my sheet. Straight to voicemail.

I try Ben's radio. Nothing.

I try his cell. Also nothing.

Okay. Okay. I scan the crowd, the vendor stalls, anywhere he might be. The man's a ghost.

Near the main tree, Derek is adjusting a spotlight, his tool belt jangling as he climbs down from a ladder. I remember the staff meet-and-greet my first night. Derek sharing his love of classical guitar for at least half an hour. Let's hope that enthusiasm translates to skill.

"Derek." I'm slightly out of breath from speed-walking across the plaza. "The carolers aren't here. Can you play something?"

He blinks at me. "What?"

"Guitar. You play guitar. There's a crowd waiting for music, the carolers are MIA, and I need something to happen in the next three minutes or we're going to have sixty disappointed people staring at an empty stage."

"I don't really know Christmas songs."

"Do you know any songs?"

"I mean, yeah, but—"

"Great. Perfect. You're hired." I'm already steering him toward the performance space. "Play whatever you want. Classical is fine. Jazz. Honestly, play 'Twinkle, Twinkle' on repeat, I don't care. Just buy me twenty minutes."

Derek looks like he wants to argue, but my desperation must convince him. He sighs, sets down his tool belt, and runs inside to grab his guitar.

I don't wait to see if he actually does it. I'm already moving, cutting through the vendor stalls toward the chalet, checking the parking lot, the staff entrance, anywhere Ben might be hiding. The hothouse, I think, but when I pass the restaurant's service entrance, I spot him through the propped-open door.

He's in the kitchen doorway, leaning against the frame with a crate of greens tucked under one arm. Lettuce, herbs, something leafy—deliveries from the hothouse, probably. But he's not delivering. He's *chatting*. With a pretty dark-haired prep cook who's laughing at something he said, her hand resting on his forearm like it belongs there.

The carolers are missing and he's flirting in the kitchen.

I push through the service entrance. The prep cook sees me first and steps back, her hand dropping. Ben turns, and his easy smile falls away when he registers my panic.

"The Silverbell Singers," I say. "They're not here."

"What?"

"The Christmas carolers. They're not here. There's a crowd waiting by the main tree and no carolers."

He frowns. "No, they should be. Maybe traffic?"

I shrug. "They're not answering my calls. Are you sure you booked them for today?"

"Of course." He shifts the crate, pulls out his phone with his free hand. "I confirmed them. I remember doing it." He scrolls through his email, confident. "I sent the confirmation on Wednesday. I remember because I was in the—"

He stops.

I watch his face change. The frown deepens, then goes slack. Something shutters behind his eyes.

"What?" I ask, even though I already know.

He turns the phone toward me. The email is right there on the screen:

CONFIRMING:
SILVERBELL SINGERS
SATURDAY 11/29, 12PM

But it's not in his sent folder. It's in drafts. It was never sent.

The prep cook has quietly disappeared. Smart woman.

Over Ben's shoulder, through the kitchen pass-through window, I see Gloria. She's seated at a table in the restaurant, a cup of tea in front of her, and she's watching us. Not moving. Not intervening. Watching. And she does not look happy.

Ben sees me looking. He turns, follows my gaze, and he exhales loudly when he spots his grandmother. When he turns back to me, whatever openness was left in his expression has vanished. His voice comes out flat.

"I thought I sent it. I was in the hothouse when I wrote it..." All at once, he blanches. "...and then Derek called about the generator, and I must have—"

"It doesn't matter what happened." I'm already pulling up the caroler contact list on my own phone. "I need to fix this."

"Let me call them. I can—"

"I've got it."

I'm walking away before he finishes the sentence, phone already pressed to my ear. Behind me, I hear him say something else—my name, another offer to help—but I don't stop. I don't turn around.

The Pine Ridge Methodist Church doesn't answer. I try the next group on the list—Holy Family Catholic from Silverbrook—and get a woman named Doris who sounds like someone's grandmother and tells me they're available tomorrow but not today, they have a potluck.

Third try: the Snowdrop High School chamber choir.

"This is Madison Lark from Winterbloom Market. I know this is incredibly last minute, but we have a performance slot open right now and I'm wondering if any of your students might be available."

A pause. "How last minute are we talking?"

"The slot started fifteen minutes ago."

A longer pause. I hold my breath.

"The drama department is rehearsing for our winter performance right now. The choir kids are involved, and they'd probably love the exposure. Can you give us fifteen minutes to get there?"

"You're a lifesaver. I will name my firstborn after you."

She laughs. "Get back to me on that when you're in labor."

I hang up and allow myself exactly three seconds of relief before heading back to the main tree. Derek is perched on a stool on the makeshift stage, playing something that sounds vaguely like "Singin' in the Rain," and the crowd has settled into polite appreciation. A few kids are dancing. One of the red-scarved women is swaying along. It's not caroling, but it's *something*. When Derek looks up, I give him the heart-hands sign and my very best smile.

Thirteen minutes later, six teenagers in matching Snowdrop High hoodies arrive with sheet music and enthusiasm. They launch into "Carol of the Bells" with the kind of earnest energy that only high school drama students can muster, and the crowd loves it. The red-scarved women are actually crying.

Crisis averted. No thanks to Ben.

*

Ninety minutes later, I'm waiting for him in the staff conference room, reminding myself to keep my cool. The caroling snafu turned out okay and I've got the paperwork for the florist right on top of my clipboard. No worries.

At two-fifteen, I'm still in the conference room. Alone.

At two-thirty, I give up and go looking.

I find him in the parking lot, coat on, keys in hand, climbing into a mud-splattered Jeep.

"We had a meeting," I say. My voice is sharp enough to cut glass and I don't bother to soften it. "Again."

He has the grace to wince. "Right. I'm really sorry, but I've got an appointment in town and I'm already late. Can we do tomorrow?"

"Tomorrow?" The caroling disaster was two hours ago. Two hours, and he's already leaving. "Ben, this is the second time you've blown me off. We're supposed to talk projections for the season. At a minimum, I need your sign-off on the flower delivery schedule before I can—"

"Then do it without my sign-off. You're clearly capable."

"That's not the point. Gloria said—"

"Gloria will understand. I'll explain. I'm sorry, I really do have to go."

And then he's in the driver's seat, engine running, backing out of the space like I'm not standing there with a clipboard and a schedule and approximately fourteen things that need his input. The afternoon light catches his profile through the window—loose dark curls, stubborn jaw, a mouth I have no business admiring when he's peeling out like that—and I'm annoyed that I notice. That I'm still noticing.

I watch his taillights disappear down the access road.

Movement catches my eye. Gloria is crossing the market plaza, heading toward the chalet. She's not looking at me—she's watching Ben's Jeep turn onto the main road. Then her gaze shifts, finds me standing in the parking lot, and holds for just a moment.

She doesn't wave. Doesn't call out. She looks at me with an expression I can't quite read, then continues toward the chalet entrance.

You're clearly capable.

Was that supposed to be a compliment? Because it felt like a dismissal. Like he was saying: You handle it. I have better things to do.

Fine. I'll handle it.

I go back to my office and do it myself. Change the floral designs from Petal and Pine, consolidate deliveries to one time a week. Update the loading zone calendar. Send the revised schedule to Lacey's email address. Done. Without Ben's input, without his sign-off, without his permission.

I'm still tapping at my keyboard at seven o'clock, finishing up the weekend projections that were supposed to be a collaborative effort. Sienna finds me hunched over my laptop, surrounded by spreadsheets and cold coffee.

"You're still here?" She leans against the doorframe. "I thought you'd be at dinner."

"Someone had to finish this."

She reads between the lines. "Ben bailed?"

"Ben bailed." I save the document and close my laptop.

"Come on," Sienna says, pushing off the doorframe to pull me out of my chair. "Judy saved us plates. You need real food, not whatever sad snack you were planning to scrounge from the vending machine."

She drags me to the staff dining room for pot roast and mashed potatoes. I eat without really tasting any of it, but after dinner, I let her declare a girls' night. We end up cross-legged on her bed, splitting a bag of kettle corn and laughing about the time she accidentally sent a love poem meant for her TA to our entire public relations class.

"I transferred sections," she reminds me, wiping her eyes. "I couldn't face him."

"You got an A in that class."

"Guilt grade. The professor felt bad for me."

For most of the evening, I let myself forget about vendor schedules and missed meetings and carolers who never showed. It's good. Easy. The way things used to be before ice sculptures ruined my life.

But later, alone in my room, my mental tally writes itself.

Missed meeting number one: opening day, eight-thirty a.m.

Missed meeting number two: today, two p.m.

Journaling at a picnic table while the rest of us worked.

Flirting with Bree. Flirting with the florist. Flirting with the prep cook.

Carolers that never came because he never sent the email.

His face, shuttering closed when he realized his mistake. Not apologetic. Not scrambling to fix it. Just—blank. Controlled. Like it didn't really matter.

And then driving away two hours later like nothing had happened.

You're clearly capable.

Yeah. I am.

I save my files and close my laptop. Tomorrow I'll handle whatever comes next, with or without Ben Bennett.

Probably without.

IT'S BEGINNING TO LOOK A LOT LIKE *Trouble*

SUNDAY MORNING'S STAFF MEETING STARTS WITH Gloria making an announcement.

"I'm implementing some adjustments for the rest of the season," she says, standing at the head of the conference table like a general addressing her troops. "In the interest of efficiency, Madison will be taking point on vendor coordination and the entertainment schedule in addition to facilities oversight. Ben, I'd like you to focus on the hothouse."

Whoa. I glance at Ben.

His jaw tightens almost imperceptibly. He doesn't argue. Doesn't protest. Just nods once, short and sharp, like he's swallowing something that tastes bad.

"Sure," he says. His voice is perfectly neutral. His eyes are not.

The meeting continues—weekend recap, upcoming events, a reminder about the children's craft fair on Saturday—but I'm only half listening. I'm watching Ben, who is very carefully not looking at me.

After Gloria dismisses us, Sienna catches my arm in the hallway.

"So," she says, voice low. "That was interesting."

"Was it? It seemed pretty straightforward to me."

That's not entirely honest. I saw his face. I just don't know what to do with the complicated knot of feelings it gave me.

Sienna gives me a look. "Gloria gave you most of Ben's job." She glances down the hallway, making sure we're alone. "He's been handling vendor coordination since Ford died last year."

Oh.

"Why would Gloria take it away from him?"

Sienna hesitates. "Fresh eyes, probably. And you're..." She trails off.

"I'm what?"

"Really good at it." She says it gently, like she's apologizing. "You solved problems in two days that have been sitting in the Deal With It Later pile for weeks. You handled opening weekend chaos like you'd been here for years."

I should feel proud. I do feel proud, a little. But mostly I feel like I accidentally stepped on a landmine I didn't know was there.

"Great," I mutter. "So now he hates me."

"He doesn't hate you. He's just..." She searches for the word. "Ben has a hard time with stuff like this. He means well, but sometimes things slip through the cracks, and then he beats himself up about it, which makes it worse, and then more things slip..." She shrugs. "It's a cycle. Gloria's seen it happen before."

"So she brought in a replacement."

"Sure. For Phoebe, who was terrible. Not for Ben. He still

has stuff to do. He just wanted to do more this year, and now…"

"Now he's doing less."

Sienna squeezes my arm. "This isn't your fault, Maddie. You're only doing your job."

Right. My job. Which apparently now includes most of what Ben used to do.

I spend the rest of the morning trying to get up to speed on my new responsibilities. The vendor files are a disaster—Phoebe's organizational system was apparently throwing papers in the general direction of a folder—and I need to understand the relationships before I can manage them.

Which means I need to talk to Ben.

I find him in the hothouse.

The door opens into a wall of warmth so sudden it's almost disorienting. After three days of snow and cold, the humid tropical air feels like stepping into another world. The quiet in here is different from the quiet outside. Softer. Punctuated by the drip of condensation and the rustle of leaves.

Ben is at a workbench near the door, transplanting seedlings into small terra cotta pots. He looks up when I enter, and whatever softness was in his face hardens into something polite and distant.

"Madison."

"Ben." I hold up the folder I'm carrying. "I need to ask you about the vendor relationships. There are notes in here I can't make sense of, and I figured since you've been handling this—"

"Was handling it." His voice is flat. "Past tense."

I take a breath. "Okay. Well. I'm handling it now, and I could use some context. Like this note about Helen at Mountain Creamery—"

"Helen delivers on Tuesdays and Fridays. Cheese boards for the chalet, samples for the tasting tent."

"The files say Fridays only."

"The files are wrong. I changed it two years ago. Phoebe probably never updated them."

"And the special pricing arrangement? There's a note here about a discount, but no details."

"She gives us fifteen percent off because we buy in volume and pay on time." He still hasn't looked up from his seedlings. "Anything else?"

I flip through the folder. "The Bergstroms—"

"Corner spot. They've been in that location for twelve years. Don't move them."

"Mrs. Chen—"

"She'll say she doesn't need help unloading. She does. Send Derek or Pete."

"Agnes—"

"Requires extensive emotional support and regular reassurance about her 'energy concerns.'" For the first time, something like dark humor flickers across his face. "Good luck with that one."

I almost want to smile at that. Almost.

"Is there anything else?" he asks. "Because I do still have *some* work left to do."

The jab lands. I feel my spine stiffen.

"Right. Thanks for your help." I turn to leave, then stop. Turn back. "You know, I asked you questions yesterday. About the delivery schedule for Petal and Pine. You told me to figure it out."

Now he looks up. "What?"

"In the parking lot. When you were leaving. I asked for your input and you said, 'Just do it without my sign-off.' So I did." I hold his gaze. "And now Gloria's decided I should keep doing it. If you're upset about that, maybe consider that I *tried* to include you. You barely answered."

Something shifts in his expression. Surprise, maybe. Or the beginning of guilt.

"That's..." He stops. Starts again. "That was one conversation."

"You also missed both of our scheduled meetings. Friday and Saturday." I'm ticking them off on my fingers now, which is petty, but I don't care. "And the carolers? The ones you 'confirmed' but never actually sent the email for? Gloria was sitting right there when I found out. She watched me fix it." I let that land. "In the few days I've been here, you've blown me off twice, disappeared when I needed you, and left me holding the bag on a crisis you created. So if you're mad that I'm doing the vendor stuff now, maybe consider that Gloria had reasons which have nothing to do with me."

His mouth flattens. "Yeah. I'm sure she does." He walks away without another word.

I wait until his footsteps fade before I let out a breath. That was probably not my most diplomatic moment. But if you leave a gap, someone's going to fill it. That's how it works.

"Okay, then," I say to the empty room. I slip out the hothouse door. Cold air smacks me in the face.

Good. I needed that.

I spend the afternoon making the rounds, introducing myself to vendors as their new point of contact.

"You're the new one," says the woman selling cat ornaments. "Ben mentioned there'd be changes."

"Ben always handled this," says the candlemaker. "He knows how we like things."

"Is Ben okay?" asks Mrs. Chen, genuine concern in her voice. "He seemed down this morning."

I smile and nod and make notes and feel, with every interaction, more and more like an invader. Everyone here has history with each other. Relationships that go back years, sometimes decades. Inside jokes I don't understand. Unwritten rules I keep accidentally breaking.

Agnes corners me near the fudge stand.

"I hope you're more understanding than your predecessor. Phoebe's aura was very muddy," she says, fixing me with a look that suggests she already suspects I'm not. "Ben always respects my energy concerns."

"I'll do my best," I say, which is apparently the wrong answer, because she sighs heavily and wanders off, muttering about the void moon.

By six o'clock, I'm exhausted and starving and ready to hide in my room for the rest of the night. Instead, I find Sienna in the staff dining room, two plates of lasagna already waiting.

"You look like you need this," she says, pushing a plate toward me. "And possibly wine. Unfortunately, all I have is water."

"Do you have Red Bull? Or whiskey?" I collapse into the chair across from her. "I just spent four hours being politely reminded that I'm not Ben."

"That bad?"

"Agnes told me Ben 'respects her energy concerns.' I didn't even know energy was a concern one could have. Aside from the waning kind that I'm currently experiencing."

Sienna snorts. "Oh, Agnes. She once asked Derek to rearrange the entire lighting grid because the warm tones were 'interfering with her chakras.'"

"Please tell me you're joking."

"I wish. She still hasn't forgiven him for refusing." She stabs a noodle cheerfully. "Of course, Derek has never quite forgiven Ben for doing the LED conversion before he was here to consult. We all hold grudges here in Christmas-town."

"Ben did the LED conversion?"

"And the sound system upgrade. And the new point-of-sale system for the vendors. When he actually finishes something, it's good. The problem is the *actually finishes* part."

I process this. "So he's...what? Brilliant but unreliable?"

"He's complicated." She takes a sip of water. "He'll have these bursts where he's everywhere at once, solving problems, charming vendors, making things happen. And then he'll just... disappear. Miss meetings. Forget deadlines. Start three projects and finish none." She sighs. "It's frustrating because you can see how capable he is, and how involved he wants to be. He's getting better. But you can't always count on him, you know?"

I think about Ben in the hothouse, carefully transplanting seedlings. Ben with the notebook at the picnic table. Ben missing our meetings. Ben charming Agnes one minute and forgetting our schedule the next.

"Yeah," I say. "I'm starting to get that."

We eat in comfortable silence for a while. The lasagna is good—I wonder vaguely if it's from Judy, who runs the café, or Chef Raúl in the restaurant—and slowly the tension in my shoulders starts to ease.

"So," Sienna says, a mischievous glint appearing in her eye. "Speaking of complicated men. Did you notice Mike was wearing a new apron today?"

"I did not notice Mike's apron."

"It had little pizzas on it. Evie picked it out." She's trying very hard to sound casual. "He told me when I stopped by for a slice."

"Just the one slice?"

"I was hungry."

"So a second slice?"

Her cheeks go pink. "Okay, fine, I went back three times, but in my defense, it's really good pizza." She points her fork at me accusingly. "Don't look at me like that."

"I'm not judging. I'm observing." I shrug and grin. "Observing that you went to the same pizza stall three times in one day."

"The crust is wood-fired! It has a very specific char!"

"I'm sure that's exactly why you keep going back."

She throws a dinner roll at my head. I catch it and take a bite, grinning.

This is what I needed. Not the coworker drama or the awkward vendor introductions or the feeling of being an outsider in someone else's story. Just my best friend, some carbs, and the comfortable rhythm of someone who's known you long enough to throw bread at your head.

"For the record," Sienna says, "Mike barely talks. To anyone. The fact that he told me about the apron is basically a marriage proposal."

"I'll start planning the bachelorette party."

"I hate you."

"You love me."

"Unfortunately, yes." She sighs dramatically. "Now eat your lasagna, you poor baby. Tomorrow's going to be another long day."

She's not wrong about that.

Later, in my room, I stare at the vendor files spread across my bed. Thirty-two businesses. Decades of relationships. A web of unwritten rules and personal histories that I'm supposed to navigate in six weeks.

I don't know what to do with what Sienna told me about Ben. The bursts of brilliance. The scattered follow-through. The way people seem to like him even when he frustrates them.

None of it changes the facts. I was hired to do a job. Gloria gave me more responsibility because she saw that I could handle it. That's not something to apologize for.

And yet.

I think about Ben's face in the staff meeting. The way he'd swallowed whatever he wanted to say and just...accepted it. Like he'd almost been expecting it. I recognized that look. I'd worn it myself, standing in Devon's office while she explained that someone had to take the fall.

I shake my head and gather the files into a neat stack. I'm not here to fix Ben Bennett. I'm here to fix Winterbloom's operations. And if that means stepping into a role he used to fill, that's Gloria's decision, not mine.

I have a job to do.

I'm going to do it.

I spend Sunday night reorganizing the vendor delivery schedule.

It's not that I think I'm better than Phoebe or anyone else who came before me. It's that I can see a problem, and I know how to fix it, and after everything that happened in Miami, I *need* to fix something. To prove—to Gloria, to myself, to everyone who decided my career should implode over a pair of hysterical ice chickens—that I'm still good at this.

The current system is chaos. Deliveries scattered throughout the day with no apparent logic, the service entrance constantly jammed. I've watched the backup on Mountain Pass Road three days in a row now. Delivery trucks stack up because there's no coordinated schedule, blocking traffic for tourists trying to get to the market.

So I create windows. Early morning deliveries from six to eight, before the market opens. Afternoons from two to four, when foot traffic dies down but before the cars start rolling in.

Nothing during peak hours. Clear time slots, organized by vendor type, with buffer time built in for delays.

It's clean. Logical. Efficient.

I present it to Gloria first thing Monday morning, and she nods approvingly as she flips through my color-coded spreadsheet.

"This is exactly what we needed," she says. "I'll send it to the vendors right away."

I walk out of her office feeling, for the first time since I arrived, like I might actually make this work. Like maybe I can figure this job out.

That feeling lasts approximately two hours.

The first complaint comes from Agnes.

Of course it's Agnes.

She finds me near the bratwurst stand, her face a thundercloud of righteous indignation. "The new schedule," she says, "has my deliveries arriving at the same time as Harriet's."

I check my tablet. "That's correct. I grouped similar vendor types together to streamline the—"

"Harriet makes candles."

"Right. You both have small shipments, so I thought you could share a window—"

"Harriet takes up the entire loading dock." Agnes says this like I've suggested she share a delivery window with a war criminal. "She brings a folding chair and supervises her unloading like it's a military operation. There's no room for anyone else, physically or energetically."

I open my mouth to point out that the loading dock can accommodate multiple deliveries, then think better of it.

"I can adjust the timing. Give you a buffer."

"A buffer won't help. She'll just start coming early." She

crosses her arms. "Ben understood this. Ben gave us separate days."

Of course he did.

I make a note on my tablet, trying to keep my voice pleasant. "I'll get it changed soon."

Agnes doesn't look satisfied, but she leaves. I take a breath. Then Mrs. Chen appears.

"The new schedule says I can't receive deliveries until six a.m.," she says, her voice tight with worry. "But Mr. Park comes at five-thirty. He has a route. He's been coming at five-thirty for twenty years."

"I can talk to the supplier about adjusting—"

"You don't understand." She shakes her head. "Mr. Park's father used to make this delivery. Then Mr. Park took over. Now his grandson rides along, learning the route. Three generations, same time, same day. You don't *adjust* Mr. Park."

Something cold settles in my stomach.

"I didn't realize," I say. "I'll fix it."

The complaints keep coming.

Judy and Chef Raúl—along with multiple members of the kitchen staff—point out that my twenty-four-hour notice requirement for schedule changes is impossible when you're dealing with fresh ingredients and mountain weather. "Sometimes my fish guy can't get over the pass until afternoon," Raúl says. "Sometimes he can only come at dawn. I'm supposed to know that a day in advance?"

I don't have a good answer for that.

By noon, I've fielded eight complaints, made twelve apologetic phone calls, and manually approved three emergency exceptions to my own system. The spreadsheet that looked so elegant this morning is now covered in red marks and crossed-out times and hastily scribbled notes. I'm standing in the middle of the market, tablet in hand, trying to figure out how to fix the situation, when Ben finds me.

"So," he says. "I hear you fixed our delivery system."

I don't look up from my tablet. I can't. If I look at him, he'll see that I already know what he's about to say.

"I streamlined it. It was inefficient."

"It was a community." His voice is quiet, but there's an edge to it. "These vendors have been working together for years. Some of them for decades. They have relationships. Agreements. History."

"I was trying to help." It comes out more defensive than I intend. Even as I say it, I hear how flimsy it sounds. The rallying cry of people who've made things worse. *I was trying to help. I meant well. I didn't know.* "The traffic backup on Mountain Pass Road alone—"

"Gets bad sometimes, yeah. And we deal with it. Because the alternative is telling Mr. Park that his family's twenty-year routine doesn't fit our spreadsheet." He shoves his hands in his pockets. "You reorganized a system you don't understand because it didn't look right on paper."

The words hit harder than they should. Maybe because I'm already thinking them myself. I'd been so sure I was right. The spreadsheet made sense. The schedule was logical. Everything looked perfect, just like my vendor order for two kissing swans had looked perfect, right up until two hysterical chickens showed up instead.

And suddenly I see it. What I've been doing since I got here.

I came in terrified. Terrified of being blindsided again, of trusting a system I didn't build and getting blamed when it failed. So I grabbed control of everything I could get my hands on. If I built it myself, I could defend it. If I understood every piece, no one could say I missed something.

Except now I've made an actual mistake. One that's entirely mine.

I finally look up from my tablet.

"I screwed up," I say. The admission hurts, but I force it out anyway. "I should have asked more questions before I changed things. I'll fix it."

Ben blinks. Whatever he was expecting me to say, that apparently wasn't it.

"I'm not trying to prove I'm smarter than everyone," I add, and I should stop there but it's been a long morning and my rattled nerves let something slip. "I haven't done this in a while. I'm rusty."

And apparently tossing out that red flag in front of my boss's grandson—who's just standing there, not interrupting, just looking at me with a blank face—apparently that frees up the rest.

"I'm only trying to prove I can do this without messing up. Because the last time I had a job, I got fired. I mean, for something that wasn't my fault, but four million people watched a video of my professional humiliation, and I've spent the last three months eating ice cream soup wondering if I'll ever work in events again."

When my mouth finally stops running, I summon the courage to glance at him.

Of course he's openly staring at me. Which sets my already hot face ablaze. But I'm surprised when he only says, "Ice cream soup?"

"It's—it's when the ice cream melts but you eat it anyway because you're too depressed to care." I rub my forehead. "That's not the point. The point is, I got scared. I saw problems and I wanted to fix them before anyone could blame me for not fixing them. And I moved too fast."

A long silence stretches between us. The market hums around us—families browsing, vendors calling out, Christmas music drifting from somewhere near the tree. Ben's expression shifts. Not pity, exactly. I'm not sure what.

"For what it's worth," he says finally, "I don't think you screwed it up. You just...didn't know what you didn't know."

"That's generous."

"It's true." He almost smiles. "Also, ice cream soup is a real thing? I thought I invented that when I was nine."

I choke out a pathetic almost-laugh. "Sorry. My patent is pending."

The corner of his mouth twitches. A crack in the wall between us, maybe.

He walks away without another word, and I get back to fixing my mistakes.

I spend the entire afternoon undoing my own work.

I call Mr. Park's grandson—Mr. Park himself doesn't do phones—and apologize profusely. I assure him that five-thirty is perfect, that Winterbloom values his family's business, that nothing needs to change. He's skeptical but agrees to continue the route. Mrs. Chen nearly cries with relief when I tell her.

I give Agnes and Harriet separate delivery days—Tuesdays and Thursdays respectively—and listen to Agnes explain for ten full minutes why Harriet's folding chair is a territorial act of aggression. I nod in all the right places.

With each conversation, each apology, each adjustment, I start to understand something I should have seen from the beginning: You can't optimize relationships like these. You can only respect them.

Late in the afternoon, I run into Agnes again. She's

packing up her stall for the day, arranging her crystals and lavender sachets with the care of someone handling precious artifacts. She studies me for a long moment. "I hear you're from Miami."

I'm not sure where this is going. "Yes?"

"Big city. Everything fast. Efficient." She says the word like it's slightly distasteful, like finding a hair in your soup. "Here, things are slower. On purpose. We know each other's children. We remember each other's losses. Efficiency isn't the point."

"I'm starting to understand that."

"Good." She nods. Her face softens into what might be approval. "Most people from outside, they don't. They try to make us into something we're not."

"I don't want to do that."

"Then don't." She pats my arm, surprisingly gentle. "You made a mistake today. You're fixing it. That counts for something." She tilts her head, considering me. "Your energy is better than it was this morning. Less...grippy."

"Grippy?"

"You were holding on too tight. To control. To being right. The mountain doesn't respond well to that. Neither do the people who live on it."

I don't know what to say to that. It's simultaneously the most nonsensical and the most accurate thing anyone's said to me in days.

"Thank you," I manage. "I think."

Agnes smiles—a real smile, warm and unexpected—and goes back to her crystals and sachets.

That evening, I sit in my room with my laptop open, staring at the spreadsheet I'd been so proud of this morning.

It's not wrong, exactly. The traffic problems are real. The backup on Mountain Pass Road is real. But I'd been so focused on fixing the visible problems that I'd missed the invisible ones I was creating. I think about what Agnes said. *You were holding on too tight.*

She's right. I've been gripping so hard since I got here—since Miami, really—that I forgot to actually look at what I was holding.

I close the spreadsheet without saving it. Tomorrow I'll start fresh. Ask questions before I make changes. Listen before I optimize. Remember that behind every line item on a schedule is a person with a story I don't know yet.

It won't fix everything. Ben still resents me, the vendors are still wary, and I'm still the outsider who showed up and immediately tried to reorganize their lives.

But it's a start.

HOW STILL WE SEE THEE *Lie*

I SPEND TUESDAY TRYING TO BE LESS GRIPPY.

It's harder than it sounds. My instinct when I see a problem is to fix it—immediately, before anyone can blame me for neglecting it. But Agnes's words keep echoing in my head, so instead of reorganizing the vendor check-in system (which definitely needs reorganizing), I watch. I ask questions. I learn that Derek always handles the north section lights first because they're the most temperamental. That Judy restocks the bakery case at exactly ten a.m. because that's when the first tour bus arrives. That Mrs. Chen likes to be greeted in Cantonese, which I don't speak, but I'm working on *zou san*.

Small things. Things that don't show up on spreadsheets.

By the time I fall into bed that night, I'm exhausted but something feels different. Less like I'm fighting the current. More like I'm learning to swim in it.

Wednesday morning, I wake up before my alarm.

This is either personal growth or altitude-induced insomnia. I choose to believe the former.

By mid-morning, I'm back at my desk in the little chaos office, working through vendor contracts. Phoebe's filing system—if you can call it that—is a nightmare of half-filled spreadsheets and invoices shoved into folders with no apparent logic. Yesterday after dinner I spent my whole night sorting through payment records and matching invoices to suppliers, trying to make sense of it all.

One bright spot: I managed to process the outstanding payments. Multiple businesses that had been waiting on checks, from contractors to florists to bulk grocery items—all handled. Most had been sitting in Phoebe's urgent folder for almost two months. I'd stayed up until almost two a.m. processing payments and now: done.

My new boss had nodded approvingly when I told her the backlog was cleared. "Efficient," she'd said, which from Gloria felt like a standing ovation. So I'm feeling almost competent when I hear voices in the hallway.

Gloria's office is two doors down from mine. Because hers is neat as can be, unlike the one I inherited, she's not embarrassed to keep her door open. I'm not trying to eavesdrop when I walk past on my way to the supply closet, but Ben's voice stops me cold.

"—just wanted you to know."

"Which vendor was this?"

"Lacey Powell. Petal and Pine."

My stomach drops. Lacey Powell. The florist. The invoice I stayed up half the night to verify, process, and pay.

"Yes, I saw her pull up a little while ago. She looked angry when she headed for the hothouse. What was that about?" Gloria's voice is sharp.

"Just an issue with her most recent payment. I took care of it. I should've been keeping closer tabs on things during the transition. She's fine now. Delivering the poinsettias as we speak."

I stand in the hallway, my blood turning to ice and then to fire. I gave up precious sleep to process that payment. I matched the invoice to Phoebe's records exactly. I've been here a handful of days. I work with what I'm given.

But that's not what Ben told Gloria. He told her there was a problem, implied it happened on my watch, and then swooped in to fix it—making himself look like the hero while I look like the incompetent new hire who can't even process a simple payment correctly.

"Thank you for resolving it, Ben," Gloria says. "We don't need vendor issues, especially not this season. It reflects poorly."

"Of course. But it's fine. I handled it before it became a thing."

Handled it. Like he saved the day from *my* incompetence.

I don't wait to hear more. I fling myself into the office that feels more like a stranger's than it ever will mine and imagine all the things I'm about to say to Ben Bennett.

After half an hour, I have calmed my rage from an inferno to a controlled burn and trust myself to remain professional—or at least not to swear. I head for the hothouse.

The smell hits me before the warmth does—sharp and green, cutting through the humid air. Ben is at the workbench again, stripping rosemary from its stems. His head snaps up when I storm in.

"If there was a problem with the florist's payment, you should have come to me."

His expression shifts from surprise to wariness. "What?"

"I heard you in Gloria's office. Telling her there was a payment issue. That you caught it and took care of it." I can hear my voice shaking and I hate it. "I processed that payment yesterday. I matched the invoice to Phoebe's abominable files exactly. But you made it sound like I screwed up and—thank goodness!—you were there to fix it."

"Madison—"

"You told Gloria you 'should've been keeping closer tabs on things during the transition.' Which is a polite way of saying you should have been keeping tabs on me. And now Gloria thinks—"

"Gloria doesn't think anything." His voice is careful, controlled. "That's the point."

"The *point* is that you went behind my back. If there was an issue with a vendor I paid, you should have told me. Let me handle it. Let me explain to Gloria what happened. Instead you just—" I gesture broadly, too angry to find the right words. "Swept in. Made yourself look good."

"Made myself look—" He stops. His eyes lock on mine. "You think I was trying to make *myself* look good?"

"What else am I supposed to think? I heard you in my boss's office explaining how you caught my mistakes before they 'became a thing.'"

His face tightens, then closes off.

"You don't know what you're talking about."

I cross the six feet between us so I can really stare him down. "So explain it to me."

"I don't have to explain myself to someone who's been here for five minutes and thinks she's got me and everything else figured out."

"I know what I heard."

"You heard half a conversation and filled in the rest with whatever confirmed the terrible things you've decided about me." His voice rises now, that easy charm stripped away to reveal something raw underneath. "You walked in here with your spreadsheets and your systems and immediately assumed that everyone here is incompetent so you had to fix us."

"You told Gloria—"

"I told Gloria exactly what she needed to hear so that *you* could keep doing your job without her questioning every decision you make!" He's fully angry now. "You're so sure you've got me figured out. The boss's lazy grandson who poaches more deserving people's credit. Who coasts on the family name. Right?"

The accuracy of it stings, but I don't back down. "If the shoe fits."

"You don't know anything about me. You don't know anything about what I do around here, or why I do it, or what I've been trying to—" He stops himself. Takes a breath. When he speaks again, his voice is level, but barely. "Forget it. Believe whatever you want. You'll only be here six weeks anyway."

We stare at each other. The hothouse feels suddenly too warm, the air thick with moisture and the heavy scent of blooming flowers I'm too furious to appreciate.

"I was hired to do a job," I say. "I can't do that job if you're going around me. If you're lying about me making mistakes."

"Lying!" For two seconds, he looks irate. And then: aloof. I'm not worth the effort. "Look. I've been invested in keeping this place running my whole life. Forgive me for not immediately trusting someone who jumps to conclusions first and asks questions never."

Neither of us backs down. Neither of us apologizes. We're standing close enough that I can see the rise and fall of his chest, the flush creeping up his neck. Close enough that if I weren't so furious, I might notice other things. Things I refuse to see.

Finally, I turn and walk out, letting the door swing shut behind me. The cold air barrels into me, and I stand there for a moment, breathing hard.

Charming. Useless. And now I can add dishonest to the list.

You'll only be here six weeks anyway.

He meant it as a dismissal. I claim it as a countdown.

Six weeks and I never have to see him again.

THE REST OF THE DAY IS A BLUR OF SMALL DISASTERS.

A server calls in sick—stomach flu, highly contagious, please don't come near me—leaving a gap in the staff that I have to scramble to fill. The generator that Derek fixed yesterday is making a concerning noise again. An influencer with forty thousand followers posts a video calling our hot chocolate "aggressively mid" and now an indignant Sienna's on a damage control mission.

And through it all, I keep replaying the hothouse conversation in my head.

You heard half a conversation and filled in the rest with whatever confirmed the terrible things you've decided about me.

No. I heard exactly what I heard. He said he should have been keeping closer tabs on me.

By six o'clock, I'm running on cranberry-orange muffins and spite. The market is beginning to wind down, families drifting toward the parking lot. I should feel satisfied. We've almost made it through another day with no major catastrophes. But instead I just feel hollow.

I've been here six days. Six days, and I've already made an enemy of the owner's grandson.

I'm walking back toward the chalet, Sienna's too-small coat pulled tight around me, when I hear it.

Crying. Soft, hiccuping sobs coming from somewhere near the center of the market.

I follow the sound and find a little girl, maybe seven or eight, sitting on the bench near the Letters to Santa mailbox. Her mother is crouched beside her, rubbing her back, looking exhausted and helpless in that particular way parents get when they can't fix whatever's wrong.

"Sweetie, I'm sure there's a reason—"

"He *forgot* me." The girl's voice is thick with tears. "I put my letter in the mailbox *three days ago* and Santa never wrote back. Sam got a letter. Lily got a letter. And I didn't get *anything*."

I stop walking.

The mother looks up and sees me. I'm still wearing my staff lanyard, and relief breaks across her face.

"I'm so sorry," she says, standing. "She's just...she was so excited about the letter program. She spent an hour writing to Santa. And when her siblings got responses and she didn't..."

"I understand." I crouch down to the girl's level. "Hi. What's your name?"

"Emma." She wipes her nose with her sleeve. "Emma Patterson."

"Emma, I work here at Winterbloom. And I can promise you that Santa didn't forget about you. Some letters just take a little longer. Especially when Santa wants to make his reply extra special. Trust me, your letter is important. *You're* important. Okay?"

She looks up at me with red-rimmed eyes. "You promise?"

"I promise. I'm going to personally tell Santa to hurry it up," I say with a smile.

The mother mouths *thank you* over Emma's head, and I nod. They walk away toward the chalet, Emma still sniffling but calmer now as she holds her mother's hand.

I stand there for a long moment after they're gone, staring at the cherry-red mailbox.

I have no idea how the Letters to Santa program actually works. I don't know who coordinates it, or how letters get assigned, or why Emma Patterson's letter fell through the cracks. I just made a promise I have no idea how to keep.

Add it to the list.

It's almost nine by the time I finally wrap things up and head back to my room. I stop by the mulled wine vendor on my way and pick up two—one for now, one for later—because it's that kind of night. I have to admit, it's better than my usual Aperol Spritz. Warmer, anyway. More appropriate for standing in the snow questioning all your life choices.

But I can't stop thinking about that little girl's face. The devastation of being forgotten. The way she'd said *he forgot me* like it was confirmation of something she'd always secretly feared.

I know that feeling. More than I want to admit.

My room is small but cozy—exposed wooden beams, a quilt that looks handmade, a window that frames the market lights below like a Christmas card.

It should feel charming. Instead it just feels lonely.

I think about calling my mother, but it's late in Florida and she'll ask questions I don't want to answer. I think about texting Sienna, but she's the early-to-bed type most nights, and anyway, what would I say? *I picked a fight with a cartoon rabbit whose grandma owns this place and now I'm drinking alone and questioning every choice that landed me here?*

I open my laptop instead. Check my email. Scroll through job listings I've already memorized, positions I'm not qualified for anymore because my name is synonymous with disaster in every event planning circle in Florida.

Four million people saw the ice chickens that toppled my career. None of them saw the seven years of hard work I put into building it.

I close the laptop. Finish my first mulled wine. Don't feel guilty when I knock back the second. Then I think about Emma Patterson's letter and pull on my coat—my thin windbreaker that Sienna mocked—and then layer her short fluffy coat over it. I add the hat and gloves she loaned me. A hat without a pom pom, because no.

I head outside.

The market is closed now, empty except for the security lights and the soft glow of the Christmas decorations that stay on all night. It's beautiful in a way I haven't let myself appreciate since I got here. Peaceful. The kind of quiet that only exists when snow is falling and the whole world is holding its breath.

The Letters to Santa mailbox glows softly in the lamplight, cherry-red paint cheerful against the white snow. The little sign beside it reads: *Write to Santa! Every letter answered.*

Every letter answered.

I don't know why I do it. Mulled wine? Exhaustion?

Maybe it's Emma's tear-streaked face, or the way I'd yelled at Ben in the hothouse. The way he'd looked at me like I was exactly the person he expected me to be. Maybe it's simply the fact that I'm standing in a Christmas market in Colorado when a week ago I was puddling onto the couch in a Miami heatwave, barely capable of thinking about the holidays.

There's a small cabinet attached to the side of the mailbox. Inside, I find a stack of preprinted letter templates—the kind that fold up into their own envelope and self-seal—and a cup of stubby pencils. I take one of each, find a nearby bench, and prop the heavy cardstock on my knees.

The bench is freezing through my jeans, and the cardstock is stiff and waxy under my numb fingertips. It's so quiet I can hear the scratch of my pencil, the soft hush of snow falling, my own breathing. Nothing else.

And I write.

Dear Santa,

This is stupid. I know this is stupid. I'm a grown woman writing to Santa on a preprinted letter template like some kind of emotional disaster.

But there was this little girl today. Emma Patterson. She's staying here at Winterbloom. She was crying because Santa forgot to write back to her, and I promised her that her letter mattered. That she mattered. And I meant it. I really did. So please make sure she gets a response?

Anyway. That's the important part. You can stop reading now.

Because I don't know why I'm still writing. But I can't seem to stop.

Here's the truth: I don't know what I'm doing here. I took this job because I was out of options. I had a career—a good one—and I lost it because of something stupid and ridiculous and not even my fault (and yes, I know that sounds like deflection but I'm almost sure it really wasn't my fault), and now I'm starting over at a Christmas market in Colorado where I'm constantly freezing and my new counterpart thinks I'm an uptight control freak who can't admit when she's wrong.

(He might not be entirely wrong about the control freak part.)

We got into a fight today. A bad one. I think he did something dishonest—I heard him do something dishonest—and I went off. I didn't ask questions. I didn't give him a chance to explain. I made up my mind and I attacked.

And now I'm sitting here replaying it and I don't even know if I was right. But that's not what bothers me most.

What bothers me most is that I used to be better than this. Before I lost my job—before everything fell apart—I was fair. I gave people the benefit of the doubt. I didn't assume the worst about everyone I met. Now I feel like I'm walking around with my fists up all the time. Ready to swing before anyone can swing first.

I came here to prove I could still do this. That I'm not the failure everyone thinks I am. But what if trying so hard not to fail is turning me into someone I don't recognize...or even like?

What if the person I was before is gone?

Anyway. I don't know what I'm asking for. I came out here to make sure Emma Patterson gets her letter, and somehow I ended up baring my soul to a mailbox. That's either the mulled wine or the altitude or both.

Thanks for listening.
Maddie

I fold the letter into its envelope, seal it, and slide it through the slot before I can change my mind.

The mailbox swallows it without ceremony. Just the soft shush of paper against metal, then the silence of the winter night.

I stand there in the snow, my breath making clouds in the cold air, feeling simultaneously ridiculous and relieved.

Snow crunches under my useless Florida ankle boots as I shuffle back to the chalet. Chafing my hands against the freezing air. Pitying whoever has to read my pathetic letter.

But at least Emma Patterson will get her reply.

SUNDAY MORNING ARRIVES GRAY AND COLD, THE kind of overcast that makes you want to stay in bed indefinitely. Unfortunately, I don't have that luxury. The market opens in an hour, and apparently we have a Santa crisis.

"Judy called. Irwin's still sick. And Gloria said Pete just called in sick, too," Sienna says when I enter the staff room. "Fever. Chills. It sounds vile."

I sip my coffee and try to look like I have useful ideas. I don't. I don't know the backup systems, the emergency contacts, the unspoken hierarchies of who can be asked to do what.

Sienna groans. "We've got four hours of Santa's Workshop scheduled today. I booked a photographer to get marketing shots."

"What about Derek?"

"Derek is five-foot-three and a size extra-small. You know I love him, but he's not going to fill out that suit."

She chews her lip. I chew mine. The staff room door swings open, and Ben walks in.

We haven't spoken since the hothouse. He glances at me—a brief, uncomfortable look—then focuses on Sienna. "I know, I'm early. Someone check the sky for flying pigs." When neither of us reacts, he adds, "Why do you look like the Christmas tree fell on someone?"

"Irwin and Pete are both sick. We need someone to wear the suit." Sienna studies Ben and his broad shoulders. "*We need someone to wear the suit.*"

A slideshow of emotions flickers across Ben's face. The most prominent one is horror. "No."

"Ben—"

"I don't want whatever janky germs are clinging to that suit!" He blanches. "Ugh. Think of the beard."

"Both those guys are old. Possibly immunocompromised. You, Ben Bennett? You're in your prime."

"That beard is primed to give me tuberculosis." He shakes his head. "Absolutely not. Find someone else."

"There is no one else. You're the right build, you're here, and you've done it before."

"Once. Two years ago. Under duress."

"Consider this duress." Sienna crosses her arms. "Ben, please. I hired a photographer. The families are already lining up. Think of the kids. Please?"

He looks genuinely uncomfortable. This is not his usual easy deflection, but something real. Like this is asking more of him than putting on a costume.

"Fine," he says finally. "But if any of the kids cry, that's on you."

Sienna throws her arms around him. "You're a lifesaver.

The suit is in the closet where we keep the—what am I saying? You know the one. You've got forty-five minutes."

Ben extracts himself from the hug and heads for the door, but he pauses as he passes me. For a second I think he's going to say something about yesterday. Acknowledge the hothouse, or the fight, or the fact that he's been pretending I'm not here.

He doesn't say anything. My stomach tightens.

Am I supposed to bring it up? I don't know the protocol for calling your boss's grandson a liar and him calling me disposable and then still having to see him at work the next day.

I should clear the air. Or salt the wound. Something.

Instead he finally says, "Try not to look so smug."

"What?" I blink. "I'm not smug. This is my neutral face."

"Then your neutral face looks smug." Something flickers at the corner of his mouth. Not quite a smile, but close.

I decide to play along. "Well, your Santa suit is going to look smug. Because you lost."

"I didn't lose. I was volunteered." He says it like it's a jail sentence.

"Volun*told*," I offer as he walks away.

He stops. Turns. Looks at me with what might be grudging respect. "Very nice."

"I have my moments."

We regard each other for a beat. It's not friendly, exactly. But it's not the hothouse, either.

He's gone before I can say anything else, and Sienna is watching me with a look I don't like.

"What?"

"Nothing." But she's smiling. "Nothing at all."

The morning rush hits before I have time to dwell on it. I throw myself into work—vendor checks, scheduling conflicts, a shipment of ornaments from Germany that arrived broken.

But Santa's Workshop is right in the center of the market, and I keep finding reasons to walk past it.

He looks cute in the suit. That is my first, most irritating observation. His shoulders fill it perfectly and he's so tall that even the padding looks good. The white beard can't hide his smile. And I have to admit, Ben has a great smile.

My second observation is less irritating and more...confusing.

He's good at this.

Really good.

I pause near the hot cocoa stall—Bree's stall, with its Instagram-perfect aesthetic—and watch as Ben lifts a tiny girl onto his lap. She's maybe four, clutching a stuffed reindeer like a lifeline, clearly terrified.

"Well, hello there," Ben says. No booming *ho ho ho,* no forced cheer. Just warm and easy, like they're old friends. "That's a beautiful reindeer you've got. Does she have a name?"

The girl whispers something I can't hear.

"Sparkle? I had a reindeer named Sparkle once! She always wanted to lead the sleigh, but Rudolph kept getting all the attention." He leans in conspiratorially. "Between you and me, Sparkle was faster."

The girl giggles, her fear melting away like snow in sunlight.

By the time she leaves, waving enthusiastically, the line has doubled. Word is spreading, apparently. The reluctant Santa is a hit.

I watch him with the next kid, and the next. A shy boy won't make eye contact. Ben asks about his shoes, which have dinosaurs on them, and suddenly the boy is launching into a detailed explanation of why T-rexes are actually his second-favorite dinosaur. A pair of twins try to test him with trick questions—"What's my sister's middle name?"—and Ben smoothly redirects: "Well, I've got a lot of names to remember. Why don't you tell me yours, and I'll make sure it goes on my very important list?"

Bree sidles up beside me to watch Ben work. "I'm so glad my stall has such a good view of Santa's Workshop. Ben has always been sexy but holy Hot Santa!" She playfully fans herself. "This is what every Christmas market needs, don't you think?" My face heats up when I find myself agreeing, but I just mumble something about him being good with the kids before making my escape.

And he is good with them, I note in near-astonishment several times throughout the day. He never talks down to them. Never rushes them. When a toddler bursts into tears at the sight of him, he doesn't call for the parents. Instead, he sits very still and starts telling a story about a snowman who was afraid of his own carrot nose, quiet and silly, until the crying stops and the toddler is staring at him with wide-eyed fascination.

It doesn't fit. None of this fits the version of Ben I've been constructing in my head—the charming lightweight, the coasting grandson, the man who can't be bothered to show up on time—or sometimes at all.

And yet here he is, making a two-year-old laugh so hard she almost falls off his lap, and something in my chest feels tight in a way I don't want to examine.

"He's good, isn't he?"

I turn. Judy from the café has appeared beside me, holding a tray of cookies shaped like Christmas trees.

"He's...not terrible," I manage.

Judy smiles. There's something knowing in it that makes me uncomfortable. "Ford—Gloria's husband—he used to be Santa every year. Ben would help him. Follow him around, hand out candy canes, learn the kids' names." She nods toward the chalet, and then at Ben. "This place grows on people. So does that one."

Before I can respond, she's moving on, offering cookies to the families in line.

I watch Ben for one more minute before forcing myself to walk away.

I have work to do. I have vendor check-ins and scheduling conflicts and a whole list of problems that need solving. I don't have time to stand around reevaluating my opinion of Ben Bennett just because he's unexpectedly patient with children.

Being good with kids doesn't mean he wasn't lying yesterday. It doesn't mean I was wrong about him.

It doesn't.

*

An envelope is waiting under my door when I finally get back to my room that night.

Cream-colored, unaddressed, with my name written on the front in neat handwriting done up in fancy gold ink. For a moment I stare at it, confused. Then I remember.

The letter. The mailbox. The mulled-wine-fueled moment of weakness that I'd convinced myself to forget.

My hands aren't quite steady as I open it.

Dear Maddie,

Thank you for your letter. It wasn't stupid—not even a little bit.

First, let me assure you: Emma Patterson will get her letter tonight. Your promise will be kept.

Now, about the rest of it.

You said you lost your career because of something that wasn't your fault. That's a particular kind of grief, the injustice of being punished for someone else's mistake. It makes you feel powerless, and when we feel powerless, we often try to control whatever we can. Schedules. Systems. First impressions.

When we've been hurt—really hurt, the kind that changes how we see the world—we protect ourselves however we can. We build walls. We wear armor. We assume the worst before the worst can surprise us. It's not a character flaw. It's survival.

But survival mode isn't meant to last forever. And the fact that you're confiding these fears about who you're becoming? That tells me the person you're afraid you've lost is still in there. Still paying attention. She's just finding her way back.

Be patient with yourself. You're not gone. You're healing. And healing is a messy, meandering road.

If you ever feel lonely again or need someone to listen, write back. The mailbox is always there.

Santa

I read the letter twice.

Then I fold it carefully, slide it back into its envelope, and sit on my bed in the quiet room.

The person you're afraid you've lost is still in there. Still paying attention. She's just finding her way back.

I think about Ben as Santa today. Patient. Present. Gentle with kids who were scared of him.

Then I think about Ben missing our meeting. Taking credit

for handling a problem I didn't know existed. Implying I need supervision.

Two versions of him. And I've spent the past week cataloging the second one so thoroughly that I almost missed the first.

The old me—the fair one, the one who existed before the swans and the firing and the ice cream soup—she would have noticed sooner. She would have held space for both versions instead of deciding he could only be one thing.

I don't know how to reconcile what I saw today with what I thought I knew. But maybe that's the point. Maybe trying is what matters.

I CAN'T STOP THINKING ABOUT BEN AS SANTA.

It's been three days since I watched him with those kids—patient and warm and so genuinely good at it—and the image keeps intruding at inconvenient moments. During vendor check-ins. While reviewing delivery schedules. At night, when I should be falling asleep.

He made reindeer sounds.

And part of me wishes that Irwin was still sick so I could watch him do it again.

Okay, not really. Not about Irwin being sick.

But Ben was really, really good.

Which is why I'm reorganizing my desk for the third time this week.

When I inherited this office from Phoebe, it looked like a paper bomb had detonated. Vendor contracts buried under Post-it avalanches. A filing system that appeared to be organized by vibes. Coffee rings on documents that should have been filed away. But thanks to my need to process this new and unexpected layer to Ben Bennett, I have spent every spare minute of the last three days excavating, categorizing, and creating systems that make sense.

Now everything has a place. Color-coded folders. Labeled bins. A whiteboard schedule that actually reflects reality instead of Phoebe's apparent philosophy of *write it down somewhere and pray.*

And yet here I am, rearranging my pen cup for the fourth time today, because my brain won't stop replaying the image of Ben Bennett making a two-year-old laugh so hard she almost fell off his lap.

My youngest niece, Rosie, is intensely shy. It always takes her time to warm up. When I'm not inhaling Christmas around the clock, I FaceTime them every week, so I know exactly how hard it is to make a scared kid laugh like that. Ben did it like breathing.

He was *good* with them. Not performatively good, the way some adults are when they know people are watching. Genuinely good. Patient and silly and present in a way that I can't help admiring.

The problem is that Santa Ben doesn't fit the narrative I've been building. Scattered, unreliable Ben—the one who misses meetings and forgets to send emails and charms his way out of accountability—that guy I understood. That guy was easy to write off.

But the man who knelt in fake snow to comfort a nervous four-year-old? Who made Sparkle the Reindeer feel like the most important character in Christmas history? Who wore that ridiculous beard without a shred of irony because the kids believed in it?

That guy is harder to dismiss.

And I don't love that my heart does something complicated

every time I think about it. I already have a weakness for people who are good with kids. I don't need Ben Bennett adding to it.

My radio crackles. "Madison? It's Chef Raúl. Do you have a minute?"

I grab the walkie. "What do you need?"

"The Fosters' anniversary party is tonight. They specifically requested the herb-crusted pork loin, but I'm short on fresh rosemary and thyme. What I've got is looking sad."

"Can you substitute dried?"

A pause that somehow conveys professional offense through static. "For a fortieth anniversary? No. I cannot substitute dried."

Right. Okay. "What about the hothouse? Ben grows herbs back there, doesn't he?"

"That's why I'm calling you. I radioed him twice. No answer."

Of course he didn't answer. The man treats his radio like a suggestion.

"I'll handle it," I say. "Give me twenty minutes."

And I'm not even disappointed that it falls to me. That I have an excuse to walk down there and see him in person.

What is *wrong* with me? Where did my perfectly reasonable grudge go? Three days ago, I had a whole mental file on this man—Unreliable, Scattered, Coasting on the Family Name—and now my stomach is doing something fluttery at the thought of watching him cut rosemary.

Rosemary. I'm excited about *herbs*.

I grab my coat—coats, plural, because I still haven't prioritized solving the Florida-girl-in-Colorado problem—and head out the back entrance toward the hothouse.

The cold hits me like a punishment. My breath hangs

white in the air. December in the mountains is no joke, and my layered situation of fuzzy cropped jacket over windbreaker over cardigan is not cutting it.

The hothouse door is substantial; I throw my weight against it to push it open. The warmth hits me immediately, but that's only part of what makes me stop in my tracks.

Because it's gorgeous. How have I not noticed before?

I've been in here, twice. Once to confront Ben about vendor relationships, once during our spectacular fight about Lacey Powell. Both times I'd been too angry to really see it. Too focused on whatever grievance had brought me through the door.

But now, with no agenda except a rosemary-encrusted anniversary dinner, I actually *look*.

The front section is pure Christmas postcard. Poinsettias in crimson and cream cluster near the entrance, their leaves like velvet. Pink amaryllis stretch toward the glass ceiling, tall and regal. Jasmine climbs a wooden trellis near the door, filling the air with sweetness so intense it's almost dizzying. Edison bulbs glow golden along the beams. I want to curl up with a book and never leave.

It's beautiful. A lush green cathedral in the middle of a Colorado winter.

But Ben isn't here.

I move deeper inside, through another set of glass doors, and suddenly I'm somewhere else entirely.

The air changes. Wraps around me like a warm bath—humid, alive. My frozen lungs expand for what feels like the first time in days. The smell shifts, too. Not Christmas anymore, but earthier. Wet soil and green leaves and a faint sweetness I can't identify. Condensation fogs the glass walls, blurring the snowy world outside into something distant and unreal.

It's a jungle back here. Seedlings under grow lights, herbs in neat rows, winter lettuces in raised beds. Somewhere deeper in, I can hear a fountain burbling. The cold I've been carrying in my bones for two weeks finally, finally starts to thaw.

This is what I've been missing, I think. Not Miami, exactly. But warmth. Green things. The feeling of being surrounded by life instead of endless white and gray.

I find Ben at a workbench in the back corner, half-hidden by a massive orange tree. He's hunched over something—a tray of seedlings, maybe—and he doesn't hear me approach.

"Ben."

He startles. Knocks over a small pot, catches it before it hits the ground. Turns with dirt on his hands and surprise on his face.

"Madison." He sets down the pot. "I didn't hear you come in."

"Chef Raúl needs rosemary and thyme for the Foster anniversary dinner. Fresh. He says what he has is looking sad."

"The Fosters. Forty years, right?" He's already moving toward a section of raised beds, wiping his hands on his jeans. "I've got both. How much does he need?"

"He didn't specify. Enough for herb-crusted pork loin for fifty, plus garnish, I'm guessing."

Ben nods, pulling a pair of garden shears from his back pocket. He starts snipping rosemary with the easy confidence of someone who's done this a thousand times.

I should leave. Mission accomplished. But the warmth is so good after days of freezing, and there's something almost hypnotic about watching him work. His hands are sure.

Focused. Nothing like the scattered guy who forgets to send emails.

"There's a loveseat in the front section. You can wait up there if you want," he says without looking up. "This'll take a few minutes. I want to get him the good stuff."

"I'm fine here." I pull off my outer two layers—it's balmy enough that the cardigan alone will do—and drape them over a nearby stool. "It's nice. Being warm for once."

He glances at me. Amusement flickers across his face. "Miami girl."

"Colorado is trying to kill me."

"Colorado is a lamb compared to actual winter states. You should try Minnesota."

"That's a hard no."

He almost smiles at that. Almost.

We're being careful with each other. Polite in a way we haven't been since before the fight. I think about what I said to him that day. The list I rattled off. Accusing him of lying. Walking out. Letting the door bang shut.

He moves to the thyme, and I follow without really meaning to. That's when I see it.

The entire wall behind his workbench is covered in color.

Sticky notes. Scores of them—maybe hundreds—arranged in columns and clusters. Some have arrows drawn between them. Others have tiny symbols I can't decipher. A massive whiteboard beside it shows a calendar grid with more color-coding, more symbols, more layers of information than I can process at a glance.

"Whoa." The word escapes before I can stop it. "What is going on here?"

Ben's shoulders tighten. He doesn't turn around. "Yeah, I know. It looks insane."

"I was going to say impressive. It looks like mission control," I say. "For a very complicated mission."

I step closer, taking it in. Purple notes, and yellow, green, and blue. Little flags in different colors. Arrows connecting tasks across columns. It's chaos—except it's not, I realize. There's a logic here. I just don't know how to read it yet.

He finally turns. Studies my face like he's waiting for the punchline.

"Seriously," I say. "I've never seen anything like it. How does it work?"

For a long moment, he doesn't answer. I can feel him watching me, trying to decide if this is genuine curiosity or something else, but I'm not sure what. Finally, something in him seems to unlock.

"Colors are categories." He points as he explains. "Green for hothouse stuff. Yellow for events. Purple for things that need my grandmother's input." He indicates a cluster of orange notes in the corner. "These are time-sensitive. Anything with a red flag means someone else is waiting on me to finish before they can move forward. And blue..." He pauses. A wry smile that doesn't quite reach his eyes. "Blue was vendor relations. Guess I should take those down."

Something twists in my chest. I did that. I didn't mean to, but I did.

The twisting gets worse.

"ADHD," he says, and it's clear he's bracing for my reaction. "On the official scale, pretty severe. I have to externalize everything or it just...disappears. If it's not written down in a place I can see it, it doesn't exist."

I freeze as something clicks into place. As everything clicks into place.

I spell it out in my mind to remember it clearly: Attention

Deficit Hyperactivity Disorder. I think about the carolers. The drafted confirmation, never sent. How easy it would be in an operation as big as Winterbloom to miss one small piece and have a big one fall apart.

He shrugs, but it's not casual. It's the shrug of someone who's had to defend this before. "This is me trying not to accidentally skip a step and blow something up."

I nod slowly. "My college roommate was the same way. She described it like her brain had too many tabs open with no way to bookmark anything."

He blinks. "That's actually a really good description."

"How long have you—"

"Since I was eight. Diagnosed young, which everyone said was lucky." He leans against the workbench, and some of the tension leaves his shoulders. "Spent most of my childhood trying to make my brain work like everyone else's. It took me until last year to figure out that maybe I should stop trying to fix it and start working *with* it instead."

I look at the elaborate system. The colors, the symbols, the arrows. The sheer amount of thought and effort that went into building this infrastructure.

"It's amazing."

"It's functional chaos. My parents think it's an overcomplicated excuse for not trying hard enough. They have a lot of opinions about what I would be able to do if I just tried harder. Followed through."

The bitterness in his voice is old. Worn smooth like river stones.

"What do you think?" I ask him.

"I think I spent twenty-five years listening to them and all it got me was a failed business and a lot of therapy bills." His gaze drifts to the sticky notes. "That's not fair. The therapy's new.

I've been back at Winterbloom for three years, and I kept thinking I could power through. But Gran can't run this place forever, and I can't keep being the guy who drops the ball. So: therapy. To help me lock in some of these habits and systems I've been building."

I think of Saturday. His appointment. The keys already in his hand, the way he'd peeled out of here. Maybe not flaking after all.

"For what it's worth, this doesn't look like someone who can't follow through." I look again at the scope of it—the whiteboard, the sticky notes, the timers I'm now noticing on the workbench. "This is a massive effort. This is trying *harder* than everyone else. It's impressive. Brilliant, even."

He stares at me for so long I start mentally cataloging all the reasons I should have kept my mouth shut.

"Trust me," I add, trying to sound lighter than I feel. "I'm an organizational nerd. I know impressive when I see it."

His voice is quiet when he finally speaks. "That is the nicest thing anyone's ever said about my brain."

"Yeah, well." I can feel my face heating up. The humid air. Definitely the humid air. "Don't let it go to your head."

"Too late."

He's smiling now—a real smile. It changes his whole face.

I take a breath. "Listen. About the other day. In here. I owe you an apology."

And the smile fades.

"Madison—"

"No, let me." I stare at a bright orange sticky note because it's easier than looking at him. "I laid into you. Threw the carolers and the missed meetings in your face when you were already down. And then with the florist payment...I'm sorry. I overreacted. I'm a little sensitive about work stuff right now, for reasons that I blurted out to you like an idiot the other day. I let that get the better of me. I heard part of a conversation and assumed the worst, and that was wrong." I swallow. Guiltily. "I was harsh. And I didn't know—" I gesture at the wall, at everything it represents.

"You didn't know because I didn't tell you." He picks up a sprig of rosemary, twirls it between his fingers. "I don't exactly advertise it. When people find out, they treat me like I'm dumb or damaged or incompetent. None of which is great."

"I wouldn't have—"

"You might have." He says it without accusation. Just fact. "You were already keeping a record on me. ADHD would've been one more item on the list."

I think about those first days, how quickly I'd written him off. How satisfying it had been to have a simple explanation for everything he did.

"You're right," I admit. "But I'd like to think I can revise my assumptions when new data comes in."

He pauses. Gives me a long, quiet look. Then he laughs. "New data. You really are an organizational nerd."

"Absolutely."

We're both smiling now. The air between us feels different than it did five minutes ago. Lighter.

Ben sets down the rosemary and picks up his shears again. "For what it's worth, I owe you an apology, too."

"For what?"

"The thing with Lacey Powell. The florist. Lacey does the floral arrangements for the chalet and I supply some of her greenery from the hothouse. That's why she came to me, but I should have looped you in. She was supposed to get eight thousand dollars, but only eighty went through." He looks at the floor. "I looked it up in the spreadsheet you uploaded—

Phoebe's old files, the ones you digitized. A couple of zeros must have gotten dropped when you processed the payment."

I feel the blood drain from my face. "What?"

He shrugs casually, working hard to downplay it. "Easy mistake. I covered the difference and told Gran that Lacey was stressed about the seasonal transition. Bigger orders for winter, tighter timelines, more pressure. Gran thinks she was venting about volume, not money."

The words land slowly, rearranging everything I thought I knew about that conversation.

"You covered for me?"

"You just started. There's a lot to learn. And Phoebe's files were a mess."

He's not looking at me. He's deliberately not looking at me, giving me space to not feel terrible about a mistake I definitely made.

"I accused you of lying." I cover my mortified face with both hands. "I accused you of lying about me and you paid eight thousand dollars out of your own pocket so I wouldn't look bad."

"I'll expense it once the holiday chaos dies down and Gran is less stressed. Perks of the family business, right? We're all dipping into the pot." He waits for the laugh that doesn't come. "Madison, it wasn't a big deal."

"Ben. That's a very big deal."

He waves it away, herb shears still in his hand. "Consider it an investment. We didn't have time to train another ops manager on the off chance my grandmother fired you."

"Ben," I say again. I feel like I may start babbling. "I'm sorry. And thank you. I can't—honestly, I can't thank you enough. Or tell you sorry enough, for that matter."

He rubs the back of his neck, then busies himself with the rosemary. "Really. Buy me a coffee and we'll call it even."

The tips of his ears are turning pink. He looks like he needs an exit ramp from my overwhelming gratitude.

It's tough to do, but I swallow my need to apologize and build him one.

"Saving my job for a coffee. So chivalrous."

"I'm a romantic." He catches himself immediately. "I mean —not romantic, I was...it was a joke."

"I got that."

"Yeah."

"Yeah."

A new kind of tension hangs in the humid air a second too long. We're not looking at each other. The hothouse suddenly feels very warm.

"Right," I say, desperate to move past the awkwardness. "Rosemary. Thyme. Chef Raúl."

"Right. Yeah." He clears his throat, all business. "Let me finish cutting these."

I watch him work. Sure hands, careful cuts. The herbs smell incredible—fresh and sharp and alive.

"You're good at this," I say. "It's the middle of winter and these guys are thriving."

"Gramps taught me." His voice softens. "He had a gift for it. Anything he touched just...grew. I'm still figuring the rest of the business out, but this—" He gestures at the hothouse. "This is where I feel like I know what I'm doing."

I look around. The seedlings stretching toward the light. The herbs in their neat rows. The whole elaborate ecosystem he's built and maintained, despite how much harder he has to work to stay on track.

"I think you know what you're doing in more places than you give yourself credit for," I say.

He looks at me then, right in the eyes.

"You, too."

For a moment, neither of us moves. The fountain burbles somewhere in the back. Grow lights hum overhead. The humid air presses close, full of green and growing things.

Then my radio crackles, shattering the moment.

"Madison? Status on those herbs?" Chef Raúl sounds impatient.

I grab the walkie. "On my way. Five minutes."

"Tell Ben to find his radio while you're at it," he fires back.

Ben looks around wildly. "Must have left it...somewhere."

"Probably wherever you left your phone. We also called," I tell him with a smile.

"ADHD," he says. "Reliable chaos."

He hands me a paper bag, carefully packed with rosemary and thyme. Our fingers touch during the handoff. I feel the tingle of the contact for longer than I should.

I should go. I am going. But at the door, I stop. Turn back.

"Ben."

He looks up from his workbench.

"Thanks. For the herbs. For...the other thing. The payment thing." I take a breath. "And for letting me see this. All of it."

He nods. There's something warm in his expression that I don't know how to name.

"Anytime."

I step back into the cold, and for the first time since I arrived in Colorado, I don't immediately feel frozen.

That night, I can't sleep.

This morning, it was Santa Ben I couldn't stop thinking about. The patience, the warmth, the way he made those kids feel safe. I organized my entire office trying to make sense of it.

Now my brain has so much more to chew on.

The sticky notes. The colors and symbols and arrows. The way his shoulders braced when he said *ADHD*, like he was waiting for me to judge. The way his voice went rough when he said *that is the nicest thing anyone's ever said about my brain.*

Seven thousand nine hundred and twenty dollars. He paid seven thousand nine hundred and twenty dollars to protect me. And I called him a liar to his face.

The thoughts keep circling, looping back on themselves, refusing to settle. I've already reorganized my desk three times this week. I need something else. I need to get them out of my head and onto something solid. Something I can look at instead of just feel.

I grab a spare piece of Letters to Santa stationery. Sit cross-legged on my bed. Stare at the blank page until the words finally come.

Dear Santa,

Thank you for making sure Emma got her letter. I'm sure that meant a lot to her. It meant a lot to me.

I'm sorry for writing again. I know you have actual children to answer. But I need to tell someone this, and you're the safest option I've got. No face to watch. No reaction to manage. Just words on a page. And your other response landed somewhere I wasn't expecting. Somewhere helpful. So thank you for that.

I misjudged someone. Badly. I had him figured out in the first week—unreliable, scattered, coasting on charm. I kept a mental tally of every mistake and used it to justify writing him off.

But it turns out he's been working twice as hard as anyone else just to stay on track. He built systems I didn't even know existed. And when I made a mistake that could have gotten me in trouble, he covered for me and never said a word.

I called him a liar. To his face.

The worst part? He's actually good at this. Not in the way I'm good at it—spreadsheets and checklists and color-coded schedules. He's good in ways I didn't know how to recognize. He sees what people need before they ask. He knows every vendor's name, their kids' names, what's worrying them this season. He built systems that look like chaos but actually work, because they work for his brain, not mine.

I've spent my whole career believing there's one right way to be organized. One right way to be competent. Turns out I was wrong about that, too.

So now I'm sitting here wondering how many other people I've misjudged because it was easier than looking closer. How many times I've decided who someone was before they had a chance to show me the truth.

I don't love what that says about me.

Maddie

I fold the letter, pull on my layers, and walk through the quiet market to the red mailbox. The slot swallows the envelope with a soft thunk.

The walk back is cold. But the swirling in my head has gone quiet, and that's enough for now.

SANTA'S RESPONSE ARRIVES THIRTY-SIX HOURS later, slipped under my bedroom door while I was working the outdoor screening of *It's a Wonderful Life*. Fire pits glowing, blankets on the benches, guests and residents of Snowdrop alike bundled up with hot cocoa watching George Bailey realize he matters.

I'll give it to Snowdrop—they take Christmas and the Letters to Santa program seriously.

The envelope is the same as before. Cream-colored, heavy stock. My name in gold ink, that same elegant, old-fashioned cursive. I sit on the edge of my bed, still wearing my layers as the cold melts away, and open it.

Dear Maddie,

You told me you're tired of being wrong about people. Of making snap judgments and then having to rebuild your understanding from scratch.

Here's something to know about first impressions:

they're not failures of perception. They're survival instincts. We make quick assessments because our brains are trying to keep us safe.

The failure isn't in the first impression. It's in refusing to update it when new information arrives.

You're clearly someone who pays attention. Who notices when reality doesn't match the story you've constructed. That's not a flaw—that's rare. Most people would rather be consistent than correct.

The fact that you're questioning your assumptions? That's not weakness. That's wisdom trying to break through.

Be patient. Trust yourself. You're learning a new way of seeing. That takes time.

Santa

The more I read it, the more helpful it seems.

Most people would rather be consistent than correct.

I think about the mental file I'd built on Ben. How satisfying it had been to slot every mistake into a pattern. How much harder it is to admit the pattern was wrong.

And I let myself consider, for only a moment, why I'm as relieved to be wrong about him as I am.

I fold the letter carefully and tuck it into my nightstand drawer, next to the first one.

Then I sleep better than I have in days.

But I wake to a blur of crises that started before dawn and haven't let up since. It's after one and I'm so hungry and under-caffeinated that I'm genuinely worried I might cry if I don't find some food. Unfortunately, Agnes finds me first.

She's planted herself in the middle of the market pathway,

arms crossed, radiating righteous fury in the direction of Harriet the candlemaker's stall.

"Her pine candles," Agnes says, like the word *pine* is a slur. "They're drowning out my soaps. Not to mention my lavender sachets. Customers can't even smell my product."

"My pine candles were here first," Harriet fires back from behind her display of elegant tapers. "Besides, I saw you move your display closer to the walkway."

"Because your smoke was contaminating my—"

"It's not smoke, it's *ambiance*—"

"Okay." I hold up both hands. "What if we create a buffer zone? Move the mulled wine cart between you. The cinnamon and clove might create a neutral aromatic territory."

I have no idea what I'm talking about. The wafting steam from the mulled wine cart goes wherever the wind takes it; plus, it's one more scent in the mix. I hold my breath, hoping they think it's worth a try.

Agnes considers it for so long I feel sure the idea is doomed. And then: "The spiced mulled wine will complement my fragrances. It's the pine that conflicts."

Harriet opens her mouth to object, but Agnes has already turned away. I meet Harriet's eyes, which she rolls before getting back to work.

Small victories.

"Aromatic territory. Creative. And very diplomatic."

My whole body jolts when Ben's voice sounds from behind me. I blame it on my blood sugar and a lack of caffeine. When I turn, I see him holding two cups of coffee from Judy's, steam curling into the cold air. He extends one toward me.

"I owe *you* coffee," I say, but I snatch it gratefully. "Remember? Seven thousand nine hundred and twenty dollars? Chivalry? Any of this ringing a bell?"

"You can owe me two." He watches me knock back a gulp from the steaming cup, then wince at the heat. "How late were you out last night?"

"Late." I take a less frenzied sip. Mmm. It's rich and dark with a hint of hazelnut. "The screening ran until eleven, and then there was cleanup, and then someone's kid lost their special stuffie and we had to search the entire lawn with flashlights."

"Did you find it?"

"Under a fire pit bench. It took forty-five minutes."

"Hero."

"I prefer heroine, but sure."

He smiles. We're doing this easier now—the back and forth, the teasing. Something shifted in the hothouse, and neither of us seems inclined to shift it back.

Good.

"So," he says. "I need your help."

He pulls out his phone, shows me a photo of what looks like a storage disaster. Boxes stacked haphazardly, tangled strings of lights, what might be a broken shepherd's crook.

"Luminary ceremony supplies. Gran wants an inventory, and I can't find the checklist from last year. I was hoping you might have come across it in Phoebe's files."

I had, actually. A spreadsheet labeled "LUMINARIES - DO NOT LOSE" in a folder called "IMPORTANT STUFF (REAL)." Phoebe's organizational system was truly something.

"I know where the spreadsheet is. But the storage room is freezing. I'm not spending two hours in there without hazard pay."

"What if I told you the stuff for the luminaries is stored in the warming hut closet, where there's a heater and Judy's miraculous turkey cranberry sandwiches?" He holds up a paper bag I hadn't noticed. "We could eat lunch there before we do the initial count."

"I'd say you're learning how to negotiate with Florida girls."

"I've been taking notes."

The warming hut sits at the edge of the skating rink, a timber-framed building with a peaked roof and wide windows overlooking the ice. Inside, there's a row of wooden benches along the walls, a potbelly stove radiating heat, and a self-serve hot cocoa station.

The place is empty. Everyone's either on the ice or browsing the market, which means we have it to ourselves.

"Over there?" he says, gesturing to the bench closest to the stove. "We'll keep you good and warm."

And it is warm. The little stove pumps out a heat so thick that—to my surprise—I need to take off my two jackets. Ben pulls off his coat and his sweater, too; apparently he runs hot enough for just the t-shirt underneath. I try not to notice the way the t-shirt fits.

I fail.

He hands me a sandwich wrapped in brown paper. The turkey cranberry is as good as promised—roasted turkey, tart cranberry relish, herbed stuffing tucked between slices of crusty bread. I make an embarrassing sound on the first bite.

"Good?" he asks.

"Don't talk to me. I'm having a moment."

He grins, an unguarded, easy grin that makes my heart do something complicated.

When I've recovered from my first incredible bite, I say, "So the luminary ceremony is called Glimmerglass, and it's a night where we do something with candles and ice..." I pause. "Fill me in. I'm not sure I understand what any of it is."

"Believe me, by the time we're done making hundreds of ice luminaries, you'll be an expert. You freeze water in molds, leave the center hollow, nest a candle inside. Everyone who attends gets one to carry out onto the frozen lake. The ice glows from within—fire and ice together." A small smile. "Gramps always said that's what life is. A series of opposite ideas and things finding a way to coexist."

I picture it: hundreds of glowing vessels scattered across a frozen lake, each one holding a small flame. Fire and light in a cradle of ice.

"That's beautiful. How did it get its name?"

"Glimmerglass? Oh, that was all Gramps." He scrunches the napkin in his hand, his eyes somewhere else. "He was a dreamer, hence the whimsical name. He always wanted to mark things, make them matter. The luminaries were his idea."

"I think I would have liked him," I say. "I like a dreamer."

He swallows wistfully. "He was a good one. He and I had a lot of plans."

"Like what?"

"Sustainability stuff for Winterbloom. Year-round growing, reduced transport costs, farm-to-table for the restaurant. Most of it hasn't panned out yet."

"Yet."

He shrugs. "I'm an optimist. Or delusional. Jury's still out."

Outside the window, a little girl in a pink parka wobbles across the ice. She stumbles, gets up, stumbles again. Her father skates backward in front of her, arms outstretched, ready to break her fall.

"So," Ben says. "Miami."

"What about it?"

"You miss it?"

I consider the question. The heat. The palm trees. The ocean breeze. The life I was building before—

"Sure," I say. "It's home. I miss it."

But even as the words leave my mouth, I'm not sure they're true. Do I miss the apartment with the broken swamp cooler? The job market that won't touch me? The version of myself who thought she had everything figured out?

Maybe I'm just disoriented. Surrounded by Christmas cheer all hours of the day. Somehow apparently enjoying it.

But Florida is home. Of course I miss it.

"What about you?" I ask. "You've always been here?"

"Grew up in Denver, but spent as much time as I could here. Left for college in Boulder. Stayed for a few years to start a business."

"What kind of business?"

He's working on a massive mouthful of sandwich, but eventually he says, "Eco-friendly packaging. Sustainable alternatives to plastic wrap, that kind of thing."

"That sounds—"

"Like a good idea that I executed terribly?" He smiles, but it doesn't reach his eyes. "Yeah. I had the vision, not the follow-through. The company folded a few years back."

"I'm sorry."

"Don't be. It taught me a lot about what I'm not good at." He stares out the window at the skaters. "I came back here after that. Tail between my legs. Gramps gave me another chance. Let me try the sustainability stuff here at Winterbloom."

"And?"

"And we lost money. Proved everyone right about me."

The words land heavy. I think about the hothouse, the produce, all those seedlings he tends.

"But you're still trying," I say.

"Gramps believed in me. Said it was only a slow start. And maybe he was right. The hothouse is taking hold, even making a profit now." He sets down his sandwich. "He always believed in me. When no one else did. When I didn't deserve it."

"You work hard. Of course you deserved it." I don't add that everyone deserves it—support from their family when they're at their lowest. I make a note to call my parents tonight. Check in. Say thanks.

"Again. He was a good one. Probably the best." He brushes a crumb off the bench, not looking at me. "The last few months, though, he started showing signs. Confusion. Forgetting things. We thought it was just age, but..."

"Dementia?"

"We never got a formal diagnosis. Three months of symptoms, and then—" He stops. Swallows. "Massive stroke. Gone in an hour."

"Ben. I'm so sorry."

"The worst part is not knowing." He goes quiet for a moment, staring at nothing. "Did he back my ideas because he really believed in them? Or was dementia affecting his judgment? Was any of it real, or was he just a dying man humoring his screwup grandson?"

"You're not a screwup," I tell him, but I don't know what else to say, so I just sit with him in the warmth, the potbelly stove crackling, and hope the company is enough.

Outside, the little girl in pink has made it halfway across the rink. Her father catches her when she trips, steadies her, lets go. She takes three wobbling steps on her own.

After a while, Ben shakes his head. Surfaces. "Sorry. That's a lot to dump on someone over lunch."

"It's okay." I finish the last bite of my sandwich, which was unreasonably delicious. "Thank you. For the food. And for...

this." I gesture vaguely at the stove, the quiet, the temporary escape from the chaos outside.

"I'm glad you came." The words hang in the air, a moment too long. Then: "We should probably tackle Phoebe's disaster closet."

"Probably."

The inventory takes an hour. We untangle fairy lights, count luminary molds, and extract boxes and boxes of votive candles jammed behind a stack of broken sleds. By the time we're done, the afternoon light is slanting low through the windows.

"I should get going. Sienna asked for help choosing pictures from her last photoshoot," I say, picking up my two outerwear layers so I can suit up.

Ben starts to pull on his own sweater, then stops. Looks at me.

"Here." He holds it out. Copper cable-knit, soft and worn. "You're going to freeze the second you walk out that door. That furry, fluffy thing you've been wearing is not a real coat."

"I'm fine—"

"Madison. Take the sweater."

I want to argue. I should argue. But the sweater is right there, soft and worn and probably still holding his warmth. And I'm so tired of being cold.

I take it.

It's heavy—thick cable-knit, the wool soft from years of washing. It smells like him. Cedar and soap and something earthier underneath, like soil after rain.

It's too big. The sleeves completely cover my hands, like I'm a little kid. I feel ridiculous.

I also feel, for the first time since I arrived in Colorado, actually warm.

"Better?" he asks, when I'm back in all my layers.

"So much better." I pause, awkward. "Thanks."

We stand there for a moment, the stove crackling softly. His eyes hold mine. I don't look away.

Then his phone buzzes, and the moment breaks.

"Judy," he says, checking the screen. "I should—"

"Yeah. Me, too."

We walk out together, back into the cold. But thanks to Ben, I'm not shivering anymore.

THE NEXT MORNING, BEFORE I PUT ON MY LAYERED jackets, I slip on a borrowed sweater that smells like cedar and soil and someone I'm trying very hard not to think about. After triaging a frenzy of early morning deliveries, I take the ten a.m. shuttle down the mountain and find my way to the community center. The Santa's Helpers are running low on stationery.

The community center is a converted church hall with stained glass windows and the faintly musty smell of old hymnals. I push through the door with two boxes of preprinted cardstock sheets and find myself in the middle of organized chaos.

Long tables stretch across the room, each one occupied by volunteers sorting through piles of letters. Children's handwriting, mostly, in crayon and pencil and the occasional glitter pen. But I spot adult letters, too, the handwriting cramped or careful or shaky with age.

A woman looks up from the nearest table. Silver hair in a

chic pixie cut, reading glasses on a chain around her neck. Sharp eyes, kind face. The look of a woman who's heard every story and judged none of them.

"You must be Madison. We spoke earlier." She rises, extending a hand. "Heloise Whitmore. I coordinate the Santa's Helpers program."

"Nice to meet you." I set down the box and look around at the frenzied pace of the volunteers. "I can see why you were running low on stationery."

"Bless you. The response has been overwhelming this year." Heloise gestures at the stacks of letters. "We're up thirty percent from last season."

"That's a lot of letters."

"And every one deserves an answer." She smiles. "That's what Ford always said. Gloria's husband, you know. He started this program fifty years ago."

I look around the room, taking in the volunteers. A man with wire-rimmed glasses and a tweed jacket is reading a letter with the intensity of someone grading a dissertation. Nearby, a younger woman with a kind face is composing a response, a ball-point pen caught between her teeth in concentration.

"That's Zeb." Heloise points to the man in tweed. "Literature professor at the community college. His responses are practically poetry. Beside him is Clara, who specializes in letters to older children and teenagers. She's a school counselor. She understands what it's like to be too old to believe but too young to stop wanting to."

At the far table, an older woman glances up, studies me for a moment longer than comfortable, then returns to her work.

"That's Dr. Sinclair," Heloise says, following my gaze. "She's one of our best writers. Very insightful."

"She's a doctor?"

"Psychologist. Semi-retired. She has a gift for reading between the lines."

Dr. Sinclair, I notice, is holding a calligraphy pen. On her desk, I spot a glass jar of burnished gold ink—the kind used to write the recipient's name on the envelope. The kind that had made my name glitter.

Of course, when I look, I see gold ink at every writer's place. Standard issue for addressing envelopes, apparently. So much for that clue.

I watch them work. Zeb murmurs phrases under his breath as he writes. Clara's adding a postscript to an envelope. Dr. Sinclair's pen moves in quick, decisive strokes.

Any one of them could have written my letter. The wisdom could have come from Heloise's years of experience, or Zeb's literary sensibility, or Dr. Sinclair's clinical insight, or Clara's trained empathy.

"How does it work?" I ask. "The matching, I mean. How do you decide who answers which letter?"

Heloise smiles. "Whoever picks it up. Volunteers take them as they're ready. It's random, really. The magic is in the response, not the system."

Random. So there's no way to trace back who answered mine.

Maybe that's better. There's something freeing about writing to a stranger—no history, no judgment, just words on a page. If I knew who it was, I'd have to see them around town. Wonder what they thought of me. Perform gratitude instead of feeling it.

Dr. Sinclair looks up again, meeting my eyes with an expression I can't quite read. There's something knowing in the tilt of her head, but I just smile and look away.

Better to let the letters stay magic.

I thank Heloise for the tour and head back to the shuttle stop. The sweater is warm against my skin—too warm, actually, for the heated bus, but I don't take it off.

I'm ready for coffee when I make it back to Winterbloom. The line at Judy's café is seven people deep, which gives me plenty of time to notice that, in between customers, Judy is looking at me with a twinkle in her eyes. It's a full-on mischievous gleam when I make it to the counter.

"Well, well. That's a lovely sweater. Very seasonal. And it matches your eyes."

Ben's copper-colored cable-knit is approximately three sizes too big for me. The sleeves stick out of Sienna's too-short fluffy coat, covering my hands. But still, who notices that?

Judy notices it, that's who.

"As a matter of fact, I recognize that sweater." She points to the three embroidered initials on the cuff—BRB—which I'd found hilarious when I noticed them last night. "I gave it to a certain someone who runs the hothouse."

"Oh. Uh..." Can I pass off the embarrassed flush I feel spreading over my cheeks as a byproduct of the cold? I exaggerate a shiver, just in case.

Judy slides my coffee across the counter with a smirk. She's already memorized my order, which has never happened to me once in Miami. I guess it's a small-town thing.

"Mm hmm." She starts to say more, but I'm saved when one of her assistants calls out that they're running low on lettuce for the sandwiches. She turns to me with a certain kind of grin. "Madison, be a dear, won't you? Run over to the hothouse and ask Ben to bring us more lettuce."

She adds a hefty dose of cream to another cup of black coffee before snapping on the lid and pushing it my way.

"No sugar with a criminal amount of cream. Now you

know how he takes it. And tell him I need the butter lettuce, not the romaine."

I grab both cups and escape before she can say anything else.

The walk to the hothouse takes approximately ninety seconds. I spend eighty-seven of them telling myself this is just business. An errand. A favor for Judy. There's absolutely no reason my pulse should be doing whatever it's doing.

It's the altitude. Definitely the altitude. *Only* the altitude.

The hothouse door is heavier than I remember, and I have to hip-check it open while balancing two coffees. The warmth hits me immediately—humid and fragrant and alive—but I'm so focused on not spilling anything that I almost walk straight into Ben.

He's standing right inside the entrance with a bag of soil over one shoulder, clearly on his way somewhere. When he sees me, he slams to a stop. The soil slides forward so he has to catch the bag.

"Hey," he says. Then his eyes drop to the two cups in my hands, and he smiles. Not his usual easy smile. Something less practiced.

"Uh, hi. Judy needs lettuce." I hold out his cup. "And I was already in line, so I decided to pay my debt. She said you take it with a criminal amount of cream."

He sets down the soil and takes it, his fingers brushing mine. Neither of us acknowledges this.

"Keep showing up like this and I might start leaving my radio off on purpose." He stops. Seems to replay his own words. "That was a joke." A beat. "Mostly." He clears his throat. "Lettuce. You said Judy needs lettuce."

Are hothouses supposed to be this warm?

"Butter lettuce," I say, because I need to say something. "Not romaine. She was very specific."

"I'll take some up. No problem."

I should go. That's what a professional person would do. A person who wasn't looking for excuses to linger in a hothouse with a man whose sweater she definitely slept in last night.

"Actually, come with me." He heads to the double glass doors leading into the back and holds one open for me. I follow him to his workbench, where he fishes up a shopping bag that he holds out to me. "I have something for you."

"You—what?"

He pushes the bag into my hands.

"It's nothing, just something I..." He shakes his head. "Just open it."

The bag is heavier than I expected, the paper crinkling under my grip. He's suddenly studying his workbench like the soil is fascinating. I reach inside. My fingers find fabric—thick, soft, the kind of weight that means warmth.

I pull out a coat.

It's beautiful. Long, deep burgundy wool, with a fitted bodice and a skirt that flares out below the waist. A coat a Victorian Christmas caroler might have worn, or the heroine in one of those old holiday movies my grandmother and I used to watch. The kind of thing I would have ogled in a store window but deemed too whimsical, too romantic, too impractical for someone like me.

"It's a reproduction, not vintage," Ben says, like I might find this a drawback. "Dorothy—she runs the thrift store in town—said it came in last week. Some company that makes vintage styles. It's got some kind of special lining that makes it warmer than it looks."

I hold it up, speechless.

"You're always cold. And you're still wearing Sienna's coat, which is too short and too...I don't know, you look miserable in it. I saw this and thought of you."

"Ben, I can't—"

"It wasn't much. Dorothy gave me the family discount. She was Gramps's favorite cousin. He brought her hothouse flowers that didn't quite make market standard. Now I do, too."

I look at him. This man who noticed I've been freezing here. Who thought of me when he saw a coat in a thrift shop. Who took flowers to an old woman because his grandfather used to. Who covered eight thousand dollars of my mistake without making me feel incompetent.

"Try it on," he says. "If you want."

I shrug out of layers of windbreaker and fluffy cropped coat so I can slip my arms into the burgundy wool. The fitted bodice nips in at my waist. The flared skirt falls a few inches below my knees. The silky liner is soft against his sweater, which is soft against the blouse sliding against my skin. I feel warm—actually warm. And not just from the coat.

I glance down at myself. I look like I stepped out of a Christmas postcard.

"Well?" Ben's voice is careful.

I smooth my hands down the front.

"I don't know what to say. It's perfect. Thank you." I meet his eyes. "Really. This is—no one's ever—"

I don't know how to finish that sentence. No one's ever just *noticed* like this. Paid attention without being asked. Showed up with exactly the right thing at exactly the right moment, expecting nothing in return.

Something about it cracks me open. The armor I've been wearing—the spreadsheets, the systems, the snap judgments about everyone I meet—it's already dented. Full of holes from ice sculptures and viral videos and a career that crumbled beneath me. But standing here in his sweater beneath this coat, surrounded by all the ways he's learned to hold himself together—

Maybe I don't need armor anymore.

"Madison." His voice is quiet.

I look up. We're close. Close enough that I can see the gold flecks in his eyes, the slight unevenness of his breathing. The way his gaze drops to my mouth and then back up again.

He reaches toward me and for a breathless second, I think he's going to lean in. Instead, his hand adjusts the collar of the coat. His thumb traces the edge of the fabric, so light I might be imagining it.

"Now you look like you belong here."

Here could mean Colorado. It could mean Winterbloom. It could mean something else.

His fingers leave the collar, skim upward now, featherlight on the curve of my neck. He hesitates there, giving me time to step back.

But I don't step back.

I forget how to breathe.

The hothouse hums around us, grow lights and fountains and the soft green silence of growing things. I can feel my pulse in my throat, right where his thumb rests.

I sway toward him. He sways toward me.

The hothouse door bangs open.

"Ben!" Gloria's voice cuts through the humid air.

He steps back so fast I almost stumble. The warmth from his hand vanishes, replaced by its phantom pressure against my skin.

"Gran." He clears his throat. "I was just—"

"I can see what you were just." Her tone is unreadable. "Judy is out of lettuce. She needs it now." Her gaze flicks between us, lands on the bag at my feet and the coat that I'm wearing, on Ben's sweater, visible at the cuffs. Her eyes sharpen. "Ben, go. Madison, I'd like to see you in my office when you have a moment."

It's not a request.

She's gone an instant later, the door swinging shut behind her.

Ben runs a hand through his hair. "I should—"

"Yeah. Go."

He hesitates. Looks at me in the burgundy coat, framed by his seedlings and his sticky notes and all the ways he's learned to make things grow. Like he's memorizing this—the coat, the moment, me standing in the middle of everything he's built.

Then he shoulders a crate of lettuce and goes, and I'm alone in the hothouse with the plants and the grow lights and a heart that won't stop racing.

I press my hand to my neck where his fingers had lingered. Six weeks. That's all this is. Six weeks. Except now, only four are left. And standing here in his sweater, in this beautiful coat, surrounded by evidence of how hard he works to hold everything together...

It suddenly feels like it might not be long enough.

GLORIA'S OFFICE IS AT THE END OF THE MAIN hallway, past the restaurant and the staff dining area and what feels like a mile of my own anxious footsteps.

I know I'm not getting fired. Probably. You don't fire someone by saying "when you have a moment" in that clipped, grandmother-knows-best tone. You fire someone by saying "we need to talk" or "clean out your desk" or "the ice sculpture was supposed to be swans, not chickens, Madison."

But I also know what she saw. Me standing close enough to count the gold flecks in her grandson's eyes, his thumb resting in the hollow of my throat.

Professional. Very professional.

Her door is open. She's seated behind a massive oak desk that probably predates electricity, reading glasses perched on her nose, a stack of papers in front of her. The office is immaculate—nothing like the chaos I inherited from Phoebe. Leather-bound ledgers on the shelves behind her, each one labeled by year in neat gold script going back decades. A bay window overlooking the market, where I can see the bustle of a day in full swing without me.

And photographs. Everywhere, photographs.

The wall beside her desk is a mosaic of family history. Ford and Gloria, young and radiant on their wedding day, her dress simple and his smile enormous. Ford breaking ground on what must be the chalet, shovel in hand, mountains behind him. A Christmas photo from the sixties, judging by the hair—Gloria in a red sweater, a serious-faced young boy beside her, a toddler in a pink dress laughing in Ford's arms.

And Ben. Ben is all over the wall.

I recognize him immediately. Same bright eyes, same easy grin, same dark curls that refuse to behave. In one photo, he's maybe eight, holding up a fish nearly as big as he is, beaming at whoever's behind the camera. In another, he's a gangly preteen with braces and a science fair ribbon, standing next to a project I can't quite make out.

He looks proud. Hopeful. Like someone who hasn't yet learned that the world doesn't always reward honest, good-faith effort.

"Sit down, Madison."

I sit.

She removes her reading glasses and folds them, setting them on top of the papers. Takes her time. A clock ticks somewhere behind me. Through the bay window, the market noise is muffled to a murmur. I resist the urge to fill the quiet with nervous chatter, which is harder than it sounds.

"You've done excellent work since you arrived," she says finally. "Sienna was right to recommend you. You're organized, you're intelligent, and you handle problems without creating new ones. That's rarer than you might think."

"Thank you." I wait for the but. There's definitely a but.

"But." She leans back in her chair. "I need to be direct with you about something, and I hope you'll receive it in the spirit it's intended."

My stomach tightens. "Of course."

"Ben is..." She pauses, choosing her words with the care of someone who's thought about this for a long time. "Ben is the best parts of his grandfather." Her voice softens when she says it, her gaze drifting to the photo of Ford breaking ground on the chalet. "The vision. The creativity. The way he sees possibility where other people see problems. Ford always said Ben would be the one to carry Winterbloom forward."

I stay quiet. This doesn't feel like a conversation that needs my input.

"He's also spent most of his life being underestimated. By teachers who didn't understand how he learned. By people who only saw the scattered surface and never bothered to look deeper. By his own parents, who—" She stops herself. Takes a breath. "By most people, if I'm honest." Her gaze sharpens. "Including, I suspect, by you. At first."

"I misjudged him," I admit. "I know that now."

"Good. Then you'll understand why I'm protective." She picks up a pen from her desk, turns it in her fingers. "Three years ago, Ben came back from Boulder. His business had failed. He was...*broken* isn't too strong a word. Not only because of the company. There was a woman. A partner, in every sense. He was passionate about their business. So was she."

She.

Not Bree giggling at him in her hot chocolate stall. Not Lacey adjusting his scarf. Someone else. Someone who mattered.

"The business started struggling. Cash flow problems. A

supplier that didn't deliver. The usual things that kill startups. It could have been weathered. Plenty of companies survive such crises. But she left." Gloria sets the pen down with a soft click. "When things got hard, she left. Taking half the remaining assets and most of his confidence with her."

My throat burns. The failed packaging company. The therapy bills. The way he'd said *it taught me what I'm not good at* like he'd memorized a script to make it hurt less.

Someone taught him that lesson. Someone who was supposed to love him.

"Ford helped him get himself back," Gloria continues. "Let him try his sustainability ideas here. Gave him projects in the hothouse. Let him fail at small things until he remembered he could succeed. It's been slow progress, but it's been real progress. He's starting to believe in himself again."

She looks out the bay window at the ice skaters whirling around the rink. Her voice wavers, slightly, when she says, "Ford died before Ben was ready. Before any of us were ready. And now Ben is trying to prove he can carry this place forward, and I—" She stops and turns back to face me. "This season matters. Not just for Winterbloom's survival. For his."

"I understand."

"Do you?" Her voice isn't unkind, but it is unflinching. "You're only here for six weeks. You have your own career, your own future. I'm not questioning your character. I've seen enough to know you're not the type to toy with someone's feelings. But I've also seen the way he looks at you. And the way you've started looking at him."

I don't have a response to that. Because she's right. And we both know it. I was standing in his hothouse ten minutes ago, heart pounding, ready to close the distance between us.

"I'm asking you to be careful," Gloria says. "Not for my

sake. For his. He's lost enough. I won't watch him lose more because someone let him fall in love with her and then left."

The words settle over me like snow, cold and quiet and heavy.

She's not wrong. I am leaving. After six weeks at Winterbloom, I'm going back to Florida to be close to my family, to rebuild what's left of my career. And Ben—with his sticky notes and his seedlings and his quiet hope that this time things might work out—Ben deserves better than someone who's already got one foot out the door.

"I do understand," I say quietly. It's not a commitment. It's not a denial. It's simply the truth.

Gloria studies me for a long moment. Whatever she's looking for, I'm not sure she finds it, but eventually she nods.

"That's all I ask." She returns to her desk, puts her reading glasses back on. Apparently I'm dismissed. "The Ballentines are checking into the Evergreen Suite at three. Longtime guests that return each year for the luminaries. Make sure the welcome basket is ready."

Just like that, we're back to business.

"It will be," I say, and leave before she can see how much this conversation has rattled me.

The rest of the day passes in a blur of tasks I barely remember completing. I personally deliver the Ballentines' welcome basket. I confirm tomorrow's vendor deliveries. I solve a crisis involving a double-booked event space and call a very upset bride-to-be who wanted the Snowdrop Room for her rehearsal dinner. I do my job, and I do it well, because that's what I know how to do when everything else feels like it's spinning out of control.

I don't see Ben. I'm not sure if that's deliberate—his avoidance or mine—but the hothouse door stays closed every time I pass it, and I don't let myself wonder what he's doing in there. I throw myself into my tasks with the focus of someone who does not have time to think about green eyes and borrowed sweaters and gorgeous burgundy coats.

But the coat is warm. Warmer than anything I've worn since I arrived. Every time I catch a glimpse of myself in a window—the fitted bodice, the flared skirt, the absolutely impractical beauty of it—I hear him. *I saw this and thought of you.*

Who does that? Who notices that someone is cold and goes out of their way to find them something so warm and beautiful?

Someone who's been hurt enough to pay attention to hurt in others.

I adjust the collar—the same collar his fingers brushed hours ago—and get back to work.

She's right. Of course she's right. I'm a temporary fix for a seasonal problem, and getting tangled up with the owner's grandson is exactly the kind of complication neither of us need. I came here to escape one disaster, not to create another.

This position lasts six weeks. I have to keep my head down, do my job, and let Ben do his in peace. Then go back to Miami with a decent reference and maybe—hopefully—some semblance of a plan for what comes next.

That's the smart move. The professional move. The move that doesn't end with me crying into a pint of Cherry Garcia.

I've already done that once. I don't need a repeat.

By the time the market closes and I trudge upstairs to my room, I'm exhausted in a way that has nothing to do with the physical labor. Gloria's words keep circling in my head. *He came home broken. She left when things got hard. He's lost enough.*

Outside my bedroom window, the market lights are twinkling like they're mocking me with their cheer. And I'm still wearing the burgundy coat, thinking of his fingers adjusting the collar, his thumb tracing the fabric and then my skin, the way he looked at me like—

Stop it.

I hang the coat in the closet. Then I take it back out and drape it over the chair because the closet feels too far away. Then I roll my eyes at myself and leave it on the chair because apparently I've lost all capacity for rational decision-making.

Maybe Santa can help.

I pull out the last letter from my nightstand drawer and read.

The failure isn't in the first impression. It's in refusing to update it when new information arrives.

I think about Ben. The version I'd constructed in my head—charming, unreliable, coasting on family connections—versus the man I'm actually starting to know. The one who builds elaborate systems to accommodate a brain that works differently. Who covers for a stranger's expensive mistake without rubbing it in. Who carries on his grandfather's tradition of taking hothouse flowers to an elderly woman who has excellent taste in coats.

I've updated my impression of him. That's not the problem.

The problem is what I'm supposed to do about it now.

Gloria's voice echoes in my head: *He's lost enough. I won't watch him lose more because someone let him fall in love with her and then left.*

And this stranger's voice, written in elegant script on cream-colored paper: *Trust yourself. You're learning a new way of seeing.*

Somewhere below, a mailbox waits to swallow whatever I write next.

Six weeks.

It's long enough to change everything. Or long enough to ruin it.

OF COURSE I WAKE UP THE NEXT MORNING WITH Gloria's voice still in my head.

He's lost enough.

The burgundy coat hangs over the chair where I left it, and for a long moment I stare at it. Wearing it feels like a declaration. Not wearing it feels like a rejection. I put it on anyway, because it's cold and I'm not about to freeze out of cowardice, but I catch myself adjusting the collar the way he did—thumb tracing the edge of the fabric—and have to stop.

The market is already humming when I step outside. Vendors setting up, early visitors clutching coffee, the sweet scent of Judy's pastries drifting through the cold air. A normal Saturday at Winterbloom.

And then I see him.

He's crossing the market toward Judy's café, and something behind my ribs does a complicated twist—half longing, half warning. Gloria's voice echoes again: *He's lost enough.*

He spots me. Stops walking. For a moment we just stand

there, twenty feet apart, the market bustling around us like we're the still point at the center of a snow globe.

Then he smiles. Not his easy, charming smile. This one is smaller. More uncertain. Like he's not sure what happened yesterday either, but he knows we've crossed into some new space.

I want to close the distance between us. I want to tell him the coat is the most thoughtful gift anyone's ever given me. I want to feel his thumb trace my collar again, settle into the hollow of my throat...

Instead, I lift my hand in an awkward wave and turn toward the vendor stalls.

Be careful. He's lost enough.

I spend the morning being careful. Which is to say: I throw myself into work with the focus of someone trying very hard not to think about anything except spreadsheets and delivery schedules and whether the pretzel vendor has enough salt.

It almost works, except Ben is everywhere. Joking with Agnes. Helping Derek with a sound issue at the skating rink. Talking to Mrs. Chen, who pats his arm in her maternal way. Crossing my peripheral vision like a magnet I keep having to resist.

But around noon, the energy in the market shifts.

I feel it before I see the cause—a subtle tension rippling through the staff, conversations trailing off mid-sentence, smiles becoming slightly fixed. I pass Judy coming into the chalet as I'm heading out and her expression tightens almost imperceptibly. But she's looking past me.

A man is striding across the cobblestones toward the entrance.

He's maybe sixty, tall and lean, wearing a cashmere overcoat that probably cost more than my monthly rent in Miami

—the nice place, not the dump I just left. Silver hair swept back from a face that would be handsome if it weren't so grim. Everything about him radiates authority. The kind that expects to be obeyed without question.

And walking beside him, shoulders slightly hunched, is Ben.

I've never seen Ben look small before. He's at least six-two, broad-shouldered and frankly, gorgeous. He has the kind of presence that usually fills the room without trying. Even when we were fighting, when I was accusing him of things he hadn't done, he held his ground—shoulders squared, those green eyes holding mine without flinching. But something about this man's presence has diminished him. Collapsed his shoulders inward. Made him look younger. Less certain.

"Madison Lark?"

I startle. The man has stopped in front of me, assessing me with pale blue eyes that miss nothing.

"Yes?"

"Ah." A thin smile that doesn't reach his eyes. "The temp. Glad you could be here this season."

Before I can respond, he's already moving past me through the big double doors, Ben trailing like a boat trapped in a rip current.

"That's Trip," Sienna says, appearing at my elbow. "Ben's dad. Gloria's son."

"I gathered." I watch them disappear through the main doors. "He seems..."

"Like a jerk?" She nods. "He runs some big investment firm in Denver. Only shows up when he wants something."

"What does he want?"

Sienna's expression darkens. "He wants Gloria to sell."

The rest of the afternoon, I catch fragments and staff

rumors of what's happening inside. Raised voices from Gloria's office, quickly muffled. Ben emerging once to grab coffee from Judy's, his jaw tight and his eyes distant. Gloria on the phone with someone, her tone clipped and professional in a way that suggests she's holding something back.

After a few hours of catching snippets of the staff buzzing with reports of what's going on inside, I may or may not have made a nosy choice to clean out the filing cabinets in my office—the last of Phoebe's chaos. I'm sorting through drawerfuls of her cryptic notes when I hear Trip and Ben leave Gloria's office and step across the hall into Ben's. The one he never uses because he prefers the hothouse. The one that shares a wall with mine.

"Your ideas are completely unrealistic." Trip's voice carries, sharp and dismissive. "Ian Preston is offering real money. Guaranteed money. Not some fantasy about sustainable greenhouses and artisanal cheese."

"It's not a fantasy." Ben's voice is quieter but firm. "Gramps and I had a plan—"

"Your grandfather was losing his mind at the end. You know that as well as I do."

The silence that follows is devastating.

"The hothouse project has potential," Ben says finally. "If you'd look at the numbers—"

"I've looked at the numbers. They're projections based on best-case scenarios that have never materialized. Just like the packaging company. Like every other idea you've had." Trip's sigh is theatrical. "Ben, I'm not trying to be cruel. I'm trying to be realistic. You can't pill your way out of a lack of follow-through."

I stop breathing.

Pill your way out.

He's talking about Ben's ADHD. The thing Ben has worked so hard to manage, building elaborate systems and now even getting professional help. And his father is using it as evidence of failure.

"That's not—" Ben starts.

"Your grandmother is eighty-three years old. She went into AFib six months ago. She can't keep running this place, and we both know you're not capable of taking over. Selling to Ian is the responsible choice."

"You mean the profitable choice."

"I mean the only choice that makes sense for everyone involved. Including you." Trip's voice softens, but I don't hear any warmth in it. "You could use your share of the proceeds to start fresh somewhere. Get away from this place and all its memories. It might be good for you."

Get away. Like Winterbloom is the problem. Like Ben's attachment to his grandfather's legacy is something to be cured.

I hear footsteps approaching and quickly busy myself with the filing cabinet. Trip passes my door without a glance, already on his phone, already moved on to the next thing.

Ben doesn't pass. He stops in my doorway.

He looks wrecked. Hollowed out. Like someone—his own father—had reached inside him and scooped out everything that makes him who he is.

"Hey," I say softly.

"Hey." His voice is rough. "Sorry you had to hear that."

"I didn't—"

"The walls are thin." He almost smiles. "This whole place is thin walls and old secrets."

I don't know what to say. Gloria's warning rings in my ears

—*be careful*—but careful feels like the wrong response to this moment. Careful feels like abandonment.

"Your father is wrong," I say instead. "About all of it."

Ben's eyes meet mine. "You don't know that."

"I know what I've seen. The hothouse. The systems you've built. The way you are with the vendors, with the kids who come through Santa's workshop." I take a breath. "I know your grandfather believed in you. And I don't think that was dementia talking."

For a long moment, he just looks at me. Then he sways slightly, catching himself on the doorframe.

"Ben?"

"I'm fine." But he's pale now, a sheen of sweat on his forehead that wasn't there a moment ago. "Just tired. It's been a long day."

"You don't look fine. You look like you're about to pass out."

"I'm not going to—" He stops. Closes his eyes. "Okay. Maybe I'm not fine."

"When did you last eat?"

"I don't remember."

"What did you last eat?"

"Also don't remember."

I'm already moving, grabbing my coat—*the* coat—and making him put on his own. I steer him toward the door. "Come on."

"Where are we going?"

"Somewhere your dad is not."

His cabin is a five-minute walk from the chalet, tucked into the trees behind the hothouse. I've passed it before without really seeing it—just another outbuilding in the Winterbloom complex. But inside, it's completely Ben.

Warm. Cozy. Unpretentious. And filled with living, growing things. It's maybe four hundred square feet, if I'm being generous. A single room with a bed tucked into one corner, a kitchenette with a small table and two chairs in another, and a shabby couch beneath one big paned window. Every available surface is covered in plants. Seedlings on the windowsills. Herbs hanging from the ceiling to dry. A massive fern cascading from a shelf above the bed like a green waterfall.

There are books everywhere, too—stacked on the floor and piled on the nightstand. Gardening manuals. Business books. A dog-eared copy of something called *When Attention Wanders* that I recognize from my college roommate as an ADHD classic.

And on the tiny kitchen counter, a mug that reads WORLD'S OKAYEST GRANDSON.

"You were right. I'm mooching off the family, like you thought. But it's not the penthouse suite I bet you were picturing." He follows my gaze to the fern over his headboard. "She came with the place. Couldn't bring myself to evict her."

"She's clearly thriving."

I look around, take in all the ways he's made this place his own. It fits.

"I was envisioning something much less alive." I gesture at the plants colonizing the place. "This makes more sense."

I find a can of vegetable soup in his cabinet, heat it on the ancient stove, and press it into his hands, but he can barely grip the mug. His fingers fumble against it, clumsy and weak. I catch it before it spills, then press my hand to his forehead. Hot. Too hot.

"When did you start feeling sick?"

"Somewhere between Gramps being senile and pills not fixing my personality," he says, making me think violent thoughts about Trip Bennett. "I said that Santa beard was a biohazard. Should've trusted my instincts."

He manages half the soup before pushing it away. His eyes are glassy now, his skin flushed, and he's starting to shiver even though the cabin isn't cold.

"You should go," he says after his temperature clocks in at nearly a hundred and two. "I don't want you to catch this."

"I've already been exposed. The damage is done."

"That's not how—"

"Ben. Lie down."

He's too tired to argue and stumbles to his bed, dropping onto it without even taking off his shoes. I debate removing them for him for at least ten seconds before telling myself to stop being a control freak and let the man sleep.

"Cold," he mumbles, even though he's still in his coat.

I find an extra blanket in the closet and spread it over him, then sit nearby on that battered couch and do my best not to be a weirdo who watches him sleep.

Except the place is small, and I forgot my phone, and there's not much to do. I borrow the ADHD book and another on ferns, but every now and then...well, he's cute. It's hard not to sneak a peek.

He looks younger like this. Softer. The tension that lives in his jaw, the watchful way he holds himself around his father—all of it's smoothed away. I think about what Gloria told me. *Broken isn't too strong a word.* Looking at him now, I can imagine it. I can imagine what it would take to break someone this stubborn, this hopeful, this determined to believe that things might work out.

Wind pushes against the windows. The cabin creaks and settles. I sit on the couch and listen to Ben breathe—rough but steady—and try not to think about anything else. After a couple of hours, he sits up, so I check his temperature again. Hotter now—nearly a hundred and three—not good.

She left when things got hard.

Not me. Not tonight.

He's asleep two minutes later, and I use my smart watch to text Sienna to let her know I'm handling a staff emergency. She responds with a string of messages:

??????????

Is it Ben???

OMG IT'S BEN

Details! Tomorrow!

Typical Sienna.

He sleeps fitfully through the evening, occasionally mumbling things I can't quite make out. I press a cool washcloth to his neck and receive an unconscious "Madison." At one point he says "Gramps" in a voice so raw my stomach twists. At another, he says something that sounds like "sorry" repeated over and over, a litany of apologies to someone who isn't here.

I wonder who he's apologizing to. His grandfather. His father. The woman who left.

Around midnight, his fever breaks. He wakes up long enough to drink some water and register surprise at finding me still there.

"You stayed."

"I stayed."

"Thank you. You didn't have to."

"I know."

He falls back asleep before he can say anything else, but

there's something in his expression—soft, unguarded—that stays with me long after his breathing evens out.

I should go. There's nothing more I can do here, and tomorrow is Sunday, another busy market day, another round of vendors and crises and professionalism.

But I don't go. I stay on the couch, wrapped in a blanket that smells like cedar and soil—like him—and watch over him until the first gray light of dawn creeps through the windows.

Somewhere in those quiet hours, I start composing a letter in my head.

Not about Ben. Not about Trip or Gloria or any of the complicated tangles of this place. About something older. Something I've never told anyone.

When Ben finally wakes up properly—groggy but lucid, his fever thankfully gone—I slip out with a promise to send up some of Judy's soup. Then I walk through an empty early-morning Winterbloom, past the skating rink where the ice gleams untouched, past the vendor stalls just starting to stir, all the way to the cherry-red mailbox at the center of it all.

I pull out a new page of stationery from the cabinet. And I write.

Dear Santa,

I need to tell you something I've never told anyone. Not Sienna. Not even my parents, really—not the whole truth of it.

When I was seventeen, my grandmother got sick. Cancer. The kind that moves fast and doesn't care how much you love someone.

She was my favorite person in the world. She taught me to bake, to organize, to make lists and check them twice. She used to say I had "an old soul and a young heart" and I never knew exactly what she meant but I loved that she saw something in me worth naming.

When she went into hospice, I wrote her a letter. A real letter, on paper, because she always said handwritten notes meant more. I told her I loved her. I told her I was scared. I told her I didn't know who I would be without her.

I never sent it.

I kept waiting for the right moment. Kept thinking I'd give it to her in person, read it to her myself. Kept putting it off because sending it felt too final, like admitting she was really going to die.

She died on a Tuesday. The letter was still in my desk drawer.

I've carried that with me ever since. Not the grief, necessarily, but the knowledge that I waited too long. That I had something to say and I was too scared to say it.

I think that's why I've preferred to be alone. Don't get me wrong, I've dated people. Decent guys, I guess, most of them. There was a man at work I saw for almost a year, another I met at a friend's wedding who I dated for six months. But I always found a reason to keep things light. To end it before it got too real. I told myself I was focused on my career, and that was true. But it was also true that I never let anyone close enough to leave a mark.

It was easier that way. Safer.

There's someone here. Someone I've been trying very hard not to care about. He makes me laugh. Real laughter, not the polite kind I've been faking for months, maybe years. He sees through my defenses every time and instead of using them against me, he waits. Like he believes I'm smart enough—sincere enough—to come around.

He's fighting for something bigger than himself. His

grandfather's legacy, this place, the people who depend on it. He could have walked away a dozen times—his family practically begged him to—but he stayed. He keeps staying.

I don't know what to do with someone like that. Someone who doesn't quit.

Tonight I watched over him until his fever broke, and I thought about how much I respect him, how much I care. About all the things I'm too scared to say.

I don't want to be seventeen years old again, hiding letters in desk drawers.

I just don't know how to be anything else.

Maddie

I fold the letter. Slide it through the slot. Stand there in the cold morning air, watching my breath fog and fade, wondering what I've just confessed and to whom.

Then I go back to the chalet to start another day.

THE PROBLEM WITH CARING FOR SOMEONE WHEN they're sick is that it creates a very specific kind of intimacy.

You see them vulnerable. Stripped of the defenses they usually wear. You see them sleep and hear them mumble in their fever dreams. You press a cold cloth to their skin and feel something shift inside you—something you'd been holding at arm's length since the moment you met. Somewhere in those quiet hours, everything changes. Because once you've seen all that, you can't unsee it. Every interaction afterward carries the weight of that knowledge. The awareness that beneath this person's surface, beneath the charm and the chaos, there's something tender and breakable.

And I don't know what to do with any of it.

The burgundy coat hangs over my chair where I left it yesterday, beautiful and impractical and chosen specifically for me. I pull it on, because the alternative is Sienna's cropped I-sheared-a-mountain-goat-to-get-this coat, and because not wearing it would be a snub I'm not capable of inflicting on Ben. Not after what I witnessed with Trip.

So I wear the coat. And every moment I'm wrapped in it, I think of him.

I'm opening the door to my office when an email notification on my phone stops me mid-stride.

SUBJECT: AN OPPORTUNITY
FROM: CAROLINE REYES

I haven't heard from Caroline in years—not since she left The Palms to start her own wedding planning company in Miami. We'd been close once. She'd trained me during my first year, taught me the difference between good enough and excellent, covered for me when I made rookie mistakes. Then she'd moved on, and I'd been too busy climbing to stay in touch.

I open the email right there in the doorway.

Maddie—

I know it's been too long. I'm sorry for that. I heard about what happened at The Palms, and I want to say right now, for the record, that anyone who's worked with you knows that disaster wasn't your fault. Devon needed a scapegoat, and you were convenient. It's disgusting, and I'm sorry.

Confetti & Co. is growing faster than I ever imagined. We've established ourselves in Miami, and now we're ready to expand. I'm opening a Naples office in January, and I need someone to lead it. Someone who can manage high-profile clients, coordinate complex events, and build something special from the ground up.

I thought of you immediately.

The position starts after New Year's. Competitive

salary, benefits, creative freedom—and you'd be running your own show. I know your parents are in Naples. This would put you right there with them.

I don't know where you've landed since The Palms, but wherever you are, I hope you'll consider this. Touch base if you want to talk.

—Caroline

I read it twice, standing in the dark of my office, before even flipping on the light.

A job. A real job, with someone who believes in me, doing work I'm actually trained for. A path back to the career I thought I'd lost. And Naples—I could see my parents and my nieces whenever I want, be there for Sunday dinners and school events and all the ordinary moments I've been missing.

This is everything I've wanted. Everything I've been desperately searching for since the ice sculpture disaster ended my life as I knew it.

So why does my stomach feel so tight?

I pocket my phone and settle into my chair. I'll think about it later. I have work to do.

That's when I see it.

A cream-colored envelope, centered perfectly on my desk.

My heart stutters. The envelope is exactly like the others—my name written in gold in that same elegant hand. But this time it wasn't slid under my bedroom door. It was placed deliberately on my workspace, positioned so I'd see it the moment I sat down.

Someone with access to staff areas left this here. But who?

I sink into my chair, fingers trembling slightly as I break the seal.

Dear Maddie,

I read your letter about your grandmother three times before I could respond. Not because it was difficult to read, although it was, but because I wanted to find the right words. You deserve the right words.

You were seventeen. Still a child, even though you probably didn't feel like one. And you were facing something no child should face: the slow, impossible loss of someone who shaped the person you were becoming.

You wrote your grandmother a letter. You put your love into words. That matters. The fact that she didn't get to read it doesn't erase what it meant. Don't forget, letters aren't only for the people who receive them. Sometimes they're more for the people who write them. A way of saying the things we can't say out loud, of making our feelings real by committing them to paper.

Your grandmother knew you loved her. Trust me, grandparents know. Not because you told her in a letter, but because you showed her every day, in a thousand small ways that words can't capture. Maybe the goodbye you wrote was never really for her. Maybe it was for you. A way to hold the feelings you couldn't speak.

Guilt is a heavy thing to carry. Heavier, sometimes, than grief. But you don't have to keep holding it. You can set it down. You can forgive yourself for being seventeen and scared and human.

Let the guilt go. The only person holding it against you is yourself.

Santa

After the fourth reading, my vision has blurred and I have

to set the letter down because my hands are shaking too much to hold it steady.

The only person holding it against you is yourself.

I think about my grandma—her soft, papery hands, her eyes the same cinnamon brown as mine, the way she called me her little organizer because as early as elementary school I was making lists of my stuffed animals and alphabetizing my picture books. I think about the letter in a box of old diaries in my old bedroom closet at my parents' house, yellowed now with age, still sealed in its envelope because I could never bring myself to open it.

I'd written to her. And then I'd waited for the perfect moment to send it, and the perfect moment never came, and then she was gone and the words were useless. A relic of a goodbye I never got to give.

But I consider it and decide that Santa's right. The letter was never really for her. It was for me. A way of holding the feelings I couldn't speak aloud because speaking them would have made everything too real.

I tuck the letter into the inside pocket of the burgundy coat, close to my heart. Then I wipe my eyes, take a breath, and try to focus on the day ahead.

I've barely started reviewing my schedule when Gloria's voice comes through the open door.

"Madison. A moment, please."

Her office door is open. Inside, I catch a glimpse of two familiar figures: Dr. Sinclair and Heloise from the community center, both bent over what looks like a ceremony program. They're laughing softly about something—old friends comfortable in each other's company.

I file this away. Both of them here in the staff area this morning. Meaning either one of them could be Santa.

"Come in," Gloria says, waving me toward the chair across from her desk. "We were discussing tomorrow's luminary ceremony."

"Thank goodness it's been so cold this year," Heloise says, which I firmly disagree with until she adds, "The lake is frozen solid, so we can do the ice luminaries."

"Last year we had to do candles on the shore instead," Dr. Sinclair adds. "It's lovely in its own way, but not quite the same."

"It's the first year we'll have luminaries since Ford..." Gloria takes a breath. Something soft crosses her face at the mention of her husband, there and gone. "He always loved to see them lit."

Dr. Sinclair puts her hand on Gloria's desk, support from a respectful distance. "Grief is a weary, winding road. But you carry on with walking it, and eventually you find new joy in what used to sting."

Something about the phrasing catches at me—an echo of words I've read before. I glance at Dr. Sinclair, but her attention is on Gloria, her expression warm with old friendship.

"Which brings me to why I asked you here," Gloria continues. "The ceremony has five traditions: Release, Hope, Remembrance, Beginnings, and Light. Dr. Sinclair speaks on Release. Sienna on Hope. Ben, if he's feeling well enough—he's still recovering—will speak on Remembrance. I close with Light."

I wait, not sure where this is going.

"I'd like you to fill Beginnings."

For a moment, I'm certain I've misheard. "Me?"

"You. Beginnings is about fresh starts. Finding hope in unfamiliar places. Who better to speak to that than someone who's actually doing it?"

"I've only been here a few weeks," I manage.

Heloise nods warmly. "Ford always said the ceremony should feel like a conversation. Different voices, different perspectives. What matters is showing up while you're still finding your way. That takes time. And courage."

Another familiar phrase.

Apparently every Santa's Helper is a poet philosopher. So much for narrowing it down.

Dr. Sinclair's gaze is assessing but not unfriendly. "New voices keep traditions from becoming museums. You'd be a welcome addition."

Gloria is watching me, waiting for an answer.

"I'd be honored," I hear myself say.

"Good." She returns to her papers, a clear dismissal. "Tomorrow at seven. Dress warmly. We'll be out on the ice."

I'm halfway down the hall before the reality hits me.

I have to write a speech. About new beginnings. And deliver it in front of the entire Winterbloom community while Ben—if he can make it—watches from a few feet away.

Sienna finds me at lunch, staring at a half-written draft that sounds wooden and false.

"I heard," she says, sliding into the seat across from me. "Gloria asked you to speak. That's huge."

"It's terrifying."

"No, it's an honor." She steals an olive off my salad. "Gloria doesn't ask outsiders to speak. Ever. Asking you means she's decided you're one of us." She grins. "You've been claimed."

"Claimed?"

"By the mountain. By Winterbloom. It's a whole thing. Very mystical. Agnes would explain it better, probably with crystals."

I smile, bigger than I've managed all day. "Thank you. I needed that."

She wanders away, and I look down at my draft, at the polished phrases that don't feel true. I'm supposed to speak on Beginnings while actively and seriously considering a job offer that would end my time at Winterbloom. That would take me back to Miami and away from everything I've started to build here.

The thought catches me off guard. Everything I've started to build here. When did I start thinking of it that way?

I shake my head and return to my draft.

What would Santa say about new beginnings?

I don't know. But I wish I could ask, because I guarantee it would be more insightful than anything I'm coming up with right now.

Tuesday arrives cold and gray, the kind of sky that makes the Christmas lights seem brighter by contrast.

I spend the morning finalizing team instructions for the ceremony and polishing my speech until every word sounds professional. By afternoon, I have five minutes' worth of remarks that hit all the right notes about fresh starts and finding your footing in unfamiliar places.

It's good. It's solid. It sounds like a speech someone should give at a ceremony full of insight and ice candles.

It just doesn't sound like me.

By six o'clock, the center of the market has been transformed. Wooden benches are arranged in an arc near the massive Christmas tree, facing the frozen lake beyond. The ice luminaries Sienna, Derek, and I had been freezing for days wait in neat rows near the shore—hundreds of them, each one a hollowed-out vessel no bigger than a cantaloupe, glinting in the last light. Staff members move among them with lighters and long matches, ready to light the candles nested inside once the speeches conclude.

Beyond the market, the frozen lake gleams silver in the twilight, its surface smooth and untouched, waiting to receive the lights.

People are already gathering. Families with bundled children. Couples holding hands. Visitors wrapped in fleece blankets provided by the staff. The energy is different than usual—quieter, more reverent. Like everyone knows they're about to witness something sacred.

I find my place with the other speakers near the front. Dr. Sinclair sits straight-backed and calm, the silver threaded through her dark hair catching the light. Sienna looks nervous but, as usual, upbeat. Gloria presides over everything with quiet authority.

And then I see him.

Ben. Standing slightly apart.

He's not wearing his usual insulated jacket. Instead, it's a black wool peacoat, sharp and fitted, the kind of thing that belongs in a magazine—and on him, it's devastating. The shoulders, the way it tapers at his waist. He looks like a problem I very much want.

His jaw is tight with something I can't read. His hands are shoved deep in his pockets.

There's nothing easy about him tonight. He's a man about to do something that will cost him.

He catches me looking. Our eyes meet, and something passes between us. Not the awkwardness I've been anticipating all day. Something raw. Honest.

I can't make myself look away. The moment stretches, weighted with everything we haven't said.

Then Gloria rises to speak, and the spell breaks.

She welcomes the crowd, her voice carrying clear and strong across the hushed assembly. She speaks of Ford, of Winterbloom, of the traditions that have anchored this community for decades. Her words are brief but weighted with meaning—the particular gravity of someone who knows exactly what she's fighting to preserve.

Then Dr. Sinclair takes her place.

Her speech on Release is measured and wise. She speaks on the burdens we insist on carrying, the old wounds we nurse, the emotions we hold long past their usefulness. I file away phrases for later consideration, but my attention keeps drifting to the man in the peacoat three seats away.

Sienna goes next. Hope. At first, her words tumble out too fast, but she finds her rhythm. If anyone was born to speak on choosing optimism, it's her. She radiates hope like light through a window. Her eyes find Mike and Evie at the edge of the crowd, and her face softens.

But now it's my turn.

I stand on legs that want to run back to the chalet. I make them walk to the platform. The crowd is a blur of expectant faces waiting to hear what wisdom this unfamiliar face could possibly offer.

My notes are folded and ready in my pocket. I've practiced them. I know they're good.

But I leave them where they are.

"I had something written. Something polished and professional. But the words felt like they belonged to someone else. So here are mine."

The crowd shifts. Settles.

"A few weeks ago, I was at my lowest point. I'd lost my job, my reputation, and my belief that hard work and good intentions would make things turn out right." I pause. "And then a friend called and offered me a chance. A temporary job at a Christmas market in Colorado. A place to start over."

I find that friend in the crowd. She's smiling.

"I didn't come here looking for a new beginning. I was looking for somewhere to hide. A pause button that would give me time to figure out what came next." My voice steadies. "But that's the thing about beginnings. They don't ask permission. They don't wait until you're ready. They just happen. In the people who take a chance on you. In the places that wake you up before you even realize you'd fallen asleep."

My gaze finds Ben without permission. He's watching me with an intensity that makes my next breath hard to find.

I look away before I lose my nerve.

"I don't know what my new beginning looks like yet. I'm still figuring it out. But I know it started here. With all of you." I swallow. "So thank you."

I step down to applause that's warmer than I expected, genuine rather than simply polite. Sienna squeezes my hand as I pass. Dr. Sinclair nods in what might be approval.

Then Ben stands. Remembrance.

He walks to the small wooden platform near the Christmas tree. No note cards. No prepared text. Just him and the crowd and the weight of everything his grandfather built.

"Ford Bennett was my best friend." His voice, still hoarse from the virus, catches on the words. He clears his throat. "That probably sounds strange. Your grandfather is supposed to be the guy who slips you candy when your parents aren't looking and falls asleep during football games. And Gramps was that, too. But he was also the person who believed in me when no one else did. Including me."

He shoves his hands deeper into his pockets. A protective gesture I'm starting to recognize.

"Three years ago, I came back to Winterbloom after some big losses. Gramps didn't give me a pep talk. He didn't tell me everything would be okay. He just handed me a pair of gardening gloves and said, 'Let's see what we can grow.'"

My eyes are stinging. I don't blink.

"Remembrance isn't only about honoring people we've lost. It's about carrying forward what they taught us. Gramps taught me that sometimes the most important thing you can do is show up—again and again—even when you're not sure you're enough."

His gaze sweeps the crowd. Lands on me.

Holds.

"He also taught me that the best things in life are the ones you don't see coming. The people who show up when you're not looking. The ones who change everything."

Is he still talking about Ford? About Winterbloom? Because he's looking at me. Only at me.

"So tonight, when you place your luminary on the ice, think about the people who shaped you. The ones who believed in you before you believed in yourself. And then carry them forward. In everything you do. In everyone you love."

He steps down. The crowd is quiet for a beat too long, sitting in that particular silence of people processing something that landed harder than expected. Then the applause comes, quieter than what came before but somehow deeper. More reverent.

Gloria rises for the final tradition: Light. Her words wash over me—something about wisdom and legacy and the responsibility of carrying forward what we've been given. I know I should be paying attention, but my thoughts keep circling back to the man in the peacoat and everything I'm not supposed to feel.

Then Gloria gestures toward the lake, and the crowd begins to move.

Our staff members work quickly now, touching long lighters to the candles nested inside each luminary. One by one, the vessels begin to glow—soft gold cradled in frosted globes, each flame like captured starlight.

Eventually I look up from lighting candles to watch the first people step onto the frozen lake. They move carefully, reverently, holding their luminaries. The ice is thick and solid beneath their feet—a foot deep, at least, more than enough to hold the crowd, yet we still make sure they go on in shifts. When they reach the spots they've chosen, they kneel and place the ice lanterns on the frozen surface. The effect is immediate and breathtaking—pools of warm light blooming against the silver-white expanse, growing as more and more people add their luminaries to the constellation.

Glimmerglass.

It perfectly fits. Ford Bennett had a way with words.

The crowd is quiet. I hear the scrape of boots on snow, the soft clink of luminaries touching ice, the hiss of matches being struck. The air smells like sulfur and candle wax and cold. I hug my arms to my chest and study the families clustered together, placing their luminaries in little groups. An elderly couple kneels side by side, their breath curling white into the cold air as they set their lights inches apart. Children slide and then stop, suddenly solemn, feeling if not understanding the weight of the ceremony.

I stand on the shore and take the beauty in as thoughts circle through my head. My grandmother. My guilt. The letter I never sent. The self-forgiveness I've never managed to find. I wish I'd saved a luminary for myself.

But I turn and, of course, there he is: Ben, with exactly

what I need. A luminary flickering in his upturned hand. The glow turning his face to gold.

"You deserve one, too." He holds it out to me.

"Thank you." The weight of it settles into my palms. Even through my gloves, I feel the chill.

The flame shimmers inside the ball's hollow center, writhing like a wish, like hope made real.

"You should place it," he says, but neither of us moves.

I look at the luminary, its edges softening where flame meets frost. At Ben, waiting.

"I know." I swallow. "I'm just not ready to let it go."

The amber glow radiates between us. He holds my eyes in the flickering light.

"Yeah." His voice drops to almost nothing. "I know the feeling."

Around us, the lake is a field of stars. Hundreds of luminaries scattered across the ice, their glow reflecting off the frozen surface until it's impossible to tell where the light ends and its reflection begins. The effect is dizzying, beautiful. Like standing at the edge of the sky.

The crowd around us has dispersed into clusters—families hugging, babies squealing, kids calling out to their excited friends.

Couples kissing.

The tree sparkles behind us. Snow starts to fall. The soft flakes catch the light like glitter.

"Madison." He whispers it.

The luminary is heavy in my hands. I should let it go.

I should let go of all of it.

"Maddie," I say instead. "People who know the real me call me Maddie."

The words hang in the air between us. An offering. An invitation.

His face softens. His whole body shifts toward me, and I can see him reaching for words—something meaningful, something that will change everything, something I want to hear so badly it terrifies me.

And I can't. I can't let him say it.

He's lost enough.

"I got a job offer."

The words land between us like stones. Ben goes very still.

"Yesterday," I continue, before I lose my nerve. "An old colleague runs a wedding planning company. She's expanding to Naples. She wants me to lead the new office." I force myself to keep talking. "It starts the week after New Year's Eve. It would put me close to my parents."

The snow falls between us. I watch a flake land on his shoulder and melt.

He doesn't say anything for a long moment. When he finally speaks, his voice is careful. Empty.

"That's...that's a great opportunity."

I nod, not trusting my voice.

"Near your family. In your field. A new beginning. Just like your speech." He's not looking at me anymore. He's looking at the lake, at the field of lights, his shoulders rigid. "Is that what you want?"

I don't answer. I can't.

His face closes off. Resignation takes over. The weary resignation of a man who's been here before.

And I can't fix it.

I set the luminary at the edge of the lake. A lone candle flickering. Solitary.

"I should go," I tell him. "Cleanup duty."

He nods and then coughs, hard and deep, the virus still rattling in his chest.

"And you should get inside and rest." I push as much humor as I can muster into my voice, trying to bridge the distance I've just created. "Operations manager's orders. No pneumonia. Not on my watch."

He smiles. It doesn't reach his eyes. "Wouldn't want to create extra paperwork for you."

"Exactly. Very inconsiderate."

The joke falls flat. We both know it.

"Goodnight, Madison," he says quietly.

Madison. Like a door clicking shut.

I head toward the chalet, toward the work and the cleanup and all the sensible reasons I should be keeping my distance. The burgundy coat is warm around my shoulders. Santa's letter in my inside pocket. Close to my heart.

Let the guilt go. That's what it said.

But walking away from him, leaving him standing there alone in the falling snow, the guilt has never felt heavier.

THE LONGEST WEEK OF MY LIFE CRAWLS BY.

I tell myself this is what I wanted. Distance. Clarity. The clean lines of a professional relationship with no messy feelings spilling over the edges.

I've seen Ben exactly four times since the luminaries—twice crossing the market, once in the hallway outside Gloria's office, once through the window of the hothouse when I was pretending not to look. Each time, we've exchanged the kind of wave you give someone you vaguely recognize. Polite. Brief. Meaningless.

It's fine. This is fine.

Caroline and I talked on the phone Thursday night. She described the Naples office—a converted bungalow two blocks from the beach, exposed brick, original hardwood floors. A team of three to start, with room to grow. The kind of clients who want elegant, not excessive. The kind of work I used to dream about before I started dreaming about survival instead.

"It's yours if you want it," she said. "I've never met anyone more organized, more capable of making chaos into something beautiful. You'd be running your own show, Maddie. And I know you'll do it well."

I should be thrilled. I should be counting down the days until I can pack my bags and start fresh in a city that actually makes sense for me, close to my family, doing the exact work I trained for and love.

Instead, I feel...untethered. Like I'm watching someone else's future take shape and trying to convince myself it's mine.

But maybe that's the lesson here. Maybe the whole Ben situation proves that I've been playing it too safe with my heart. I've identified the problem now: there's a hole there that needs filling, and Ben—charming and warm and disconcertingly attractive—tapped into it. And that's all this is. A vacancy sign that lit up when someone worth noticing paid attention.

So maybe I'll fill it with someone who lives in Florida when I'm back where I belong. Someone I can actually keep.

Before I can talk myself out of it, I open my laptop and type a reply to Caroline.

I'm in. Let's talk details after New Year's.

I hit send before the doubt can creep in. There. Done. A decision made. A future secured.

It's Monday morning, and I'm reviewing vendor schedules for the third time when a knock on my doorframe makes me jump.

It's Ben who's standing there, which makes me jump again.

He's in his usual Patagonia jacket and he looks tired. The kind of tired that lives behind your eyes even when you've slept enough hours.

"Got a minute?" he says. "Emergency meeting."

My stomach drops. "What kind of emergency?"

"The Ian Preston kind." His mouth tightens. "Judy heard something. Gran wants us in her office now."

He's gone before I can ask anything else.

I grab my notebook and follow.

Gloria's office feels different today. The photographs on the wall—Ford breaking ground, Ben with his science fair ribbon, decades of family history—seem to watch us all. Ben is standing at the bay window, arms crossed, staring out at the market. He doesn't turn around.

Gloria is behind her desk, reading glasses perched on her nose, phone pressed to her ear.

"Yes, I understand. No, we haven't made a decision yet." A pause. "I'll call you back, Frances."

She ends the call and sets the phone down with deliberate care.

"That was my daughter. She runs a cattle operation in Montana. Very successful. Very strategic. Very opinionated." The ghost of a smile. "She's concerned." Gloria gestures to the chair across from her. "Thank you for joining us, Madison. I need your perspective."

Need. Not want.

"Of course." I sit, hyperaware of Ben's presence to my left. The distance between us feels physical. Measurable. "What's going on?"

"Judy came to see me this morning. She heard from a friend who works at the county clerk's office that Ian Preston is preparing to make an offer on the Alpenglow property."

"Alpenglow?" I frown. "So not Winterbloom?"

"Our assumption is now that he wants both." Gloria removes her glasses and sets them on the desk. "He's been buying up houses in town for years—converting them to vacation rentals, squeezing out the locals. If he's going after Alpenglow and Winterbloom, it changes everything."

"If he gets both properties, he'll own a big chunk of the valley," Ben says. He still hasn't turned from the window. "Enough to reshape the entire town. Luxury condos. Chain hotels. Everything that makes this place special, gone."

The bitterness in his voice is old. Bone-deep. This isn't just about business for him. This is about his grandfather's legacy. Everything Ford built.

"The Holloway family still owns Alpenglow," Gloria continues. "They've discussed selling, but they're hesitant. Picky about buyers. They want someone who'll honor what the place meant to them."

"So we have a chance," I say. "If we move fast."

"That's what I'm hoping." Gloria leans forward. "Ford and Ben had been making plans. They felt combining the properties would be smart. We could create one year-round destination instead of two struggling seasonal operations."

"The numbers work," Ben says, and then stumbles, like he's expecting a blow. Like he's heard this dismissed before. "I mean—I have projections. They're rough, but the fundamentals are—"

"I believe you," I say.

He turns from the window. His expression is guarded, but there's a flicker of something underneath. Surprise, maybe. Or hope.

"Madison, you have experience with large-scale hospitality operations," Gloria says. "The business side of making places like this work. I need your help putting together a proposal the Holloways can't refuse."

I don't hesitate. "Where do we start?"

"First, I need you to see the property. Understand what

we're working with." She glances between Ben and me. "Ben can take you at two."

The silence that follows is awkward enough that I'm certain Gloria notices. Her expression stays studiously neutral, but her gaze sharpens. I feel heat creep up my neck, like I've been caught doing something wrong.

"If that works?" Ben asks. His voice is hesitant. Careful. And no matter how lightly he says it, I suspect all three of us know this isn't really about the time.

"That works," I say.

He nods once and disappears before I can say anything else.

Gloria watches me for a moment. She doesn't comment on whatever tension she's observed, but I feel the weight of her attention.

"Thank you, Madison," she says simply. "For staying in this fight."

I nod and head back to my office, trying not to think about how much harder this just got.

At two o'clock, I find Ben waiting in the lobby, keys in hand.

"Ready?"

"Ready."

His Jeep is parked by the staff entrance—a mossy green Wrangler with faded paint and a scratch along the passenger door. Inside, it's cleaner than I assumed it would be. No fast-food wrappers or scattered papers. Only a battered notebook on the backseat and a parking permit dangling from the rearview mirror.

He pulls out of the lot, and I grip the edge of my seat before I can stop myself.

Ben, as usual, notices. "You okay?"

"Fine." I force my fingers to relax. "Sienna drives in this

snow like she's auditioning for a car chase movie. I've been conditioned to expect death around every curve."

His mouth twitches. "I promise not to plunge us off any cliffs."

"That's very reassuring. Thank you."

"I try."

It's not much. A flicker of warmth, there and gone. But something cracks open between us, just a little, just enough to make the silence feel less suffocating.

He drives the way I'd hope someone who grew up in the mountains would drive—steady, slow, respectful of the snow-packed roads. Nothing like Sienna's cheerful chaos behind the wheel. I find myself relaxing despite the awkwardness, trusting that he actually knows what he's doing.

"Turn's coming up," Ben says. "Right past those aspens."

Alpenglow emerges from the trees, and my breath catches.

It's beautiful. Not in the grand way Winterbloom is beautiful, but in a different way entirely—a mid-century time capsule with a soaring roofline and walls of glass angled toward the slopes. The kind of place where movie stars came to ski in the sixties. Teal shutters. Clean angles and soaring beams. A vintage neon sign that probably glowed with "VACANCY" in better days. Hand-painted lettering on the windows advertising hot cocoa and slope-side service. Massive picture windows that would flood the interior with mountain views and natural light.

I love it instantly.

"Oh," I breathe. "It's perfect."

Ben glances at me, surprise in his eyes. "You think so?"

"Are you kidding? Look at those colors. That sign. Those windows." I'm already cataloging the original stonework, the rounded corners on the check-in awning. It's a postcard from another era. A love letter to the past. "This is exactly the kind of place I'd want to stay. Who wouldn't love it?"

"I doubt Ian Preston does." Ben's voice goes flat. "He'll want concrete and marble. Gold fixtures in the bathrooms. Something that looks like every other luxury resort in every other mountain town."

"That would be a crime."

He parks the Jeep and cuts the engine. "So the Holloways built this place in 1955. It's always been a family operation, like Winterbloom. Arthur Holloway and his wife ran it together for forty years before their son took over. My mom used to come here on vacation when she was a teenager."

"Really?"

"That's how my parents met, actually." A small smile tugs at his mouth. "Dad was working at Winterbloom and liked to sneak off to girl-watch at Alpenglow. Mom was staying here with her family. She wiped out at the bottom of the bunny slope and he happened to be walking by."

"That's adorable."

"It's something." The smile fades. "Neither of them is particularly sentimental about anything in Snowdrop anymore. But I like knowing the connection is there."

We get out of the Jeep. The cold hits immediately—sharper up here, with a wind that cuts through my coat. I tug the burgundy wool tighter at the throat and follow Ben toward the main entrance.

"What happened to the Holloways?" I ask as we trudge through knee-deep unplowed snow.

"Arthur and his wife passed in the late nineties. Their son Robert took over. Bachelor, no kids, ran the place by himself until he died six years ago. That's when it closed. The Holloway grandkids—Robert's sister's kids—inherited it." Ben approaches a side door, jiggling the handle in a specific way until it clicks open. "Gramps and I used to come up here and poke around. This door's been broken for years."

Inside, it smells like dust and decades. Our footsteps echo too loud off the high ceilings. Somewhere deeper in the building, a window rattles against the wind. And the lodge is frozen in time. Sheets cover the furniture in the lobby, but I can see the bones underneath—teal vinyl chairs, a boomerang-shaped coffee table, a reception desk with original Formica countertops. The massive stone fireplace has a vintage clock mounted above it, hands frozen at ten past three. And the enormous picture windows! Even grimy with years of neglect, they frame the mountain views like art.

"This is incredible," I say, running my hand along the check-in counter. "And a major selling point. Mid-century modern is huge right now. You preserve this aesthetic, update the infrastructure, and you've got something very few businesses can offer."

He's watching me with an expression I can't quite read. "You really see it, don't you? What this place could be?"

"I see it." I turn to face him fully. "I love it. This place deserves to be saved."

Something passes between us. For a moment, we're not two people pretending to be strangers. We're co-conspirators. Believers in the same cause.

It's a dangerous thing.

But Ben clears his throat. He gestures deeper into the lodge. "I'll show you the rest."

We reach the door to the restaurant, and he hesitates. His hand moves toward it—stops—moves again. The universal awkwardness of a man who can't decide whether holding a door open is chivalrous or patronizing when things are already this complicated between you.

He finally commits, pulling it open right as I step forward to do the same.

We collide. My shoulder hits his chest. His hand lands on my arm to steady me. We both jump back like we've been burned.

"Sorry—"

"No, I—"

"After you," he manages, gesturing stiffly.

My face is on fire. I walk through the door without looking at him.

He leads me deeper into the property—through the restaurant with its original diner booths, past the ski rental shop with its vintage wooden skis mounted on the walls, out onto the deck overlooking runs that sweep down the mountain like white ribbons.

"The chairlifts need maintenance, but they're not shot," he says. "Six months of focused effort and this place could be operational."

"You've really thought this through."

"Gramps and I had lots of plans. What we'd fix first. Where we'd put the new amenities. How we'd tie it all together with Winterbloom." He shoves his hands in his pockets. "I have notebooks full of ideas. Terrible spreadsheets that don't make sense to anyone but me." He glances at me. "But you might be able to figure them out."

The respect in his voice catches me off guard.

"Show me," I say.

"Now?"

"We have work to do, don't we? But maybe somewhere warmer than this deck."

At that, he finally really smiles.

The Snowdrop Brewing Company is a converted mining building with exposed brick and mismatched furniture. Ben orders a pale ale. I get a spiked hot apple cider because my hands are still frozen from Alpenglow and also I need something to do with them.

He spreads his notebooks across the table—three of them, characteristically stuffed with sticky notes and folded papers and margins crammed with his handwriting.

"Fair warning. You've already been exposed to my chaotic organization. These are probably worse."

I picture his wall of sticky notes, the color-coded systems that looked random until you understood the logic. "When you know how to read it, it's not chaotic at all. I told you I thought it was brilliant."

"You were being nice," he says, but I shake my head.

"I am not *nice* about organizational systems, Ben," I say, and he kind of smiles but I'm not joking. "It's brilliant."

"Most people think it's a mess."

"Then most people aren't paying attention."

He's quiet for a moment, thumbing the edge of a notebook, back and forth, and keeping his gaze on the table. But when he finally looks up, there's a weight in his eyes that I wasn't expecting. Regret, possibly. I only think so because I suddenly feel it, too. I shove it away as he slides the first notebook toward me.

I start paging through. He's right that it's unconventional. Ideas jump between sections, cross-references point to pages that don't seem to exist, and his handwriting shifts between neat and completely illegible depending on, I realize, how exciting the idea was. How fast he had to get it down before it leapt out of his mind or another one crowded it out.

But underneath the chaos, there's a real vision here. Sustainability initiatives. Revenue projections. A detailed breakdown of how the hothouse could supply both kitchens. Integration plans that would make the two properties feel like one destination while preserving what makes each unique.

"This is good," I say, and I mean it. "Ben, this is really good."

"You don't have to—"

"Augh, stop it. I'm not being nice. I'm right." I tap the page showing his sticky-note system for tracking seasonal operations. "This is creative. And this..." I flip to his cost-reduction analysis. "This shows you understand the business side, not just the vision."

He's quiet for a moment. "That's what Dr. Sinclair says. That I should stop apologizing for how my brain works. To own it."

"Oh. Dr. Sinclair is your therapist?"

"Yeah. She's great. Really helpful."

Dr. Sinclair. His therapist. Who also happens to be a Santa's Helper, who also speaks at the lantern ceremony, who also says things that sound remarkably like the letters I've been receiving.

I file this away and keep my expression neutral.

"She's right," I say. "So listen to her. These systems—the sticky notes, the notebooks, all of it—they're not chaos. They're solutions. They're something to be proud of."

First relief hits his eyes, then that same regret. A blink. He looks away. And finally: "So where do we start?"

We work for two hours, translating his notebooks into something that might resemble a formal proposal. I ask questions. He explains. Slowly, carefully, we build a framework—

talking about projections and partnerships and timelines instead of everything we might rather say.

It's almost comfortable. Almost.

But every time our hands brush when we reach for the same paper, we flinch apart like the contact stings. Every time I catch him watching me and he looks away, I remember the frozen lake, full of flickering light. The name I offered him that he refused.

Goodnight, Madison.

Professional. Distant. Exactly what I asked for.

That night, I sit at my desk with a sheet of stationery.

This will be my last letter to Santa. I've decided.

I've found what I was looking for when I started writing. Clarity. Direction. A path forward. I know where I'm going. I'll be okay.

Even if my heart hurts when I pick up my pen.

Dear Santa,

Thank you.

I know that's a strange way to start a letter, but I'm not sure I've ever actually said it. Thank you for reading my rambling confessions. Thank you for writing back. Thank you for being patient with someone who showed up in your mailbox full of grief and confusion and ice-sculpture trauma.

This will be my last letter to you—not because you haven't helped, but because I think I've finally found my footing. I know where I'm going now.

There's a job waiting for me in Naples. A good one,

with people who believe in me, doing work I'm actually trained for. It's close to my parents, my brother, my three little nieces. It's everything I thought I wanted when I first came here.

The strange thing is, I'm not cold anymore. I don't know when that changed. Maybe it was the coat someone gave me—burgundy wool, beautiful, chosen specifically for me by a man who noticed I was freezing. Maybe it's the hothouse, where winter-blooming flowers grow against all logic because that same man decided they were worth the effort. Maybe it's Judy's coffee and Sienna's hugs and the way this whole town shows up for each other like it's nothing, like that's just what people do.

Snowdrop started to feel like something I wasn't expecting. Like home.

But home isn't a place you stumble into for six weeks. Home is where you build a life. And I don't know how to build a life somewhere I was never supposed to stay.

So I'm going to take the job in Florida.

But first, I'm going to fight for this place. For Winterbloom, and for the old ski lodge next door that's been sitting empty for years, waiting for someone to remember how beautiful it could be. For the people who've built their lives here—the vendors and the staff and the families who come every year to make memories in the snow.

For a man who's been carrying his grandfather's dream on his shoulders, trying to prove he's enough to see it through.

Ford Bennett planned to pass Winterbloom on to his grandson. That grandson deserves to own it someday. He can run it well. I believe that now. And I can help set him up to thrive the way he was meant to. I can do that much before I go.

I've learned something these past few weeks. Sometimes protecting someone means walking away. Sometimes the kindest thing you can do is not let them love you when you can't promise to stay.

It hurts more than I expected. But I think it's right.

Thank you for listening, Santa. For all the letters, all the wisdom, all the gentle reminders that I'm allowed to forgive myself for being human.

I hope you know how much it helped.

Maddie

I fold the letter and tuck it into my pocket.

Tomorrow I'll drop it in the mailbox on my way to the chalet.

Tonight, I pull out my laptop and start turning Ben's chaotic notebooks into a proposal that will hopefully save everything he loves.

Everything he loves.

It's the least I can do.

Chapter 17
Deep and Crisp and Even

We start in my office because it's neutral territory.

That's what I tell myself, anyway. Neutral territory. Professional distance. Two colleagues working on a business proposal, nothing more. Never mind that, once again, one of those colleagues is wearing a sweater that belongs to the other, or that the last time they really talked, one of them announced she was leaving and the other said *goodnight, Madison* like she was already gone.

Professional. We're being professional.

Ben arrives at nine with coffee and his notebooks. He sets my cup on the desk without comment—my favorite honey oatmilk latte; Judy must have tipped him off—and spreads his materials across the small conference table I've wedged into the corner. The sticky notes have multiplied since I last saw them, a rainbow explosion of ideas and cross-references.

"I organized them by category," he says, not quite meeting my eyes. "Green for Alpenglow infrastructure, blue for

Winterbloom integration, yellow for community partnerships, purple for things we need Gran to approve."

"That's good. That's really smart."

"I've been working on it."

We're so polite it hurts.

I pull up the spreadsheet I started last night, the one I built from his chaotic notebooks that translates his brilliant mess into something the Holloways might be able to read. Revenue projections. Renovation timelines. A detailed breakdown of how the two properties could operate as one destination while preserving what makes each unique.

"This is incredible." Ben leans over my shoulder to look at the screen, close enough that I catch the scent of his soap and that particular warmth that is specifically, undeniably, unhelpfully, all him. "You did all this last night?"

"I couldn't sleep."

"You—"

A knock on the doorframe. Derek's head appears.

"Hey, sorry to interrupt. Two delivery drivers are about to come to blows over who gets to use the loading dock first. Can you sort them out?"

I glance at Ben. He waves me off. "Go. I'll keep working on the partnership list."

The loading dock standoff takes twenty minutes to untangle—one driver had the wrong time on his manifest, the other was early, neither wanted to back down. By the time I get back to my office, Ben has made progress on the community outreach section, but Agnes is hovering in the doorway with a complaint about Harriet the candlemaker again.

"She says my space heater is making her candles soft. Impossible. I'm six feet from her, at minimum. And my sound bowls don't resonate properly if they're too cold."

"It is a pretty big heater, though. Can you angle it toward the back wall instead of her booth?"

"Then my feet will be cold."

"Agnes."

"Fine. But if my bowls sound flat at the sound bath demonstration, I'm telling everyone why."

Agnes leaves, quiet but probably not content. But ten minutes later, I'm called by a vendor who's convinced someone stole her cash box. Then I handle a parking lot fender-bender that somehow becomes my problem when both drivers insist a Winterbloom employee witnessed it. A lost child. A burst pipe in the maintenance closet. A faucet leak in the women's restroom.

When I finally make it back to my office, it's been three hours and Ben is still there, still working, still patient.

"Sorry," I say, dropping into my chair. "This is impossible."

"It's fine. You do still have another job." He almost smiles. "I've just been sitting here pretending to be useful."

"You are useful. That partnership list is—" I lean over to look at his notebook. "Wait, you added the credit union?"

"They've been supporting local businesses for years. Seemed like a natural fit."

Another knock. This time it's Sienna.

"Sorry, sorry, I know you're busy." She's holding her phone like it personally offended her. "But Bree posted a behind-the-scenes reel that accidentally shows the storage area where we keep the broken decorations, and now I have fourteen comments asking if Winterbloom is 'falling apart' and I need to do damage control immediately."

"Can you just—"

"I need you to approve the response language. Gloria's rules."

I approve the response language. Sienna disappears. Ben and I get approximately seven minutes of actual work done before Mrs. Chen appears with questions about her daughter's upcoming wedding reception, which isn't even happening at Winterbloom but somehow requires my input anyway.

By one-thirty, I want to scream.

"This isn't working," I say, after the fourth interruption in twenty minutes—this time a vendor dispute about parking spaces that somehow escalated to involve threats of calling the mayor. "I can't focus. Every time we get momentum, someone needs something."

"That's because you're good at your job." Ben stretches, his shoulders popping audibly. "Everyone knows you'll actually solve their problems."

"That's not a compliment right now."

"It's a little bit of a compliment."

The door opens again. This time it's Heloise from the community center, wrapped in a gorgeous hand-knit shawl.

"I heard about the proposal," she says, settling into the chair across from my desk like she plans to stay awhile. "Gloria mentioned you're trying to build community support."

"We are." I try not to sound as frazzled as I feel. "We're working on it. Or trying to. Between emergencies."

Heloise's eyes crinkle with understanding. "The holidays are always chaos. But I wanted to suggest something. The proposal will be stronger if it includes endorsements from established local businesses. People the Holloways know and trust."

"We were just talking about that." Ben holds up his notebook. "I've got a list started."

"Good. Make sure you include Hank Morris. He owns Snowdrop Brewing Company—the brewery where you two were working the other day." She gives us a knowing look that makes me wonder exactly how small this town is. "The Morrises have been part of Snowdrop for forty years. If he signs on, it sends a message."

"I know Hank," Ben says. "We've talked before about collaborating on a signature brew for the restaurant."

"Perfect. He respects your grandfather's legacy. Appeal to that. A local business owner vouching for the plan will carry weight with the Holloways."

Ben is already writing in his notebook, logging the task in his complicated system. I watch him add a yellow sticky note—community partnerships—with Hank's name and a series of symbols I'm starting to recognize: a star for high priority, a speech bubble for follow-ups, an exclamation point for time-sensitive.

"You should handle the outreach," I tell him. "The town knows you. They trust you. I'm still the outsider."

His eyes fill with surprise. "You sure?"

"I'm positive. You're amazing with people."

His thumb stills on the edge of the sticky note. For a second he looks like he wants to argue, or maybe thank me, but he does neither. Only nods once and adds another symbol—a checkmark inside a circle, which I've learned means *needs documentation.*

"The merchants' association might help, too," Heloise continues. "And don't forget Dr. Sinclair. She's on the town council, you know. Her endorsement would—"

My walkie crackles. "Madison? We need you at the skating rink. A kid took a bad fall. Medics are on it but the parents are upset. They're asking about liability."

My stomach drops.

"Go," Ben says. "I've got this."

By three o'clock, we've managed maybe forty-five minutes of actual collaborative work, scattered across six different sessions interrupted by twelve separate crises, including one tourist who would not accept that Winterbloom does not and will never offer helicopter tours.

"Haven't you heard the phrase never say never?" Ben tells me. "We're working on expanding year-round, you know."

"This is ridiculous," I say, dropping my head onto my desk. The cool wood feels nice against my overheated face. "We're never going to finish this proposal."

"We need to work somewhere else." Ben's voice is careful. Measured. "Somewhere people can't find you."

I lift my head. "Got any ideas?"

He doesn't answer right away. When he does, he's looking at his notebook instead of me. "My place? It's quiet. No foot traffic. And I have all my other reference materials there. The stuff from Gramps, the original plans we made together."

His notebook. A convenient place to look when you're pretending you haven't just suggested something weighted with everything neither of you will say.

His cabin. Where I watched him sleep off a fever while his father's awful words echoed in my head. Where I sat on his battered couch and thought about my grandmother and wondered what in the world I was doing with him.

"That makes sense," I hear myself say. "Logistically."

"Logistically," he agrees.

We're both terrible liars.

I beg Sienna to triage all but the true emergencies and Ben and I set off. The walk to his cabin takes five minutes. Five minutes of crunching through snow and barely talking, the trees dark around us, the only sound our footsteps and the creak of branches overhead. The afternoon light is already fading—winter days are short up here, the sun dipping behind the mountains by four—and the path through the trees feels private in a way the market never does.

He unlocks the door and holds it open. I step inside, and the plants, the cheerful disorder—the Ben-ness of the place—wraps itself around me.

"I forgot how very *you* this cabin is," I say.

"Is that a compliment or a diagnosis?"

"Both." I run my fingers along the edge of a leaf—something broad and tropical-looking that shouldn't be thriving in a Colorado winter. "You keep things alive. That's not nothing."

"Well, you kept me alive the other night. Thank you for staying. I don't think I ever said that."

"Oh, you did," I tell him, and I let myself turn wicked. "You were asleep when you said it, but you did thank me."

A mortified look spreads over his face. "My mouth likes to run in my sleep. Did I say anything so embarrassing we'll have to cut off all contact?"

"You apologized a lot. To someone who wasn't there."

He goes still. "Well, I have a long list. Had to start somewhere."

He's deflecting. I recognize the move, having made it myself a hundred times. I let it go. Some doors aren't meant to be forced open.

We settle into work, and slowly, gradually, the awkwardness starts to thaw.

Maybe it's the cabin itself, small and warm and filled with evidence of who he really is—not the scattered flake I'd first assumed, but someone who nurtures things, who keeps trying. Maybe it's the blessed absence of walkies crackling and vendors complaining and crises demanding attention. Maybe it's just that we've been circling each other for so long that exhaustion finally wins out over caution.

Whatever it is, by the time we've been working for an hour, we're actually talking. Not only about the proposal. About everything. He tells me about Ford's original vision for Winterbloom, how it started as a Christmas tree farm and grew into something neither of his grandparents expected.

I tell him about event planning, about the satisfaction of making chaos into something beautiful, about how the swan disaster didn't just cost me my job—it marked me. One Google search and I'm the woman who ruined a celebrity wedding.

"That's not who you are," he says. "One bad day doesn't define you."

"It does when it's the first thing anyone sees."

"Then they're not looking hard enough." He's studying me like he means it. Like he's proving it, right now. The moment stretches a second too long before he glances away, then he's back with a smile. "Besides, I'm the last person to judge someone for a spectacular public failure."

"Is that what we're bonding over? Professional disasters?"

"Worse things to have in common."

We grin.

And we keep working. He makes coffee—terrible coffee, from a machine that looks older than both of us—and I don't complain because he made it for me and that feels like something.

"Give me one minute," he says somewhere around nine, standing and stretching and giving me a quick look at his healthy abs. "I think I have more of Gramps's papers in the Jeep. Be right back."

Be right back. BRB.

The laugh escapes before he reaches the door.

He stops. Turns. Lets out a long-suffering sigh. "Oh, come on. You, too?"

I hold up my wrist, the cuff of his sweater folded back to show the embroidered initials.

"I have heard every possible joke. I promise you. Every single one."

"Judy embroidered this. She knew exactly what she was doing."

"Judy thinks it's the funniest thing she's ever heard. Maybe because she remembers me as a kid, always saying that very same thing while running in a hundred directions." He shakes his head, but he's smiling now. "Every Christmas she asks if I want a new one with my full name instead. Every Christmas I tell her absolutely not."

"Because BRB is better?"

"Because Buford Rudolph Bennett stitched on anything any*where* is worse. There's no winning. There's only choosing your defeat."

"No, it's perfect," I say, clutching my stomach because it's starting to ache with laughter. "It's the most perfect thing."

"It's a life sentence."

"It's a perfect life sentence."

His eyes are smiling at me. "At least you waited a few weeks. Most people can't hold out."

"I was being polite."

"You were biding your time."

"That, too."

I'm wiping my eyes now. And he's watching me. The laughter has faded from his face, replaced by something softer. More intent.

"I missed that," he says.

"Missed what?"

"Your laugh. This whole week—" He stops. Starts again. "We've been so careful with each other. I missed the you who laughs."

The cabin feels even smaller suddenly. Closer. The glow from the fireplace catches the gold flecks in his eyes, and I remember standing in the hothouse with his thumb against my throat, standing close to him as the luminaries lit up the lake.

Then I remember Gloria's words and my new job in Naples and all the reasons I need to keep my distance.

"Ben—"

"I know." His voice is strained. "I know you're leaving. I know there's a job in Florida and your family and a whole life that makes sense. I wouldn't ask you to—" He swallows. "I just want you to know that this week has been hard. Not seeing you. Not really talking to you."

"It's been hard for me, too."

The admission costs me. I watch it land—see his surprise, the hope he's trying not to show.

"Yeah?" he whispers.

"Yeah," I breathe.

He leans forward. Not closing the distance, but narrowing it. I can see the question in his eyes, the one he's not quite asking. The one I'm not sure how to answer.

"Madison—"

His phone buzzes. Once, twice, three times in succession.

We both freeze.

He pulls it out, glances at the screen. Frustration flickers across his face. And then his dark humor.

"Gran and her sixth sense for terrible timing," he says. "She wants to know when we'll have this draft ready."

Of course she does. Right on cue, she's here to remind me: I should know better. He's lost enough.

"We should probably—"

"Yeah. We should."

I swallow a sigh as Ben texts Gloria, then slips out to his Jeep for the missing papers. The moment breaks apart like morning frost, delicate and irretrievable.

But something has shifted. The careful distance we've been maintaining all week has broken apart, too. And I don't think I can stand to patch it back together.

By eleven o'clock, we have a working draft of the proposal. It's rough. It still needs polishing, and Gloria's review, and the community endorsements Ben will spend the next few days gathering. But it's real. It's something we built together.

"This is good," I say, scrolling through the document on my laptop. "We've got it, Ben. It works. It's good."

"You're the one who made it make sense." He's leaning back in his chair, watching me with an expression I'm trying not to analyze. "I just provided the chaos."

"Your chaos is underrated."

"I'll put that on my tombstone."

I laugh, and it comes out softer than I mean it to. This is the problem. This right here.

I should go. It's late, and tomorrow will be another long day of operations management and crisis prevention and all the things that have nothing to do with Ben Bennett and his textable initials and the way he's been looking at me across this small table.

I gather my things—my laptop, my notes, the burgundy coat. "So. Tomorrow?"

"Tomorrow." He leans back in his chair. "I'll reach out to Hank first thing. And the merchants' association."

"Perfect. I'll polish the presentation and we can—"

"Get ready for the staff Christmas party you're in charge of?"

I stop. The party. Tomorrow night. Vendors, staff, the whole Winterbloom operation.

I completely forgot.

"That was a test," I say. "You passed."

"You forgot."

"I was focused on the proposal."

"You forgot." He's smiling now—that slow, warm smile that's becoming a problem.

"It's your fault. You're very distracting."

The smile deepens. "Noted."

And there it is—that glow spreading through my chest, the easy rhythm of us. I pull on the coat and step back before I let it go any further.

"I should go. Big day tomorrow."

Hurt flickers across his face. He noticed the shift. But he doesn't call me on it. Just stands.

"I'll walk you back."

"You don't have to."

"It's eleven o'clock and twenty degrees. I'm walking you back."

I don't argue.

Outside, the cold hits sharp and clean after the warmth of the cabin. The market is closed for the night, the vendor stalls dark and silent, but the Christmas lights still glow along the pathways—thousands of tiny white stars strung through the trees.

Snow crunches under our boots. We don't talk much. We don't need to. There's something easy about the silence now, despite everything. I keep catching myself smiling. I should stop. I don't.

The chalet comes into view, golden light spilling from the windows. We stop in front of the big double doors, and I turn to face him. His cheeks are red from the cold. Snowflakes catch in his hair.

"So," he says. "Tomorrow. The party. Try not to forget again."

"I'll do my best."

He's watching me—my arms wrapped around myself, my breath blooming white in the air between us.

"I'll bring coffee. You're still shivering."

"I'm always shivering. It's a permanent condition now."

"Then I'll keep bringing coffee." His eyes hold mine, steady despite the cold. "Goodnight, Maddie."

I feel it land, soft and sure. Maddie. Oh.

"Goodnight, Ben."

I watch him walk back toward the path, hands in his pockets, shoulders braced against the wind. He turns once, catches me still standing there, and grins.

I slip inside before I can do anything stupid.

My bath water is too hot. It's boiling me alive. Glorious.

I sink lower, letting it lap at my shoulders as steam curls toward the ceiling. My muscles ache from weeks of running between crises. My brain aches from days of wrangling years of ideas and handwritten notes into a polished proposal. From wrangling my own internal war between my head and my heart.

I should be getting ready. The party starts in two hours and I'm the one who's got to make sure it doesn't fall apart. But I give myself five more minutes in the heat, replaying last night behind my closed eyes.

Firelight flickering over the walls of his cabin. Ben's smile when I said he was distracting. The walk home beneath the stars and a thousand tiny Christmas lights. *Goodnight, Maddie* and how he turned back to catch me still standing there, watching him go.

I'll keep bringing coffee.

Such a small promise. Such a dangerous one.

Because I want that, so much. But here's the knowledge that's surfaced in this quiet: I can't promise him anything. Not really. There's a job waiting for me in Florida. A career I've worked my whole adult life to build. Parents who are already planning Sunday dinners, nieces eager to see my face outside of a phone screen. A whole life that makes sense.

And Ben, who's devoting himself to saving this place, deserves someone who wants to build their life around that legacy, too. Not someone who might leave.

He's lost enough.

Gloria's voice, always Gloria's voice.

And she's right; the logistics don't add up.

But right now, my heart doesn't care about logistics. My heart wants things that don't fit into spreadsheets or five-year plans. My heart wants this man, Ben, who talks in his sleep and coaxes tropical plants through a Colorado winter and looks at me like I'm answering a question he's been asking for years.

My heart wants to stay.

But upending everything for someone I've known for roughly a month...

That's not romantic. That's reckless.

Which means I shouldn't start something I can't promise to see through.

Or does it mean I'm so busy protecting him from hypothetical future hurt that I'm hurting us both right now?

Enough.

I pull the plug and watch the water drain, then start getting ready for a party I'm supposed to be running.

The champagne sequined skirt was an impulse buy three years ago—a sample sale splurge I never got around to wearing.

Now I shimmy into it and watch it catch the light, throwing sparks across the walls.

I pair it with a cream cashmere sweater I bought myself after my first big promotion, back when promotions still happened to me. I take my time with my hair, leaving it down in the messy waves I was born with instead of my usual five-minute blowout or functional bun. I put on actual makeup—smoky eyes, a deep red lip. An effort I haven't made since Miami.

And then I check my reflection. For the first time since arriving in Colorado, I look like someone who belongs at a Christmas party instead of someone who's been shivering for a month straight.

Like someone worth turning back for.

I grab the burgundy coat, just in case, and head downstairs.

Christmas Eve. The market closed at four so everyone who wanted to come could be here—the local vendors and staff as well as the out-of-towners who stay on site. Tomorrow we rest. Tonight we celebrate.

The Evergreen ballroom has been transformed.

I designed this on paper three days ago, scribbling notes between proposal revisions and hoping the décor team could translate my vision without me hovering. They did more than translate it. They made it perfect.

Pine garland drapes every surface, thick and fragrant. Candles glow on the tables, along the windowsills, clustered on the mantel. They're shimmering inside frosted glass globes like tiny ice luminaries throwing warm light over the walls. Fairy lights crisscross the ceiling so the whole room glimmers like a jewel box. The world outside is silver-cool, but in here, we're wrapped in gold.

I breathe in cinnamon and clove from the mulled wine

station, butter and sugar from Judy's dessert spread, woodsmoke from the fireplace crackling in the corner. Christmas music plays softly beneath the hum of conversation —Nat King Cole, Bing Crosby, the classics.

I designed this. The luminaries inspired my vision, and my team made it real. Seeing it all together—it's magic. The kind of magic I used to create at The Palms. The kind I could create here. For real. Not a six-week stopgap, but something built to last—events that draw people to Winterbloom year-round, not only at Christmas.

The thought isn't new. It's been circling for weeks, every time I walk the grounds and see what this place could be. Spring weddings in the meadow. Fall retreats when the aspens turn gold. Alpenglow transformed into a venue that makes brides weep.

I've imagined it. I've caught myself imagining it multiple times. And I always shut it down.

Because Caroline is offering me a sure thing. An ally who knows my work, who understands what really happened at The Palms. Resources. Connections. A client list I helped build. In Florida, I'd be stepping back into a life that already has a shape.

Here? I'd be betting everything on an out-of-the-way venue with a shoestring budget and weather that could derail any outdoor event. I'd be starting from scratch in a place most people have never heard of, with no reputation to fall back on —just the wreckage of the one I used to have.

But I'd also have Ben.

I file that thought away before it can take root.

"Ho ho ho." Sienna appears at my elbow, stunning in emerald velvet that highlights the auburn in her dark hair. "You look like the Christmas angel on top of the tree. A hot Christmas angel."

"That's not a compliment anyone has ever wanted."

"Take it anyway."

Her attention drifts past me, and I follow her gaze to a table near the tree. Mike is crouched beside Evie, studying the drawing she's holding up like it's a masterpiece. Tinsel glints in her dark curls. He nods at whatever she's explaining, completely serious, like her crayon reindeer is the most important thing in the room.

Something in Sienna's face softens. Only for a second. Then she catches me watching and the mask snaps back into place.

"What?" she says.

"Nothing."

"It is nothing."

"I didn't say it was something."

"Good." She takes a long sip of her wine. "Because it isn't."

I let it go but file it away with a smile, because I know *a something* when I see it.

"Speaking of things that aren't things," she says, her tone going deliberately casual, "I have a surprise for you later. Don't ask what it is because I'm not telling."

"That's ominous."

"It's festive. I can be trusted." She glances over my shoulder and her eyes light up with mischief. "Ooh. Sexy heir of the Christmas market at twelve o'clock. Almost certainly headed your way. Which reminds me that I have cookies to sample."

She vanishes into the crowd before I can respond.

I turn.

Ben is standing near the entrance, still in his coat, holding two cups and scanning the room. He finds me and goes still.

His eyes trace the sequins, the sweater, the hair, and when they come back to my face something in them makes me stand a little straighter. A smile tugs at the corner of his mouth—not his usual easy grin, but private. A smile that's just for me. Warm and certain in a way that makes my heart flip.

He crosses the room and the crowd seems to part for him. Or maybe I'm just not seeing anyone else.

"I promised I'd keep bringing coffee." He holds out one of the cups.

"At a party with an open bar and Judy's mulled wine?"

"A promise is a promise."

I take it, tingling at the way his fingers brush mine.

"You look—" He stops. "That's a lot of sparkle. Every time you move, you throw light around the room. It's distracting."

"Funny. That's my line for you."

"Thought I'd see how it felt from this side. I get it now."

We're standing too close. I can smell his soap, something clean and evergreen. I should step back. Create some professional distance. Remember that I'm leaving in less than two weeks and he's Gloria's grandson and this is exactly the kind of complication neither of us needs.

I don't step back.

Someone calls Ben's name from across the room—Hank from the brewery, waving him over. He grimaces apologetically.

"Duty calls," he says. And then he adds, as he's backing away, "Hold on. I'll, uh, be right back."

He says it straight-faced, but his eyes are laughing.

"Did you just BRB me? Out loud? With your actual mouth?"

He grins, and it does something inconvenient to my pulse. Then he's gone, swallowed by the crowd, and I'm left holding a cup of coffee I don't need with a heart that won't quit racing and a smile I can't suppress.

For a while I get caught up in party preparations—making sure Judy doesn't spend all night fussing over the food, confirming the relief schedule for the workers manning the front desk—and we lose each other in the chaos. Every time I look for him, he's somewhere else—laughing with Derek, helping Mrs. Chen carry her coat to the rack, being the version of himself that everyone in this town loves.

And then I spot him near the Christmas tree.

He's shed his coat somewhere, and the charcoal sweater underneath fits him properly for once—no stretched cuffs, no soil stains, no evidence of the hothouse clinging to the wool. Just simple, well-made cashmere that shows off his shoulders and arms and that tight stomach in a way I'm not prepared for. He's laughing at something, his whole face open with it, and seeing it makes something bloom in my chest.

Until I see who he's laughing with.

Lacey. Lacey from Petal and Pine, with her easy smile and deep-rooted investment in this place. Tall and blonde and completely at ease in his world. She reaches out and touches his arm—casual, familiar—and my stomach drops.

They look good together. Natural. Like two people with a community in common. Two people who could share a vision and build a life that makes sense.

She'd be good for him, I think, and it hurts more than I expected. She understands the hothouse. She's committed to Snowdrop. She's not leaving for a job in Florida in two weeks.

She wouldn't make him lose someone else.

And neither will I.

I turn away before he can catch me watching, slip out of the room before he can see whatever this realization has done to my face. The back hallway is dim, the party music fading to a muffled hum as I pass Gloria's office, then Ben's, then push through the door to my own at the end of the row. Close enough to hear the celebration. Far enough to be alone.

My office is quiet. Dark. I flip on the desk lamp and sink into my chair, telling myself I just need a minute. Just a breath before I go back out there and smile through the rest of the night.

That's when I see the envelope.

Cream-colored. Heavy stock. My name in gold, in that elegant, old-fashioned script I've come to recognize.

My hands are trembling as I break the seal.

Dear Maddie,

You wrote to say goodbye. That you've made your choice, and this would be your last letter.

I won't try to change your mind. That has never been my place. But I want to leave you with something to carry with you.

Fear is a liar, a clever one. It doesn't always arrive shaking and obvious. Sometimes it wears a sensible coat and speaks in practical tones. "This is the smart move," it says. "This is what makes sense." And we believe it, because wisdom sounds so much better than fear.

You told me about your grandmother. The letter in the drawer. You've carried that weight for years—the knowledge that you waited too long, that fear led to a choice you've always regretted.

But carrying a lesson is not the same as learning it.

You wrote that Snowdrop started to feel like home, which surprised you. I wonder if it surprised you because

Naples is truly your home—or because you've decided not to ask yourself where you belong.

Sometimes belonging sneaks up on us. It doesn't announce itself with trumpets and certainty. It arrives quietly, in borrowed coats and late-night conversations and the slow realization that people are making room for you at the table.

The question isn't whether you've found something real. The question is whether you'll let yourself keep it. You say holding back is the responsible choice. But what if it's just fear wearing a sensible coat?

Whatever you decide, make sure you're the one deciding. Not the version of you that's still protecting herself from things that might hurt. You've earned the right to trust yourself.

Santa

My eyes keep snagging on the same line: *Fear wearing a sensible coat.*

Is that what this is? Have I been calling it practicality—calling it protecting him—when really it's just fear in disguise?

I think about Caroline's offer. The salary, the title, the chance to rebuild everything I lost. I think about Sunday dinners with my parents and watching my nieces grow up and a career that finally makes sense again.

I think about Ben. The way he looked at me across the room tonight. The way he said *goodnight, Maddie* like it was a promise. The way I've spent weeks telling myself I shouldn't want him when the truth is I've wanted him from the moment I paused long enough to see who he really is.

I fold the letter carefully and slip it into my desk drawer.

I'm heading down the hall when I register the light spilling from under Gloria's office door.

It's late for her to still be working, and she should be at the party. I tap lightly. "Gloria?"

No answer. The office is empty.

Her reading glasses sit on her desk next to a half-finished cup of tea, still faintly steaming. I'm about to turn away when I see it.

A bottle of ink. Gold ink, the metallic kind that catches the light. The same gold that's been inscribing my name on cream-colored envelopes for weeks.

Beside it, a piece of paper. A scrap of handwriting—not a letter, just some notes. But the script is unmistakable. That same elegant, old-fashioned cursive. The same hand that's been writing to me since I first poured my heart out to a mailbox in the snow.

Gloria.

Gloria is Santa.

I sink into the chair across from her desk, my mind racing.

Gloria is the one who warned me about Ben. That day in her office, with Ford's photographs watching from the walls, she told me Ben had lost enough. She told me not to start something I couldn't finish.

And then she spent weeks writing me letters about fear and courage and trusting myself.

How does that make sense?

She warned me away. And then she—what? Coached me toward him?

But that's not right either. The letters never told me what to do. They only ever asked me to look at myself. To question my fear. To trust that I'd know the right thing when I was ready to see it.

I stare at the gold ink, trying to make the pieces fit.

And then, slowly, they do.

The warning wasn't to stay away from Ben. It was to be sure. *The stakes are high. He's been hurt. Don't treat this carelessly.* And the letters weren't interference. They were building me up. Here's how to trust yourself. Here's how to be brave. Here's how to stop hiding letters in desk drawers and start saying the things that matter.

Gloria wasn't warning me away. She was inviting me to stay—if I could figure out how to choose it.

I stand up so fast the chair scrapes against the hardwood.

Ben. I need to find Ben.

I rush into the dim hallway and nearly collide with someone. Him.

Of course it's him, always showing up at the exact right time, always bringing me whatever I need. Which this time is just...him.

He catches my arms to steady me and doesn't let go.

"You disappeared. Are you okay?"

"I needed a minute." The words tangle in my throat. "But I was coming to find you."

"Well." A hint of a smile. "Here I am."

Here he is. And I'm so sick of talking myself out of this. I'm so tired of being afraid.

The hallway is dim. The party sounds distant, muffled, like it's happening in another building. His hands are warm through my cashmere sleeves.

"I've been really stupid."

His brow furrows. "Okay."

"Your grandmother told me about Boulder. She warned me to be careful—a completely reasonable warning to make sure I think everything through—and I turned it into some kind of purity test. I convinced myself that if I couldn't guarantee you forever, I shouldn't start something with you at all."

Understanding dawns in his eyes. "Maddie."

"I know. Thinking about it now, it's ridiculous. I've been treating you like you're fragile. Like you couldn't handle it if I didn't have everything figured out. Like—"

"Like a damaged neurodivergent whose past screwups and chaotic brain make him need protecting." He lifts his brows. "I told you."

I shake my head, annoyed with myself. "Sorry. I thought I was better than that."

"You are. But it's something most people have to learn."

I bite my lip, feeling the weight of letting him down. Then I look up and meet his gaze. "Consider me educated. For good."

He slides his palms down my arms to take my hands in his. "So listen. My grandmother—that was sweet. Bossy and unnecessary, but sweet. I'm thirty-two years old. I know how relationships work. And I know that sometimes they don't." He shrugs. "We can start this without knowing how it turns out. That's actually how dating works."

"Right." I take in the way he's looking at me, amused and incredulous with something soft underneath. "I know that."

"Do you?" He's smiling now. "Because you've been spiraling about forever when I'd have settled for a coffee date."

"You already bring me coffee."

"So we're ahead of schedule." He shifts closer. The space between us narrows. "Don't try to be logical. Be honest. What do you want?"

The question hangs there. Simple. Terrifying.

But I manage to answer it truthfully.

"You," I tell him. "I want you."

All the good things flood into his face—relief and joy and something more. Something that makes my breath catch.

"Good. Then I think you should kiss me. Right here in this hallway."

His voice is low and teasing. Mine is an uptight squeak.

"Here? Outside your grandmother's office? Now?"

His thumb brushes my cheekbone, traces over my chin. Then it slips down my neck to the hollow of my throat, and my pulse jumps against his touch like it's trying to reach him.

"Right now." He's looking at my mouth with heat in his gaze, but then the heat turns to mischief. "Don't worry. We might hate it. Then we can laugh at how you've wasted all week spinning out."

I watch the humor dancing in his eyes, and I know. Oh. I know.

"We won't hate it," I say, pulling his face to mine. "We won't ever want to quit."

It's soft at first, the way our lips brush. Careful, like a question we're offering each other, like one last chance to change our minds.

Then his mouth opens against mine, and I answer by sliding my hands up his chest, by pulling him closer. He makes a sound low in his throat as I press against him and something shifts. The kiss goes from question to answer to *finally*.

His hand moves to the back of my neck, fingers tangling in my hair, tilting my head so he can kiss me more deeply. His other arm wraps around my waist, pulling us so firmly together that I think I feel his heartbeat thudding against mine. He's warm—so warm—and real and *here*, and I stop thinking about all the reasons this is complicated.

I stop thinking.

His teeth catch my lower lip, gentle, deliberate, and the

sound I make is embarrassing. Or it would be embarrassing, if I cared. I don't. I care about the way his fingers tighten in my hair when I press closer. The way his breath hitches when my hands slide over his back. The way he kisses me like he's memorizing me, like he's going to make sure it lasts.

When we finally break apart, we're both breathing hard. His forehead drops to mine. His hand stays tangled in my hair, like he can't quite bring himself to let go.

"So," he says. "Do we hate it?"

"Hate it." I'm smiling so wide it hurts. "Truly terrible."

"The worst."

"But we should probably try again. To confirm the results."

"Rigorous methodology."

"Exactly."

He kisses me again. This time there's no hesitation—just his mouth on mine, certain and unhurried. Like he's been thinking about this as long as I have and now that it's happening, he wants to do it right. His hand slides from my hair down my spine, palm settling on the small of my back, and I arch into him without meaning to.

"Maddie." My name, low and breathless against my mouth. "I've wanted to do this since the hothouse."

I can't help laughing at that.

"Which day in the hothouse? The one where I called you lazy or the one where I called you a liar?"

He laughs with me, but his voice is low and soft when he says, "The one where you saw me, like no one else ever has."

We stay like that for a while. His heartbeat against mine. His breath soft on my temple. His arms around me like he's not planning to let go.

"We should get back," I finally say. "Someone's going to notice we're both missing."

"Let them."

"Ben."

"Fine." He sighs, dramatic, but doesn't let go. "But I'm holding your hand when we walk back in. And I'm not going to be subtle about looking at you."

"Good."

"And if anyone asks, I'm telling them we were—"

"Uh, you'll tell them we were discussing vendor contracts."

"Very thorough vendor contracts," he says in a low voice.

Heat shimmers through me again. "The most thorough."

He grins and kisses me once more—quick, almost chaste, except for the way his hand tightens on my hip.

Then he takes my hand, laces his fingers through mine, and leads me back toward the party.

The Evergreen ballroom is still glowing. Judy and Irwin are dancing near the dessert table. Derek is waxing poetic about speaker placement. Sienna catches my eye from across the room and her face does something smug that implies she wants all the details. And Gloria...

Gloria is watching from beside the fireplace. When she sees us together, she raises her glass—just slightly—and nods. A benediction.

Ben sees it, too. He squeezes my hand. "Ready?"

"Ready," I say.

And I finally mean it.

LET NOTHING YOU *Dismay*

On Christmas Day, I wake up to a photo of the hothouse at dawn.

The light is slanting through the glass walls, turning everything gold and green. A French press sits on a potting bench, with two mismatched mugs and a little bouquet. Underneath it, Ben has written:

> Merry Christmas. Come for breakfast when you wake up.

He made breakfast. At—I check the timestamp—six forty-seven on Christmas morning. He made breakfast. For me.

I debate whether to respond with a hearts-for-eyes emoji (it's sappy, but I feel sappy, but is it too sappy?) before getting sick of myself and just pressing send. He sends back a red heart, followed immediately by:

> That was from the plants. I'm playing it cool.

I'm smiling at my phone like an idiot when another text arrives.

GLORIA:

Madison, I hope I'm not overstepping. The family is arriving for Christmas dinner at five, and I'd like you to join us.

Given our timeline with the Holloways, we'll need to discuss the proposal, and I want Trip to hear from an outside professional voice. It will carry weight he can't dismiss.

I read this three times.

An outside professional voice. Translation: Trip will try to steamroll his son, and Gloria wants backup.

I think about the last time I saw Trip Bennett. The way Ben's shoulders collapsed under his father's judgment. The thin walls between our offices and the conversation I wasn't supposed to hear.

You can't pill your way out of a lack of follow-through.

My teeth clench.

I'll be there. What can I bring?

Just yourself. And perhaps your most diplomatic smile.

I send her a confirmation before racing to get ready for a hothouse breakfast. Ten minutes later, I'm walking in the cold morning air wearing a burgundy coat that still makes my stomach flip. The market is quiet, closed on Christmas Day, and a new snow from last night has softened everything into silence. My boots crunch a fresh path across the white.

When I push open the hothouse door, the warmth hits me first. Then the smell—earth and green things and something yummy. And then Ben, standing at the potting bench with a mug of steaming coffee and a smile, both for me.

I close the door behind me, and we're alone in this glass-walled world.

And then I just...stand there.

Because what's the protocol here? We kissed at a Christmas party like a Hallmark movie cliché. We said things. Intense things. And now it's morning and he's made me breakfast and I don't know if I'm supposed to walk over and kiss him or play it cool or—

"You're doing the thing," he says.

"What thing?"

"The thing where you're calculating the exact right move and the math isn't mathing."

"I don't—" I stop. "Okay. Maybe."

He sets down the mug and crosses to me. "Let me help."

And then his arms are around me and his mouth is on mine and it turns out the protocol is just this: his hands settling on my waist, and the calculations in my head dissolving into nothing.

"Merry Christmas," he murmurs.

"Merry Christmas." I pull back enough to look at him. "You made me breakfast."

"I made you mediocre eggs and stole day-old pastries from Judy's." He grins. "Don't get too excited."

We eat perched on stools at the potting bench, surrounded by Ben's elaborate systems of sticky notes and seedling trays. The eggs are good. The coffee is not, but it's from him which makes it perfect. And somewhere between my second cinnamon roll and his third cup, he reaches into his pocket and produces a small wrapped box.

"Don't freak out. This isn't a big deal."

I stare at it. "Ben! I didn't get you anything." The words come out more distressed than I intend. "I was so busy trying not to want to be with you—and then last night happened, and I—"

He presses his finger to my lips.

"Maddie." He's smiling. "Just open it."

Inside the box, nestled in tissue paper, is a small brass compass, with a worn patina and a glass face that's slightly scratched. On the back, engraved in delicate script:

Find your way home.

"It belonged to Gramps." Ben's voice is quiet. "His dad gave it to him when he left for Colorado. I know you're still figuring out where you're going. I just thought—maybe you could use something to help you find your way. Wherever that ends up being."

My throat is tight. "I can't take this. It's a family heirloom."

"No, I want you to have it." His eyes meet mine, serious. "You're fighting to save Gramps's legacy. He would've wanted you to have it, too."

I close my fingers around the brass, feel the weight of it—prized, priceless—in my palm.

"Thank you." It comes out in a whisper. "I love it."

"Good." He kisses my forehead, then my nose, then my mouth. "Now. What were you saying about not getting me anything?"

I laugh, the tightness in my chest loosening. "I said I didn't have time. But I have plans."

"Plans?"

I lean closer, lips brushing his ear. "I thought maybe later..." I whisper the rest.

The sound he makes is extremely satisfying.

"That's—" He clears his throat. "That's better than a compass."

I give him a second. He seems to need it. But eventually I wave my hand in front of his face.

He blinks. Twice. "Sorry. I was—"

"Yeah, I know where you were. Fast-forwarding through family dinner to get to dessert."

He laughs, but his expression shifts to something more complicated. "Speaking of family dinner, I heard you're coming. You sure you want to do that?" He fixes his eyes on a flowering tree nearby. "You could do something fun with Sienna. Frankly, you could spend the day cleaning toilets and have a better time."

"Gloria asked me to be there. She wants an outside voice on the proposal—someone who can talk numbers and strategy without Trip dismissing it as family loyalty." I pause. "She also implied you might need backup."

"She's not wrong. You know how some birds peck their young to death? My dad does that, too, except he pecks with suggestions about why I should be more like him." His mouth twists. "The birds do it to save resources for the stronger babies. But I'm an only child, so I've never been sure what that says about me."

"I think it says a lot more about him. I'm glad I'll be there. You've done good work, Ben. Really good work. Someone should make sure your family hears about it." I squeeze his hand. "Also, I'd love an excuse to fight your father, so there's that."

Ben's eyebrows shoot up. "Oh?"

"'*You can't pill your way out of a lack of follow-through.*'" I don't bother hiding the edge in my voice. "I heard that through the wall, you know. And I've been composing my rebuttal ever since."

His smile turns wicked. "I'd pay very good money to watch you deliver it."

"I've got a whole speech prepared. Very eloquent. Very profane."

"Now I'm looking forward to dinner."

We're both grinning, and for a second I let myself imagine it—me telling Trip Bennett exactly where he can shove his opinions about his son.

Then reality settles back in.

"Except we need him," I say. "Or at least, we need him to not actively sabotage this. So. Diplomatic smile it is."

"Diplomatic smile," he agrees, and kisses me, which reminds me to break some unhappy news.

"So, sadly, I think we should keep this quiet at dinner. The...us thing."

"The us thing?"

"You know what I mean. If they know we're together, everything I say becomes the opinion of your—" I stumble. "Your...the person you're...kissing."

"Girlfriend." He's grinning now. "I think the word you're looking for is girlfriend."

"Am I...is that what you'd call me? Your girlfriend?" I bite my lip to keep from smiling too big.

"Would you prefer paramour? Lady friend? Romantic entanglement?"

"I'd prefer to get through dinner without your dad deciding I can't be objective."

The grin fades slightly, but he nods. "Yeah. No, you're right. If he thinks you're biased, he won't hear a word you say."

He squeezes my hand. "One dinner. I'll be very professional. Give off extremely platonic energy."

"And after that?"

"After that, you can sit on my lap at the staff meeting and I'll make an announcement over the PA system."

I laugh, then lean over and kiss him, soft and quick. "Thank you."

"Don't thank me yet. Wait until you've survived dinner."

Gloria's private quarters occupy a quiet wing off the main chalet. When she opens the door and Ben's shoulders relax, I understand that I'm stepping into his childhood safe space.

It's not large, not showy, but it's so deeply lived in that even the air inside feels softer. Warm wood floors covered by old Persian rugs, worn thin in the paths between furniture. Built-in bookshelves stuffed with decades of reading—spines cracked, pages flagged. Books that were loved, not put out for display. The furniture is mismatched in the way that means each piece was chosen for a reason, kept for a memory. A leather armchair with a permanent indent. A stack of seed catalogs on the side table, one significant year out of date.

I think about Ben as a kid, escaping to Ford and Gloria's place from what was likely a tense home in Denver. Fleeing here after Boulder, to a place that still felt like unconditional love. That idea makes me fall in love with it, too.

While Ben helps Gloria with some poinsettias he brought, I wander to the stone fireplace, to the photographs crowding the mantel. Ford is in almost all of them. Young, with floppy dark curls and a dashing grin, both of which he passed on to Ben. Mid-twenties with his arm around a bright-eyed Gloria. A little red-haired girl smiling from his shoulders. Muddy and laughing with a teenage Ben, both of them surrounded by plants.

And Trip, too, looking softer and kinder in his younger days. One at maybe eight years old, gap-toothed and sunburned, proudly holding a hiking stick that's taller than he is. Another of his wedding day, his face hopeful in a way that seems impossible to reconcile with the man I met earlier. One who walks into rooms expecting to get his way.

Ben comes to stand beside me as I study the photos. "That's your mom?" I ask, nodding toward the woman in the wedding picture.

"Patricia Evelyn Penelope Ashworth Bennett, Esquire." His voice is dry. "Trish, unless you're getting paid by the syllable."

"Trish and Trip," I say, rolling my eyes. "So we've got Buford Rudolph Bennett the Third—Trip—and his wife, Patricia Eight-Middle-Names Ashworth Bennett, or Trish. And then there's little Buford the Fourth, of course." I bump his shoulder with mine. "Can I get a flowchart for reference?"

"Gran tried to save me. She suggested breaking the Buford chain with Ryan or Justin. My father said they lacked gravitas."

"You were a *baby*."

"A baby with insufficient gravitas." He shrugs. "I'm lucky I came away with Ben. The Bennetts don't do nicknames. They do legacies. It's exhausting."

"Just so you know, if this thing between us goes so far that we're naming kids, I'm instituting a cap. Two names with two syllables, max. Maybe three if it's really pretty."

Surprise, then humor, then a laugh he can't stifle. "Agreed. And no Roman numerals. Buford Rudolph ends with me."

"Deal." We shake on it, and he hangs onto my hand.

"Did we just negotiate our hypothetical children's names?"

"Consider it a preview of my project management skills."

His laugh is so deep that I glance around. Gloria's still in the kitchen. No one else has arrived. I tug him behind the white-lit Christmas tree in the corner.

"What are you—"

I kiss him. Just once. Quick and firm and smiling against his mouth.

When I pull back, he reaches for me again: "Okay, but one more," which becomes two, and then three and then—

The front door bangs open. Ben reluctantly concedes that we have to emerge from behind the tree.

First comes Frances, who is exactly the kind of woman who terrified me when I first started in events—loud, focused, suffers no fools—yet is fortunately the kind I work best with now. She's stomping snow off her boots in the foyer and looking around like she's still appraising livestock on her ranch. Red hair shot through with white, freckles across weathered skin, the kind of tan you get from spending your life outdoors. No makeup. No jewelry except a battered but very good quality watch. She catches my eye and nods once, like we're already past the small talk.

"Madison Lark? The one who's been keeping this place running while my mother overextends herself?"

"I've been helping where I can."

Frances snorts.

"Diplomatic." She strips off her coat, revealing a flannel shirt. "I look forward to hearing your take on all the fuss. Trip calls twice a week with doom-and-gloom predictions. Mother calls three times a week telling me to ignore Trip. I'm here to see who's exaggerating more."

It's blunt. I kind of love it.

"You'll be impressed," I say. "Ben's work on the Holloway pitch has been exceptional."

"Good. Show me." She's almost smiling. "I like that you didn't hedge. Most people hedge."

Ben's parents arrive ten minutes later. Trip sweeps into the room with the same air of authority that expects the world to rearrange itself around him. Trish is elegant and polished with a smile like a scalpel.

Trip greets me with the same warmth from our first meeting, when he called me a temp. As I take my seat at the table across from him, I hear his words echo through my head: *You can't pill your way out of a lack of follow-through.*

Ben is sitting at the place next to mine, so he sees my hand curl into a fist.

"Easy, tiger," he murmurs. His voice is light, but I can feel tension radiating off him, too. "It's just dinner."

"It's not just dinner," I whisper, looking at Trip's grim, self-satisfied face. "It's a war council."

"Okay, it's a war council. But the food will be good."

The dining room looks like a magazine spread. Long table, good china, candles flickering. Gloria presides at the head, regal in burgundy silk. Frances sprawls at the other end like she's in a barn, completely unimpressed by the formality. And Trip and Trish sit side by side, a united front of cashmere and judgment.

Dinner unfolds in courses, and I watch the family dynamics play out like a chess match. Gloria holds court with quiet authority. Frances asks frank questions and doesn't bother with small talk. Trish smooths over rough edges, redirects conversations that get too heated. And Trip...Trip chips away at Ben with surgical precision.

It's never overt. That's what makes it devastating.

"The hothouse is certainly productive," he says over the soup course. "Manageable scope. Low stakes."

"Ben's sustainability initiatives have been remarkably

successful," Gloria says. "Last year, the hothouse turned a profit for the first time in years."

"Profit margins at that scale are almost decorative," Trip says pleasantly. "Not that there's anything wrong with that. Small wins matter."

I watch Ben absorb *small wins*. Watch his mouth tighten, then release. He takes a sip of water and says nothing.

By the main course, I've counted four of these small cuts. The hothouse is *a nice hobby*. Ben's vendor relationships are *sweet*. His infrastructure planning is ambitious for *someone without operations expertise*. Each one delivered warmly, reasonably, the way you'd praise a child's art project before quietly throwing it away.

And Ben takes it. Every time. Shoulders curling inward, voice growing quiet, confidence eroding bite by bite.

When we finally get to the proposal, I walk them through the key points: the Alpenglow Lodge acquisition, year-round revenue, community partnerships.

Frances listens intently, asking sharp questions about projections and timelines. Trip listens with the expression of someone humoring a kid.

"The ideas Ben has developed are genuinely impressive," I say. "The vendor relationships, the supply chain optimization, the infrastructure planning—it's comprehensive work."

"Ben has always been good at making plans," Trish says. "It's the execution that tends to be the challenge."

"Boulder was years ago," Gloria says. "Ben has grown considerably since then."

"Has he? I hope so. I genuinely do." Trip's voice is concerned, fatherly—which makes it worse. "But hope isn't a business strategy. We're talking about a significant expansion, a major financial commitment. That requires someone who can follow through consistently, day after day, without—" He pauses delicately. "Without accommodation."

Without accommodation. Like Ben's ADHD is a weakness to be managed, not a difference to be understood. I can't let it go.

"I've worked with dozens of hospitality professionals, and Ben's ideas for building Winterbloom and Alpenglow into a year-round operation are among the best I've seen. Dismissing them because of how his brain works is—" I stop myself from saying *jackassery*. Regroup, Maddie. "—is missing the point."

"The point being?"

"The point being that he's good at this. Really good." The doubt on Trip's face sends the rest tumbling out: "You might see that if you stopped looking for reasons he'll fail."

The table has gone quiet. Frances is watching me with interest. Gloria's expression is carefully neutral. Trish looks at Trip. And Ben—Ben is staring at his plate, shoulders tight, bracing for impact.

Trish tilts her head, studying me. "You've been here how many weeks?"

"I've been here long enough to see what's working."

"Long enough to evaluate a complex operation and determine that a man with a history of incomplete projects is the right person to lead a major expansion?" She's not hostile, I realize—*she's cross-examining me.* "That's a significant conclusion for someone in a temporary position."

"I'm providing a professional assessment," I say carefully.

"You're providing a passionate defense." Trish leans back, arms crossed. "I've sat through enough depositions to know when someone's invested beyond their role."

I feel my neck grow hot—my signature tell. "I believe in the proposal."

"You believe in Ben." It's not an accusation. It's an observation, clinical and precise. "That's not a criticism. But if we're making decisions about this family's future, we should be clear about what's influencing them."

I open my mouth. Close it. Look at Ben.

"Oh, for God's sake." Frances sets down her glass. "They're into each other. Quit dancing around and come out with it."

The words land like a thunderclap.

Trip's eyebrows rise. Trish's expression flickers with what looks like satisfaction—case closed. Gloria takes a calm sip of wine. And Ben is fully staring at me.

"I—" I start.

"Don't bother denying it," Frances says. "You've been defending him like he's yours to protect. Nobody fights that hard for a six-week job."

But I didn't claw my way to the top of Miami hospitality to fold at a dinner table. "The plans are solid. The projections are, too."

"But your interpretation of it might not be," Trip says. "Love makes us see what we want to see. Since our family has millions riding on this deal, if you're in love with my son—"

I glare at Frances—*thanks for that*—then turn to Trip. "I care about him. I won't pretend otherwise. But even if you think I'm some lovesick temp, what I feel doesn't change the data."

"Except we hired a consultant, not a girlfriend." Trip doesn't look at me—he's looking at Ben. "Perhaps we should find one who can be objective."

"Stop." Ben's voice is low but firm. The whole table turns. "Gran brought Madison in because she's an expert in corporate hospitality. She's managed projects at a property five times Winterbloom's size. You can question my capabilities all you want. I've heard it plenty. But questioning her professionalism is out of line."

Something flashes across Trip's face—surprise, maybe, at Ben pushing back. Trish leans forward.

"Ben, we're not trying to insult anyone. We're trying to protect you." Her voice softens. "We've watched you pour yourself into things before. We've watched it fall apart. We don't want to see that happen again, especially with a property as valuable as this."

"So your solution is to make sure I never try anything?" I can see his hands trembling below the table, but his voice is steady. It makes me proud. "That's not protection. That's a cage."

He pushes back from the table. I start to rise with him, but he catches my eye. The smallest shake of his head. *Stay. Finish this.*

"Gran, thank you for dinner." He's already moving toward the door. "I need some air."

The silence that follows is suffocating. Every instinct I have is telling me to follow him, to wrap my arms around him and say his dad is wrong. But Frances is leaning forward, watching me with sharp eyes, and I realize: Ben left because he couldn't sit there anymore. But I can.

I can stay in the fight. And I will see it through.

Frances's voice cuts through the silence, sharp and impatient.

"He's right, Trip. You should give him a chance. You've been picking at him all night. *Small wins. Nice hobby.* Every time he opens his mouth you find a way to cut him down." She shakes her head. "Dad believed in him. Mother believes in him. This woman who has no reason to lie believes in him. Maybe the problem isn't Ben. Maybe it's that you decided who he was years ago and you've never let him be anyone else."

Silence.

Trip's face has gone carefully blank. Trish puts a hand on his arm.

Frances takes a swig from her glass and turns to me. "The ski season projections. Walk me through them."

The rest of dinner pivots to logistics. I guide them through Ben's ideas—the numbers, the timelines, the partnerships—and back them up with forecasts and facts. When at last the coats are being gathered, Frances catches my arm.

"You've got a spine," she says. "And so does Ben, apparently. That's new. And encouraging. He's the only one who cares about this place the way Dad did. That matters more to me than Trip's anxieties."

Gloria appears as I head for the door.

"Well," she says. "Eventful."

"I'm sorry. I was trying to stay professional."

"You were magnificent." She pats my arm. "Ford would have adored you."

I slip out of Gloria's quarters and head for the hothouse, certain I'll find Ben there. But he's nowhere. Not the hothouse. Not his cabin. Not anywhere I check, until I wander past the front desk and spot the library nook. It's tucked into a corner near the entrance, shielded from the wind by a tall bookshelf. A small fireplace crackles. Two worn armchairs face each other across a low table stacked with books. And in the deep window seat, framed by falling snow, sits Ben.

He looks up when I round the corner. His expression is complicated—gratitude and worry tangled together.

I sink onto the window seat beside him. "Found you."

"I wasn't hiding. Much." He attempts a smile. "Gramps

built this space." He runs his hand along the worn wood of the window frame. "I came here as a kid when everything felt too loud. Sat in this exact spot and watched the snow and pretended I was somewhere else."

"Where did you pretend to be?"

"Anywhere my father couldn't explain why I'd disappointed him."

My chest aches. "Ben."

"I'm fine. I'm used to it. You—" He stops. Shakes his head. "You didn't have to tell them all that."

"Yes, I did."

"But you were right. Now he doubts your credibility."

"Yeah, well, it means less to me than you do." The words come out simpler than I expected. "I couldn't just sit there and let him talk to you like that. Like you're a problem to be solved. You're brilliant and hardworking and so smart."

He lifts our joined hands and presses his lips to my knuckles. "Thank you. When you say it, I can almost believe it."

"Then I'll keep saying it until you do." His smile is small but real. "Frances is on our side. Or at least, she's not on your parents' side. That's something."

"Frances is a wild card. But she listens. That's more than I can say for them."

"Your dad was never going to be convinced. Not by me, not by data, not by a choir of Christmas angels singing the praises of sustainable hospitality."

"Probably not." He's really smiling now. "But you were impressive, standing up to him like that."

"Someone had to."

"No one ever has. Not for me." He's looking at me with something unguarded in his expression.

I reach up and brush his hair back from his forehead. I don't have words for this. So I don't use any.

The kiss that follows starts soft, but the reality that we're not just pining anymore—that I can kiss him whenever I want—turns it into something else. His hands slide around my waist. Mine curl into the front of his shirt and pull him against me. The fire crackles. Snow falls past the window in thick white drifts. I shift closer, and closer still, until we're embarrassingly tight in this public, albeit secluded, space.

When we finally break apart, I'm breathing hard. "What am I doing, making out in this window? I *am* a lovesick temp."

"No one saw. The bookshelf almost hides us. Besides, one person has walked by since we've been sitting here."

"Your parents are here somewhere. If your dad saw us, he would definitely think my opinion is worthless."

"He thinks everyone's opinion is worthless except his." He traces his finger over my lips. "So, lovesick temp? Is that your title now?"

"I panicked during dinner. I couldn't think of anything else."

"You could've said devoted consultant."

"That sounds worse."

"Passionate project manager?"

"Now you're making it dirty."

His grin is devastating. "Am I?"

"Ben."

"Maddie. You did promise me a gift," he says, pulling me close to whisper in my ear.

"We're in your grandfather's library nook," I tell him primly.

"He'd approve. He was a romantic."

"You said that about the hothouse, too."

"He was romantic about a lot of things." His mouth finds the spot below my ear that makes me shiver. "And this is a very nice window seat."

"We are not—" But I'm laughing, and his hands are firm through my sweater, and when he kisses me again, I forget my argument.

The window seat is, admittedly, very nice. Wide and deep, with worn cushions that have probably seen decades of guests curling up with books and cocoa. Right now it's seeing something significantly less wholesome, and I can't bring myself to care. Ben's mouth is on my neck. My fingers are in his hair. The snow keeps falling, the fire keeps crackling, and for one perfect suspended moment, nothing exists except this.

His fingers trace the skin just under the hem of my sweater, and I make a sound that's not appropriate for a public space, and—

"THERE'S MY BABY! MERRY CHRISTMAS!"

I freeze.

That voice. I know that enthusiastic, boundary-free, over-the-top voice.

I turn my head slowly, the way you might if you'd just heard a bear in the woods.

"Mom?"

Ben and I break apart so fast I nearly fall off the window seat. My sweater is twisted. His hair is a disaster. We look, objectively, like two people who got caught in some shenanigans.

Because we were.

My mother is standing in the opening to the library nook. She's wearing a Christmas sweater featuring sequined llamas in Santa hats, with actual battery-operated lights twinkling around the hem. The llamas appear to be dancing. Or possibly having seizures. It's hard to tell.

Behind her, my father's face has tightened in a way that used to make subcontractors sweat. His eyes move grimly from Ben's disheveled hair to his untucked shirt to his hand on my waist, which he immediately drops.

Behind both of them, Sienna is grinning with the unhinged delight of someone who has orchestrated chaos and lived to see it unfold.

"Surprise!" Sienna does jazz hands. "Look what Santa brought you!"

Beside me, Ben has gone completely still. I can feel the exact moment his soul leaves his body.

My mother, however, is anything but still.

"Oh, my baby!" She pulls me against her and hugs me while she bobs up and down. "You look so pretty and so happy, honey. And I'm so glad we get to see you for Christmas!"

I give her a squeeze—I *am* glad to see her, despite my mortification—but then she steps back and turns her gaze to Ben.

"And you must be the young man who put that bloom into her cheeks." She doesn't wait for a response, just sweeps forward, arms outstretched and llamas twinkling. She pulls Ben into a hug, the lights of her sweater flashing against him, and holds on like she's known him forever.

"I—" Ben stands there with his arms half-raised, clearly unsure whether to hug her back or turn and flee. "Mrs. Lark, I'm so sorry, this isn't—we weren't—"

"It's Linda," she says, pulling back so she can beam at him.

Ben blinks. "Uh, Ben. Ben Bennett."

"Ben Bennett!" Mom is gripping his arms, examining him with open approval. "An alliterative name! I'm Linda Lark, so I understand the curse of the double consonant. We're practically family already."

"Mom." I've recovered enough to be horrified. "Can you maybe not—"

"And just look at you." She's studying him like he's a particularly enticing dessert. "Talk about tall, dark, and handsome! With these nice arms and that movie star jawline...No wonder my Maddie was kissing you like that."

"Mom!"

"What? I have eyes, Madison Grace." She winks at Ben. "Don't let me stop you. We can come back in ten minutes."

Ben's face goes the color of the holly berries on the mantel. "That's not—I mean—we don't—"

My mother laughs, utterly delighted. My father remains utterly silent.

"Ray." Mom gestures him forward. "Come say hello to Maddie's young man."

Ray Lark is a quiet man. He's built like he spent forty years working with his hands because he did, as a general contractor. He's been retired for six years but he still believes that reputation is everything and a hand shaken is a pledge that runs deep. Right now, he's looking at Ben with the same watchful gaze he's turned on every guy I've introduced to him since high school—the one that says he has opinions.

Ben straightens, smoothing his shirt before holding out his hand, trying to save this first impression. "Mr. Lark. I'm pleased to—this isn't how I wanted to—"

Dad takes his hand. Shakes it once. Drops it without a word and turns to me. "Maddie-bird. You doing good?"

"Hi, Daddy," I say, because although I usually call him Dad, in this moment it might not hurt to soften him up. As I step into his arms, I meet poor Ben's panicked eyes. Maybe some folksy charm will break the tension. "How are y'all even here? You were supposed to be at Aunt Karol's in Tampa."

"Oh, Aunt Karol..." Mom waves a hand, llamas swaying. "Plumbing disaster. Very dramatic, she's down to one bathroom. You don't want the details. So we thought, 'Why not reach out to sweet Sienna and surprise our girl?' Of course, we didn't realize you've been having such an adventure."

I look at Sienna, who mouths *you're welcome* with absolutely no remorse. "We stopped to eat after leaving the airport and I mentioned you had a new friend," she says. "Lucky us—we got dinner *and a show.*"

I narrow my eyes at Sienna then, but my mom doesn't even pause.

"A Christmas romance! At a Christmas market! It's like you're starring in a Hallmark movie, Maddie."

"It's not a Hallmark—" I look at Ben, still shell-shocked. At my father, who's watching him suspiciously while pretending to examine the crown molding. At my mother's twinkling llamas and Sienna's smirk. Actually, yeah, it is a Hallmark movie. With a plot that makes the main character shake her head in despair.

"Let me help you with your bags," Ben says, remembering how to be a functional human. "And let's see if we can upgrade your room. We've got some nice suites on the top floor. If one is open, it's yours."

"That's so sweet of you, Ben." Mom loops her arm through his like they're old friends.

I fall into step beside my dad, who breaks a long, uncomfortable silence by huffing, "He's nervous." He grunts. "He should be, after that performance."

An hour later, my parents are settling into their top-floor suite and Ben is stressing in my office. He's sitting on the edge of my desk with his head in his hands.

"That was—"

"I know."

"Your mother saw us—"

"I know."

"And your dad—" He looks up at me, genuinely stricken. "Maddie. He looked at me like I was a nail and he was a hammer."

"He looks at everyone like that."

"Really?"

"He's a contractor. He spent forty years evaluating whether people were going to waste his time. It's his default setting."

"Even with you?"

"Well, no. Not with me." I lean against the wall opposite him and grin. "I'm his baby girl."

Ben goes pale. "He's never going to approve of me now. I'm the guy he caught mauling his baby girl on Christmas."

"First of all, there was no mauling. We were two adults kissing—enthusiastically—in a beautiful, almost-private setting. Because adults are allowed to do that." I cross to him, take his hands. They're cold. "Second, my dad takes time to warm up to people. It's not personal. It's just the Ray Lark way."

"What do I do? How do I fix this?"

"You don't fix it. You just let him see who you actually are."

"What if who I actually am is a nervous wreck who can't form full sentences around him?"

"Then he'll know you care." I squeeze his hands. "Listen. There's a Ray Lark Operating Manual. Don't root for the Gators. He went to LSU. Don't assume anything about his politics because he's an old white guy from Florida. The only thing besides construction he'll talk your ear off about is local school board elections. And don't mention kissing his daughter. For at least—" I consider. "Forty-eight hours."

Ben stares at me. "Okay, but now I'm afraid to even be in the same room as you."

"Yeah, that's rational."

"I'm serious. What if he sees me look at you wrong? What if he can tell I'm thinking about—" He stops himself.

"About what, Ben Bennett?"

"Nothing. Pure thoughts only. I'm a monk now." He

straightens up, putting actual physical distance between us. "Honestly, I should probably not touch you until they leave. When do they leave?"

"December thirtieth. Morning flight."

"That's four days away."

"Five, technically."

"Maddie." His voice is pained. "I can't be near you for five days and not—"

"Not what?"

He gives me a look that makes my stomach flip. "You know what."

"Interesting." I take a step toward him. "So if I were to, say, take your hand right now—"

"Don't." But he's smiling.

"Or lean in really close—" I press against him.

"Maddie."

I let my lips brush his neck. "Or whisper something in your ear while my parents are watching—"

"You wouldn't."

"I absolutely would." I grin at him. "My dad's watching you like a hawk anyway. Might as well give him something to see."

"You're evil."

"Yeah, well. I learned from Linda Lark."

He laughs despite himself, and some of the tension leaves his shoulders. "Your mom is terrifying. In the best way. She just—adopted me. Within thirty seconds."

"She collects people. You're part of her crew now."

"I can think of worse fates."

I lean against the desk beside him. "For what it's worth? She already loves you. The alliterative name thing alone guaranteed it. And my dad will come around. He just needs to see you in your element."

"My element being…?"

"This place. The hothouse. The work you do here. He respects people who build things. Who work with their hands and care about craftsmanship. Sound like anyone you know?"

Ben considers this. "You think talking about joinery will win over your dad?"

I give him a real kiss, right on the mouth, because no one is watching and because I can.

"I think you being yourself will win over my dad. The joinery is a bonus."

Over the next few days, I watch Ben try very, very hard.

He gives my parents the full tour—the market, the vendor stalls, Santa's workshop, and the hothouse that makes my mother gasp when she walks through the doors.

"Oh, Maddie!" She clutches my arm. "It's Florida in here!"

"I know. There's even an orange tree in the back. I come here when I'm cold."

"I'm never leaving." She wanders toward the poinsettias, the sequined reindeer on today's sweater twinkling against all the green. "Ben, this is extraordinary. You grew all of this?"

"Some of it. Most of the established plants are my grandfather's." He holds open the door to the back section. "The orange tree is older than me. But I've been building up the herb garden and the seedling program." He leads her toward the herbs and vegetables, pointing out different varieties. "These tomatoes are a new heirloom strain I've been experimenting with. And the lettuce—we supply the chalet restaurant and the café year-round now."

"Your grandfather must have been proud."

Something softens in Ben's face. "I hope so. He built this

place as a wedding gift for my grandmother. She was an Arizona girl, and he said she needed somewhere warm if she was going to survive the long Colorado winters."

Mom sighs, delighted. "That's the most romantic thing I've ever heard." She looks at me meaningfully. "It makes me think of the two of you."

Ben grins at this, then immediately aims an unsettled glance at my dad.

My dad, however, is not looking at Ben or me or the plants. He's looking at the structure—the beams, the joints, the way the glass panels fit together. I watch him run his hand along a support post.

"Hand-cut, these mortises and tenons," he says, almost to himself.

Ben turns. "Yes, sir. My grandfather did most of the original work himself. We've had to repair sections over the years, but we've tried to match his methods."

"You can't match this with modern shortcuts." Dad traces a joint with his thumb. "This is craftsmanship. The kind that takes time."

"That's what Gramps always said. Shortcuts show. Even when you can't see them."

My father looks at Ben then—really looks at him, for the first time since the library nook. I see a change in his expression. A shift in the contractor's assessment.

"Good philosophy," he says. "Smart man, your grandfather."

Ben's whole face lights up. "He was. I learned everything from him."

"These joists need resealing." Dad points to a section near the back. "Water damage, probably from condensation. You let that go another year, you'll have rot."

"I've been meaning to—" Ben stops. Pulls out his phone. "Actually, can you show me exactly what you mean? I want to make notes."

For the next twenty minutes, I watch my father and this man who is apparently now my boyfriend examine structural elements and bond over wood preservation. When they finally emerge from behind the massive orange tree, they're both looking considerably more relaxed.

"This is good work, son," Dad says, clapping Ben on the shoulder. "Real good work."

Ben's eyes go suspiciously bright. He swallows hard. "Thank you, sir."

"Ray."

"Ray." Ben says it like he's been handed a gift. "Thank you, Ray."

My mother catches my eye across the hothouse and smiles.

The days of their visit blur together in the best way. Mom befriends every vendor in the market. She charms Judy within minutes, trading recipes and opinions on unsalted butter. She attends three of Agnes's sound bowl demonstrations and emerges from each one "spiritually renewed." She adopts Mrs. Chen, Derek, Mike, and approximately half the regular visitors. She wrangles Sienna an invitation to Evie's birthday party next month.

She also keeps buying me things.

"Maddie." She appears at my office door on day three, holding up gloves and a matching knit hat by its nonsensically huge pom-pom. "I found these at the most darling little stall."

"Mom. A pom-pom?"

"Oh, you'll look adorable. Try it on," she says, already wrestling it over my head. She holds up her little compact mirror.

The thing is: I don't hate it.

The wool is a soft alpaca blend, and the dusty rose color sets off my complexion. The pom-pom is admittedly ridiculous. But also kind of...cute?

"See?" Mom is beaming. "You look darling. Very Colorado chic."

"I look like something a cat would play with."

"You look like someone who's finally letting herself have a little fun." She adjusts the hat on my head, pulling it down over my ears. "Besides, you need warm things if you're going to stay."

"Mom, I'm not—the job in Naples—"

"The job in Naples is fine, if that's what you want to do." She takes my hands, her smile morphing to something more serious. "But this place suits you, Madison. He suits you."

"We've only known each other for—"

"I know. I'm just saying. He's a good one." She squeezes my hands and we have a moment. Then she turns the moment preposterous by adding, "Your father and I would love a grandson, you know. Your brother keeps producing girls—lovely girls, we adore them all—but a boy would be nice. A little Ben Junior."

I choke on nothing. "Mother."

"What? He's got good genes. Those broad shoulders and gorgeous green eyes—"

"First of all, a Ben Junior would have to be Buford Rudolph the Fifth. So, no."

Mom's eyes go wide with delight. "Buford Rudolph the Fifth?"

"Ben is the Fourth. It's his legal name. And the family curse."

"I love it. I love everything about it." She's cackling now.

"Can't you imagine it? Little Buford the Fifth, running around at Christmas—"

"There is no Buford the Fifth. There will never be a Buford the Fifth."

"Never say never, Maddie-bird."

I look at myself in the mirror again—pom-pom hat, flushed cheeks, the lights of my mother's Christmas tree cardigan flashing behind me.

"Fine," I admit. "The hat is cute."

In between all the family activity, Ben and I keep polishing the Holloway proposal, which—it's official—we're presenting on the thirtieth. It's genuinely coming together, with the revenue projections perfected, the community partnership section strengthened, and endorsement letters from local businesses arriving in beautiful stacks. We're reviewing a hard copy in my office when our hands touch.

We look at each other. Alone time has been hard to find, and I'm starting to forget what kissing him feels like.

"Five-minute break," I whisper.

He glances at the closed door behind us. "I don't think—"

I pull him toward me and let my lips brush his. He makes a sound of surrender and his hands find my waist and for about thirty seconds everything is perfect until—

"There you are!" Mom stands in the doorway, twinkling snowflake sweater aglow. "Ben, I need your opinion on which scarf to buy your grandmother."

Ben has leapt away from me like I'm on fire.

"Yes! Scarves! I can help with scarves." He practically runs to the door. "Show me the options."

This happens multiple times over the next two days. Once behind the Christmas tree in the main lobby, where we have approximately ninety seconds of privacy before Mom appears, exclaiming over Bree's hot cocoa. Once in the hallway outside Gloria's office, where Ben pauses to brush snow from my hair and Mom materializes like she's been summoned.

"How does she do that?" Ben asks, looking genuinely haunted. "Is she tracking your phone?"

"She doesn't need to. She's got years of practice catching me in the act."

He raises an eyebrow. "In the act of what, exactly?"

"Wouldn't you like to know." I grin at him. "She's not trying to catch us. She just can't help herself. She loves this too much."

"Our suffering?"

"Our romance. She's living vicariously. We're her Hallmark movie now." I pat his chest. "Welcome to life with Linda Lark. Can you handle the full experience?"

He looks at me—really looks, with that warmth I'm starting to depend on—and says, "For you? I can handle anything."

The night before my parents leave, Sienna arranges a special last-night-at-Winterbloom experience: a horse-drawn sleigh—dark wood, velvet cushions, lanterns hanging from posts—that takes us through old growth pines heavy with snow and frozen meadows glittering under the stars. Ben points out landmarks—the aspen grove where Ford proposed to Gloria, the tree he fell out of when he was nine—until we arrive at a clearing. A heated glass yurt has been set up, glowing from within like something out of a dream. Fairy lights wrap around the frame. A fire pit crackles nearby. Inside, through the transparent panels, a table is set with real china and cloth napkins and flickering candles.

"Chef Raúl and Judy collaborated on the menu," Sienna

says as we climb out of the sleigh. "Four courses plus s'mores after, because I know Linda Lark loves her s'mores."

Mom hugs her so hard Sienna squeaks.

We talk about everything and nothing. Ben tells stories about growing up here, about Ford teaching him to fish in the lake, about Gloria's strict policy on proper table manners. My mom tells stories about me as a kid—embarrassing ones, obviously, because that's what mothers do—and Ben files each one away with a laugh.

After dinner, we move outside to the fire pit for s'mores. Mom immediately takes charge, stacking her creation with a ridiculous amount of chocolate.

"What's the point if you don't do it right?" she says when Dad looks skeptical.

The fire crackles. The stars are impossibly bright, and the yurt glows behind us like a promise. Ben's hand is warm in mine.

Mom, Dad, and Sienna are having an intense discussion about marshmallow-toasting technique—Dad prefers the golden-brown slow roast, Sienna only likes them barely cooked, Mom is a "stick it in the flames until it's torched" kind of gal—and for a moment, Ben and I are almost alone.

"Sneak away with me," I murmur. "Just for a minute."

"They'll notice."

"They're arguing about marshmallows. They won't notice anything."

I pull him toward the edge of the clearing, just far enough that we're in shadow but can still see the fire. The sky overhead is thick with stars. Our breath plumes in the cold air.

"Hi," I say, and then I kiss him. Soft at first, then deeper when he pulls me in. His hands cup my face, cold from the winter air but heating up against my skin. I make a small sound against his mouth, and he smiles into the kiss—

"Ben! Madison! You're missing the s'mores!"

We break apart. Mom is waving from the fire pit, a flaming marshmallow on her stick.

"Coming!" I call back.

Ben drops his forehead to mine. "Fifteen more seconds."

"Mmm. Twenty."

"If you negotiate like this with the Holloways, we'll be in trouble."

"You're not the Holloways. And you love it."

"I really do." His eyes find mine in the starlight, and something in his expression makes my breath catch.

We walk back to the fire hand in hand. Later, after my parents have headed to their room, I stand with him on the wide chalet porch. Snow is falling lightly. The market is dark except for the Christmas tree, still glowing.

"So," Ben says. "Your parents."

"My parents."

"They're incredible. You know that, right?"

I lean against the railing, watching the snow. "They're a lot. I know *that*."

He comes to stand beside me, close enough that our arms touch. "The way they are with each other. The way they are with you. The way they just—welcomed me in, like I already belonged."

His voice catches on the last word. I look at him.

"I've never had that." He's staring at the Christmas tree, not meeting my eyes. "Parents who look at each other like that. Parents who make home somewhere you want to be."

I think about what I know of his parents. The constant

pecking. The two-on-one. The implication that he's not quite enough.

"You should have it." I take his hand. "You are kind and smart and you work so hard, because you really care." I squeeze his fingers. "My parents see that, too. That's why they already love you."

He's quiet for a moment, and then he says, "Your dad called me son. Twice."

"I heard."

"That's—" He shakes his head. "That's more than my actual father has made me feel in years."

I don't have words for the ache in my chest. So I just lean into him, letting him wrap his arms around me as the snow falls around us.

After a few silent minutes, he whispers, "I've loved being part of this." He brushes snow from my hair—the same gesture that got us interrupted days ago—and this time, no one materializes. "The chaos. The warmth. The feeling that I finally fit. All of it."

"Even the pom-pom hat?"

"Especially the pom-pom hat." He grins. "You look adorable in it, by the way."

"I look like a cat toy."

"A very cute cat toy." He kisses me again, slow and sweet, with snow melting on our skin. When we finally break apart, I'm shivering—from the cold or the kiss, I'm not sure.

"We should go inside," I say.

"Probably."

Neither of us moves. He pulls me closer, chin resting on top of my head.

The Christmas tree glows in the dark. The snow keeps falling. And I stand there in Ben's arms, wearing a pom-pom hat, feeling like maybe—for the first time in a long time—I'm exactly where I'm supposed to be.

Fall ON YOUR KNEES

THE LOBBY OF WINTERBLOOM CHALET WAS BUILT TO impress. Soaring ceilings, that giant antler chandelier, the stone fireplace big enough to roast a whole pig. This morning, though, it feels like a very large space in which to have a nervous breakdown. So it's helpful that it's quiet—too early for guests and most of the staff—leaving us to rehearse our proposal in peace.

Ben is pacing in front of the fire like he's trying to wear a groove into the hardwood.

"Revenue projections for Year Two assume a fifty percent increase in lodging bookings based on expanded event programming and the Alpenglow acquisition." He flips through his notes. Frowns. "Fifty percent. Is that too aggressive?"

"You're turning a six-week operation into a year-round resort with a ski lodge. Fifty percent is likely underselling it." I'm curled in one of the leather armchairs, laptop open but eyes on him. "Own the number. Keep going."

"Right. The acquisition creates opportunities for—" He stops. Drags a hand through his hair. "I've said opportunities three times in two minutes. I sound like a brochure."

"You sound like someone who's done the work." I close my laptop and stand, crossing to where he's frozen mid-stride. "Hey. Look at me."

He does. His eyes are a little wild.

"You know this business," I tell him. "You know this community. You've spent years building relationships with every shop and restaurant owner in Snowdrop, and they're showing up for you. Forty-seven letters of support—commitments to host events, send customers your way, and make this town a year-round destination. That doesn't happen because someone wrote a good proposal. That happens because people believe in you."

"What if I freeze up? What if I get in there and Dad's voice in my head is louder than mine and I—"

"Then you check your notes. That's what they're for. And you remember that you developed the plan and you know the answers." I run my hands down his lapels. "Your grandfather believed you could do this. Gloria and I believe in you. It's time you start believing, too."

The wild look settles into something softer. More focused. "Thank you."

I let myself admire him—the charcoal suit he clearly needs to wear more often, the dark curls tamed into sexy waves. I smooth an invisible wrinkle from his shirt, letting my hand linger against his chest. "I can't stop thinking about how good you look in this suit, which is very inconvenient timing."

His eyes fill with unapologetic heat. His gaze travels down my black sheath dress—my best *I'm-a-serious-professional* armor—and then up again, slow enough to make my skin prickle. "You should talk. You're going to distract the entire Holloway family."

"That's the plan. I distract, you dazzle."

"Teamwork."

"Very professional."

"United front." He pulls me closer. "We have twenty minutes before we need to actually be professional. Any ideas?"

"One or two."

The kiss starts soft, like it should when you're kissing in a public place. But despite all best efforts, it doesn't stay that way. His hand slides up my back and I forget for a second that, even though we're tucked into a corner of the empty lobby, anyone could walk in. I forget that the Holloways are arriving in less than an hour, that my parents are upstairs packing—

"Ben."

We spring apart.

Trip is standing in the entryway, Trish beside him.

Oh, right. I also forgot that Ben's parents are on their way.

"Dad." Ben steps back from me, straightening his jacket. "Mom. You're early."

"Traffic was lighter than expected." Trip crosses the lobby in measured steps.

He's in a suit that undoubtedly has a pedigree. Trish's tailored black wool suggests she might depose someone.

"We were hoping to talk before the Holloways arrive," she says.

"We were going over the presentation—"

"That's what I want to discuss." Trip settles into one of the leather armchairs by the fire like he owns the place. Which, I suppose, he partially does. Trish perches on the arm of his chair. I hover near the couch, unsure whether to stay or go.

"Ben." Trip's voice is gentle. Almost warm. "Are you sure you want to do this?"

Ben blinks. "What do you mean?"

"This proposal. This plan." Trip leans forward, elbows on his knees, hands clasped. The posture of a concerned father. "I've read the numbers. I've seen your projections. And I'm wondering if you've really thought through what you're asking of yourself."

"Gramps and I were planning this for years. Of course I've thought it through."

"Yes, but he's gone." Trip's brow furrows with what looks like genuine worry. "And you'll be carrying this on your own."

"Your father's right." Trish's voice is measured. Lawyer-precise. "Ford had decades of experience. A partner. A support system. You're proposing that you take on a major acquisition while also running the day-to-day operations here at Winterbloom. That's a lot for anyone, Ben. Let alone—"

She stops herself. But the end of that sentence hangs in the air anyway.

"We're worried," Trip says, picking up where she left off. "We're worried that you're setting yourself up for another very public failure. And I have to ask—after Boulder, is that really what you want?"

The words land softly. That's the cruelty of it, and maybe the tragedy, too. He really believes he's helping. I can see it in his face—he thinks this is love. But protection that sounds like doubt still leaves a bruise.

"Boulder was different," Ben says. His voice is steady, but I can see the effort it takes. "I made mistakes. I know that. I didn't stay on top of the details, I didn't respond fast enough when things started going sideways. But I learned from it. I've built better systems. I know what I did wrong and how to do it differently."

"I hope that's true. I really do." Trip pauses. "But I've watched you your whole life, Ben. I've seen the ideas that fizzle out, the projects that get abandoned, habits that work for a month and then fall apart. You have vision—you've always had vision—but vision isn't execution. And execution requires consistency. Follow-through." He shakes his head slowly. "Those have never been your strengths."

I think he really means it as help. It lands like a verdict.

"I've built systems that work—"

"You've built workarounds. Clever ones, I'll grant you. But this isn't a hobby greenhouse or a packaging startup you can walk away from when it gets hard. This is a multi-million-dollar acquisition with real consequences." Trip's gaze slides to me, then back to Ben. "And I notice your proposal leans heavily on Ms. Lark's expertise. What happens when she goes back to Florida? When it's just you trying to hold all the pieces together?"

"The proposal is Ben's." The words are out of my mouth before I can stop them. "Every strategy, every projection, every partnership. I organized the document. He built the business plan."

Trip's gaze settles on me. Cool. Assessing. "With respect, Ms. Lark, you've been here a few weeks. I've known my son for thirty-two years."

"Then maybe it's time you start appreciating what he's capable of."

Trip stands. Straightens his jacket. When he speaks again, his voice is low and serious.

"Ben, I'm not trying to hurt you. I'm trying to protect you. From another Boulder. From the humiliation of standing in front of this family and this community and falling short." He pauses. "You did Boulder with a partner. Someone to share the load, to catch what you missed. And it still fell apart." His eyes flick to me, then back to his son. "Here, you'll be on your own."

The words hit their target. I watch Ben absorb them. Watch the doubt flicker back into his face.

And something certain rushes through me.

I'm already stepping forward, a vision taking shape at the edge of my thoughts. They're the same images I've been pushing away for weeks. Spring weddings in the meadow. Fall retreats when the aspens turn gold. Alpenglow and its mid-century magnificence—a venue that will make brides weep.

These are not the kind of weddings I used to plan in Miami. Not all spectacle and swan ice sculptures, not brides more worried about the photos than the marriage. These are personal. Authentic. Meaningful. People who come to us because the mountains mean something to them. Who want real celebrations instead of productions.

I've shut these thoughts down every time they popped into my head. Because Caroline's offer is a sure thing, and this...this is a gamble.

But I look at Ben, and the answer is clear.

I've never been more ready to bet on myself. And on this man I know and trust.

We're better together, in every way. He catches a spark and fans it into something people believe in. I work the logistics to make it real—the budgets, the timelines, the thousand details that turn a dream into a plan.

Ford had the vision. Gloria built the scaffolding.

That could be us. I want it to be us.

And watching Trip chip away at Ben's confidence,

watching Ben fight to hold onto himself—watching him hear *you'll be on your own* and believe it—

That's not going to work for me.

Ben catches my eye. "Maddie. Don't."

"Don't what?"

"I can see you thinking. And I'm not letting him guilt you into anything."

I stand up straight. "He's not guilting me."

"He's implying you're the only thing standing between me and failure." Ben's voice is tight. "You're not making decisions because you feel sorry for me."

I think about Santa's letters—*fear is a liar in a sensible coat*. I think about the letter I wrote my grandmother and never sent, and how I've spent twelve years telling myself that was a failure when really it was just fear. Fear of saying the thing I wanted. Fear of wanting it at all.

And I know: I'm not afraid anymore.

I step toward him.

"I don't feel sorry for you. I feel sorry for him. You're brilliant, and I know this will work. So I'm in. Not because you need me—you can do this yourself. But because this idea will work and because together, we work. You see possibilities and I turn them into plans. We've been proving that since my first day. And here, together, we can build something real." I hold his gaze. "I've fallen in love with Winterbloom and I've fallen in love with you. Sorry for blurting that out in front of everyone before I'd even properly said it to you. But it's true."

The words land in the silence. He's so still that, for one horrible moment, I think I've broken him. But then a smile takes over his face, relief and joy and something raw underneath, and he closes the distance between us in two steps.

He takes my face in his hands, tilts my chin and looks into my eyes.

"I think it was proper. I think it was perfect." His voice is rough. His fingers trace the curve of my lips. "Same, by the way. Falling, have fallen, will continue to fall. Any way you phrase it, I love you, too."

He kisses me. Soft. Certain. Unwavering. And I forget, again, that we're standing in the lobby, that the Holloways are coming, that Trip and Trish are watching with whatever expression people wear when their son declares his love for the help. Perhaps most importantly, I forget about Linda Lark.

"Oh, *Ray*. Ray, are you hearing this?"

My mother is standing at the base of the stairs, one hand clutching my father's arm, the other pressed to her heart. Her eyes are wet. She is beaming like she just witnessed a royal wedding.

She's already moving toward us, heels clicking on the hardwood.

"That was the most romantic thing I've ever seen. And I've seen *The Notebook* fourteen times."

She pulls Ben into a hug.

"Welcome to the family," she murmurs. "I know you'll treat her right."

Dad is quieter about it. He crosses the lobby at his own pace, stops in front of Ben, and extends his hand. "You're a good man, Ben. I've seen enough to know."

Ben swallows. He nods once, sharp, like he doesn't trust his voice.

"Declarations of love," Trip says. His tone is light, almost amused, but there's an edge underneath. "Very romantic. But I don't recall seeing that section in the business proposal."

The words land like ice water. Mom's smile falters. Ben stiffens beside me.

But Dad doesn't even turn around. He's still looking at Ben when he speaks.

"I've been in contracting forty years. Built my company from nothing. Hired hundreds of workers." He releases Ben's hand but doesn't step back. "You know what I've learned? You can teach someone to read a blueprint. You can't teach them to care about the work."

Now he turns. Faces Trip directly.

"Your son notices things. The joinery in this chalet—he knows who built it, when, what techniques they used. He sees the craft in things. That's not common." Dad's voice is steady. "And he shows up. Every day I've been here, he's been working. Not talking about working. Working."

Trip's expression flickers. He's not used to being challenged. Certainly not by a contractor from Florida.

"Thanks for your input, Mr. Lark," he says, in the tone of a man closing a meeting.

Dad doesn't flinch. He pins Trip with a look I've seen my whole life—a look that, without a word, has shamed grown men into redoing shoddy work.

Trip breaks first. Looks down and fiddles with his cuffs.

"You're welcome," Dad says.

Mom leans close to Ben. She means to whisper, but Linda Lark has never successfully whispered in her life.

"Don't you worry about him. Your ideas are going to work." She pats his arm. "Your dad is just acting like an A-S-S."

She spells it out. Loudly. Trip absolutely hears.

Ben makes a sound that might be a laugh or might be a sob. I grab his hand and squeeze.

Outside the double doors, I see Sienna's Subaru pull up. She waves at us.

"We should get going," Dad says, checking his watch. "Your mother needs her airport coffee."

The goodbyes are warm and chaotic—Mom hugging Ben and me twice, Dad shaking Ben's hand again with that same meaningful look. Both of them ignoring Trish and Trip.

"You call us," Mom says, gripping Ben's hand as she pulls me into one last hug. "The second you know anything. We want to hear it from you two."

"We will."

"And you—" She points at Ben. "Take care of my girl."

"You know I will."

They disappear through the front door in a flurry of rolling suitcases and last-minute waves. The lobby feels suddenly emptier. Quieter.

The moment breaks when Frances's voice echoes from the hallway.

"They're here."

The Holloways are a trio of siblings in their late forties or early fifties—two brothers and a sister, all with the same sharp cheekbones and wary eyes. Gloria greets them in the lobby with the gracious warmth of a woman who's been hosting guests for sixty years, but I can see the strain around her mouth. Frances flanks her. She's exchanged the barn wear for a surprisingly sharp pantsuit that makes her look like she eats corporate boards for breakfast.

Our delegation heads toward the Columbine Room. I catch Trip's eye as we file in. His expression is unreadable.

"Ready?" I murmur to Ben.

He takes a breath. Squares his shoulders. "Ready."

And he's better than ready. He presents our proposal beautifully.

Ben stands at the head of the long mahogany table, and from the first sentence, I can see the Holloways leaning in. He walks them through his vision—Alpenglow restored to its mid-century glory, integrated with Winterbloom to create a year-round destination. He talks about sustainability initiatives and community partnerships. He talks about honoring what their grandparents built. He talks about giving it a future that respects its past.

He doesn't stumble. He doesn't lose his place. The notes he glances at are just anchors—he knows this material cold because he's lived it, dreamed it, built it in sticky notes and notebooks and late nights in the hothouse.

When he gets to the community letters, his voice thickens.

"Forty-seven local businesses signed on to support this proposal. Not because we asked them to—because they believe in what Snowdrop is, and what Winterbloom and Alpenglow can become together." He fans the letters across the table. "The brewery. The bookstore. Every vendor in our market. The public schools. The Methodist church." He looks up at the Holloways. "Your grandparents built something people loved. We want to protect that. Grow it. Make sure it's still here for the next generation."

I watch the Holloways exchange glances. The sister, Margaret, has tears in her eyes. One of the brothers, the younger one, is nodding slowly.

Gloria speaks last. Her voice is steady, but I can hear the emotion underneath.

"Ford and I built Winterbloom because we believed this valley was special. Your grandparents believed the same thing. They were our neighbors, our friends, our partners in helping to make the town of Snowdrop the haven it is." She pauses. "My grandson has Ford's vision and my stubbornness. I trust him to carry this forward. I hope you'll trust him, too."

The room falls quiet.

The older brother, Paul, exchanges a look with his siblings. "Would you give us a few minutes to discuss?"

"Of course." Gloria rises with grace. "Take all the time you need."

We file out into the hallway. The door clicks shut behind us.

Frances is the first to speak. "That was exceptional work, Ben." Her voice is brisk, but there's warmth underneath. "Your grandfather would have been proud."

Ben blinks. "Thank you, Aunt Frances."

Even Trip nods, once. "The community letters were a smart touch."

It's not an apology. It's not even a full compliment. But from Trip, it's something.

Ben catches my eye. We walk a few steps down the hall, out of earshot.

"You were incredible," I tell him quietly, pulling him into my arms. "Everything you've been working toward—they saw it. All of it."

"We don't know yet, though."

"I know." I step back and take his hand. "Whatever happens in there, you did everything right."

He exhales. Some of the tension leaves his shoulders. "I couldn't have done it without—"

The door opens. Margaret leans out. "We're ready."

We file back in. Gloria looks drawn as she takes her seat, though her smile doesn't waver. Under the table, I rest my hand on Ben's arm, just a beat.

The older brother, Paul, clears his throat. "Thank you. This is—" He looks at his siblings. "This is a beautiful proposal. It's clear you've put a lot of thought into it."

"We have," Ben says.

"The thing is..." Paul hesitates. "We met with Ian Preston last night."

The temperature in the room drops.

"His offer is significantly higher," he continues. "And he's agreed to honor our family's legacy. He wants to build a memorial performance hall named for our grandparents. And his vision includes a commitment to realizing our grandfather's dream of—"

"Competing with Vail," James, the younger brother, finishes. There's something in his tone. Skepticism, maybe. Or sadness.

Margaret speaks up. "James has concerns about the Preston proposal."

James shrugs. "Granddad only wanted to become Vail when Vail started to cut into Alpenglow's customer base. He liked what Snowdrop represents. Small. Personal. A real community." He looks at Ben. "Your proposal understands that."

"But we voted, and Margaret and I sided with Ian Preston," Paul, the older brother says. Not unkindly. "The financials aren't close. His offer gives us security. Certainty." He turns to Gloria. "I'm sorry. I know this isn't what you wanted to hear. But we've decided to go with Ian."

The words hang in the air.

I reach for Ben's hand under the table. His fingers are cold.

"I understand," Gloria says. Her voice is calm. Measured. But her face has gone pale. "Thank you for hearing us out."

She starts to stand, and I see her hand reach for the edge of the table. Not to push herself up. To steady herself.

"Mother?" Frances is already moving.

Gloria's other hand goes to her chest.

"I'm fine," she says, but she's not fine. She's gray, and she's gripping the table like it's the only thing holding her up.

"Gran!" Ben's chair scrapes back.

Gloria's knees buckle.

Ben catches her before she hits the floor. Frances is there a second later, easing her down, shouting for someone to call 911. The Holloways are on their feet, frozen. Trip pushes past them, phone already in his hand.

I drop to my knees beside Ben. Gloria's eyes are closed. Her breathing is shallow.

"Gran, stay with me." Ben's voice cracks. "Stay with me. Help is coming."

I take his free hand. Hold on tight.

The ambulance takes seven minutes to arrive. It feels like seven hours.

THE WORLD IN *Solemn* STILLNESS LAY

CHAPTER 22

HOSPITALS HAVE A PARTICULAR SMELL. ANTISEPTIC and anxiety and the vending machine coffee no one actually wants but everyone drinks anyway because it gives you something to hold.

I've been holding the same cup for over an hour. It went cold ages ago.

The waiting room is the usual fluorescent purgatory—molded plastic chairs in institutional beige, a TV mounted in the corner playing cable news on mute, a wilting ficus that either Ben should steal or someone should put out of its misery. Frances is on her phone in the corner, speaking to someone in low, clipped tones. Trish is sitting with her ankles crossed and her hands folded, the picture of composure except for the way she keeps checking her watch.

And Trip is pacing.

He's been pacing since we got here. Back and forth across the same twelve feet of tile, his dress shoes clicking out a rhythm that's slowly driving me insane. Every few passes, he stops. Looks at Ben. Opens his mouth like he's about to say something.

Then he starts pacing again.

Ben is sitting next to me. Close enough to touch if I reach out. But he hasn't looked at me since we got here. He hasn't looked at anyone. He's just...still. Hands loose in his lap. Eyes fixed on some middle distance only he can see.

I've watched him spiral before. I've watched him pace and fidget and talk too fast when the anxiety gets loud. This is different. This is the opposite of spinning out.

This is shutting down.

"She was fine this morning," Trip says, and it's not clear if he's talking to us or to himself. "She was *fine*. And then—"

He stops. Drags his hand through his hair. For a moment I see Ben in the gesture, and something in my chest aches.

"She's been under enormous stress," Trish says. Measured. Careful. "Running Winterbloom is too much for her."

"Exactly." Trip's voice sharpens. "And this ridiculous proposal that's been consuming her energy. The pressure of—" He stops in front of Ben. "I told you this was too much for her. I *told* you."

Ben doesn't look up.

"Trip." Frances's voice cuts across the room. She's lowered her phone, watching him with hard eyes. "Not the time."

"When, then? After the next collapse? After she—" He can't finish that sentence. Won't. "She's eighty-three years old. She went into AFib six months ago. And we've been letting her run herself into the ground over a ski lodge and a dream that should have stayed in the past."

"That dream was hers, like it was Dad's," Frances says flatly. "And now it's Ben's. You don't get to rewrite that because you never believed in it."

"I believe in protecting this family. Which apparently makes me the villain."

"Right now, it's making you a bully. There's a difference."

Trish stands smoothly, inserting herself between them. "This isn't productive. We're all worried. We're all scared. Let's not say things we'll regret."

Trip turns away from Frances. His gaze lands on Ben again, and something flickers across his face—frustration, maybe, or something uglier wearing a mask of concern.

"Ben. Say something."

Nothing.

"*Ben.*"

"What do you want me to say?" Ben's voice is flat. Hollow. He still hasn't looked up. "You're right. You've always been right. I pushed too hard and now she's—" He swallows, hard. "I don't know what you want me to say."

"I want you to take some responsibility."

I'm on my feet before I realize I've moved. "You can stop now."

He turns that hard gaze on me. "Ms. Lark. With respect, this is a family matter."

"With respect, you're kicking him while he's down and it's not helping anyone." My voice is steadier than I feel. "We're all terrified. But blaming Ben isn't going to change what happened, and it's not going to help Gloria recover."

"She wouldn't need to recover if—"

"If what? If Ben and Gloria had given up like you wanted them to?" I take a breath, tell myself to dial it back. "I was there. Gloria asked me to help them with this because she wanted it, too. It matters to her. I know you disagreed, and I know you're scared. But this isn't Ben's fault."

Trip's jaw tightens. For a moment I think he's going to keep pushing. Then Trish touches his arm, and he deflates.

"Fine." He turns away. Resumes pacing. "Fine."

I sit back down. I want to take Ben's hand, but something in the way he's holding himself tells me not to.

"Hey," I say. "She'll be okay."

He doesn't respond.

"Ben. Look at me."

He does, finally. And the emptiness in his eyes makes my stomach drop.

"I should have seen it. I was so focused on the presentation, on proving myself, I didn't see how tired she was. How much this was costing her."

"None of us saw it."

"She's my grandmother. I should have." He looks away again. "But that's the problem with me, right? I miss things. I get so locked in on what I'm doing that I don't notice what's happening around me. My dad's not wrong about that."

"Ben—"

"Gran is in there because I couldn't let go of a dream that was never going to work. The Holloways said no. It's over. And now she's—" He stops. Swallows. "I keep making things worse."

An ache throbs behind my ribs. Now I do reach over and take his hand. He lets me, but he doesn't squeeze back. His fingers are cold and limp in mine.

We sit like that for what feels like hours. Trip paces. Trish watches. Frances makes more phone calls. The ficus continues its slow decline.

And then the door opens, and a doctor in blue scrubs steps into the waiting room.

She's maybe sixty, with tired eyes and graying hair pulled

back in a practical twist. When she sees Frances, her expression softens with recognition.

"Frances. I thought I might see you here." She crosses to us, clasping Frances on the arm.

"Ana," Frances says. "It's been a while."

"Too long. I was sorry to hear about Ford." She turns to include the rest of us, but speaks to Trip. "I'm Dr. Reyes. I've been treating your mother. I've known your family for years—Gloria and Ford hosted the hospital's holiday party at Winterbloom back when I was a resident." A small smile. "Your father made the best mulled wine I've ever had."

"How is she?" Trip cuts in. "What's happening? Is she—"

"She's stable." Dr. Reyes holds up her hand, preempting the flood of questions. "We've run tests. Her heart rhythm is back to normal, and there's no sign of a heart attack. What she experienced was a syncopal episode—essentially, her body's response to acute stress. Her blood pressure dropped suddenly, which caused her to lose consciousness."

"But she's okay?" Ben can barely get out the words. "She's going to be okay?"

The doctor's expression softens slightly. "She's resting comfortably. We'd like to keep her overnight for observation, given her history of AFib and her age. But yes, we expect a full recovery."

The relief that washes through the room is almost physical. Frances closes her eyes briefly. Trish squeezes Trip's arm. Even Trip's shoulders drop an inch.

"However." The doctor pauses, and the relief curdles. "I need to be direct with you. Mrs. Bennett is eighty-three years old. She has a cardiac history. And based on what she's told me about her current workload..." She shakes her head. "This was a warning. If she continues at this pace, the next episode may not be as benign."

"What are you saying?" Frances asks.

"I'm saying she needs to step back. Significantly. Whatever responsibilities she's been carrying, she needs to delegate them or let them go. Her body is telling her—loudly—that it can't sustain this level of strain."

The words settle over us like wet snow. Heavy. Final.

Gloria's days of running Winterbloom are over.

"Can we see her?" Ben asks.

"One or two at a time. She's tired, so keep it brief." The doctor gestures toward the double doors. "Room 114, down the hall to the left."

Frances moves first. "I'll go. Trip?"

Trip nods, a complicated look passing over his face. For a moment, he's less like a man who's been pacing and blaming and more like a son who almost lost his mom.

He catches Ben's eye.

"We'll discuss next steps when she's home," he says. "But at least this takes some pressure off. The Holloways made their decision. Ian Preston will handle the transition. She can get some rest."

He says it like it's a kindness. Like he's offering Ben an out.

Ben doesn't respond. But something in his face shutters closed, and I watch the last flicker of hope go dark.

Frances and Trip disappear through the double doors. Trish settles back into her chair, pulling out her phone—probably drafting emails about estate planning or power of attorney or whatever lawyers think about in hospital waiting rooms. Her suit is still immaculate. Not a wrinkle. Some people fall apart in a crisis; Trish Bennett finds a more efficient way to sit.

Which leaves me and Ben alone. Or as alone as you can be

in a room with fluorescent lights and a dying ficus and a mother who's fixated on her phone.

"Hey." I touch his arm. "That's good news. She's going to be fine."

He nods, but his eyes are somewhere else. Somewhere I can't reach.

"Ben. Talk to me."

"I just..." He stands abruptly and walks to the window—a sad rectangle of glass overlooking the parking lot, where gray sky presses down on gray asphalt. I follow, stopping a few feet behind him.

"I keep thinking about Gramps," he says quietly. "The last few months, before he died. I knew he was getting worse. I knew we were running out of time. And I kept telling myself I'd say everything I needed to say. That there'd be a right moment."

He's not looking at me. He's looking at his own reflection in the glass, or more likely through it, at something only he can see.

"There wasn't," he continues. "He went fast at the end. One day he was laughing at something I said, and a day later he was gone, and I never—" He stops. Swallows hard. "I never got to tell him what he meant to me. Not really. Not the way I should have. I keep thinking about Gran in there, and what if —" He stops. Swallows hard. "What if I'd lost her today without ever saying the things that matter? Without her knowing how much I—"

He turns to face me. His eyes are red-rimmed, raw in a way I've never seen. My heart lurches toward him, and the words are already organizing themselves in my mind—that I understand, so fully, what he's trying to say; that I know how he feels, and how much it hurts, and how he should tell Gloria now, while he has the chance—when his next words stop me cold.

"I know you understand. The letter you never sent to your grandmother." He exhales, shaky. "That kind of regret, it devastates you."

The cold spreads. Crystallizes.

"What did you say?"

He blinks, confused by the shift in my tone. "I just meant —I know you've been through something similar. With your grandmother. The letter you wrote but never—"

"How do you know about that?"

The confusion on his face flickers into something else. Something that looks a lot like fear.

"Maddie—"

"How do you *know* about that, Ben?" It comes out too loud, but I can't help it. "I never told you. I never told anyone until I got to Winterbloom." I stop. The pieces are rearranging themselves in my head, clicking into place like a lock I didn't know I was picking. "I only told one person about that letter. And it wasn't you."

He's gone pale. "Let me explain."

"You wrote the Santa letters." The words come out flat. Almost calm. The eye of a storm. "It was you. You wrote all of them. This whole time."

"Maddie, please, just let me—"

"You read everything." My voice cracks. "About my job. About my grandmother. About—" I stop, because the next part is too humiliating to say out loud. About falling for *him*. About being scared to let him in. About all the ways I'd convinced myself to trust again.

I wrote those things to a stranger. Someone anonymous. Safe.

Except it wasn't a stranger. It was him.

While he was giving me sweaters and coats and making me believe he saw me. While he was kissing me. While I was falling in love with him.

It was always him.

"You knew." I can barely get the words out. "You knew everything I was feeling, everything I was afraid of, and you just—what? Used it to become exactly what I needed?"

"No." He steps toward me. "That's not—Maddie, I never—"

"I trusted you." I step back. "I trusted you, and you've been lying to me the whole time."

He flinches like I've hit him.

And I'm done.

I turn and walk toward the exit, my vision blurring. Behind me, I hear him say my name—once, twice—but I don't stop. I can't stop. If I stop, I'll have to look at him, and if I look at him, I'll see the way he smiled at me in the hothouse, the way he traced the collar of that beautiful coat, the way he whispered *I love you* in front of everyone like it was the truest thing he'd ever said. I don't want to see that.

I don't want to see him.

The automatic doors slide open. Cold air hits my face, sharp and clean after the stale hospital smell. I stand on the sidewalk, shaking, not sure where I'm going or how I'm getting there.

That's when Sienna's Subaru pulls into the parking lot.

She spots me immediately, her face shifting from concern to alarm as she takes in whatever I look like right now. She's out of the car before the engine stops.

"Maddie? Oh no, Maddie, is Gloria—"

"She's fine. She's stable." The words come out mechanical. Rehearsed. "They're keeping her overnight but she's okay."

"Then why do you look like—" She stops. Studies me. "What happened?"

I can't explain it. Not here. Not now. Not with Ben somewhere behind those glass doors.

"Can you take me home?" My voice breaks on the last word. "Please. I need to go."

Sienna doesn't ask any more questions. She puts her arm around me and guides me to the car.

I don't look back.

THE *Silent* STARS GO BY

ONE SURPRISING TURN OF EVENTS: SIENNA DOESN'T ask questions. She must sense that I have no words for this moment. Instead she drives, gently, without terrifying me, which I know is a gift she's giving me. The radio plays something soft and forgettable. I stare out the window at the darkness rushing past and try to make all these shattered pieces fit.

Ben wrote the Santa letters.

Ben has been writing to me this whole time.

Every letter I wrote—every midnight confession about my fears, my failures, the grandmother I've always silently believed I let down—he read them. He knew exactly what I was struggling with, exactly what made me vulnerable, and he never said a word. He let me fall for him while holding a cheat sheet to my heart.

My eyes burn. I blink hard and focus on the trees blurring past the window.

"Do you want to talk about it?"

"No."

"Okay." She puts her hand on my arm. "But I'm here when you do."

I nod, not trusting my voice. The rest of the drive passes in silence.

When we pull up to the chalet, the windows are glowing warm against the dark. It's late, and through the glass, I can see guests lingering by the fireplace, a couple sharing a bottle of wine at one of the small tables. Normal people having a normal evening, the kind I thought I was building toward a few hours ago.

"You sure you don't want company?" Sienna asks as I reach for the door handle.

"I'm sure." I push my mouth into something I hope at least looks grateful. "Thank you. For the ride. For everything."

"Call me if you need me. I mean it." Her face is worried, but she smiles for me anyway. "I've got vats of mulled wine on standby if you want it."

I slip out of the car before she can see the tears starting again.

The lobby is warm and smells like cinnamon and woodsmoke—the signature Winterbloom scent I've grown to love. Judy is behind the café counter, and when she sees me, her face creases with concern.

"Madison, honey. How's Gloria? Is she—"

"Stable." The word comes out steadier than I feel. "They're keeping her overnight for observation."

"Oh, thank goodness." She presses a hand to her chest. "Irwin hasn't sat still since we heard. Let me go tell him."

She disappears through the back door, and I stand there for a moment, watching the space where she was. Judy, who learned my coffee order on my first day. Who slipped me pastries when I was working late. Who embroidered BRB on

Ben's sweater because she thought it was the funniest thing she'd ever heard.

I'm going to miss her.

The thought hits like a sucker punch. I'm going to miss all of them. Judy and Irwin and their quiet devotion. Derek and his convictions about speaker placement. Agnes and her cosmic vibrations. This place became something I didn't know I needed.

And now I have to leave it behind.

I cross the lobby quickly, keeping my head down. A few guests glance up as I pass, but no one stops me. I'm almost to the stairs when I spot Derek adjusting the Christmas lights on the massive tree, muttering to himself about color temperature.

"Looking good," I say, because even heartbroken I care about this place.

He turns, and the cheerful greeting he starts to offer falters. "Hey. You okay?"

"Just tired," I tell him. "Thanks."

He hesitates. "Ben called a few minutes ago. He wanted to know if you made it back."

The name lands like a blow. "Well." I shrug. "Yeah. I made it."

"Should I tell him—"

"Don't tell him anything." It comes out sharper than I intended. Derek's eyebrows lift, and I force myself to soften. "Sorry. I just—need some space. I'm really tired."

"Sure. Yeah, of course." He's looking at me like he knows there's a story, but he's smart enough not to ask. "Get some rest, okay?"

I nod and escape up the stairs before anyone else can be kind to me.

My room is dark and quiet. I lock the door behind me and lean against it, finally letting myself fall apart.

The tears come in waves—hot and messy and undignified. I slide down until I'm sitting on the floor with my back against the door, knees pulled to my chest, sobbing like I haven't since the morning my grandmother died, the letter I never sent rotting in my drawer.

I trusted those letters. I trusted them with things I've never told anyone—my fears about who I was becoming, the way I've been building walls so high I couldn't see over them anymore. And the whole time, Ben already knew. He'd read it all in my own handwriting, every vulnerable confession I thought I was offering up to a stranger.

My letter to my grandmother. I kept that secret locked away for twelve years like something shameful, like it was proof that when it really mattered, I couldn't follow through. That I was too afraid to be vulnerable, even with someone I loved, and that gut-wrenching shame is why I've never allowed myself to fully commit—to anyone.

Until him.

And the worst part is, I wrote about it to Santa *because of him*. Because I was sitting in his cabin watching him sleep off a fever, feeling things I wasn't ready to feel, and I needed help sorting through the questions in my own heart. I confessed in that letter that I'd never felt this way about anyone. I asked whether I should let myself fall for Ben.

I asked *him* whether I should let myself fall for *him*. And he never said a word.

I have never felt like a bigger fool.

How much of what we had was real? When he said the right thing at the right moment, was it because he understood me—or because I'd handed him the playbook myself?

The anger flares, hot and welcome. Anger is easier than grief. Anger has edges I can hold onto.

I push myself up from the floor and scrub at my face with my sleeves. The burgundy coat is still keeping me warm, but it's his coat, and I can't stand the weight of it anymore. I shrug it off and throw it over the chair harder than necessary.

Then I flip on the lights, grab my suitcase from the closet, and start shoving in clothes without bothering to fold them.

I don't have a plan. I don't have a flight booked. I don't even have a car to get out of town. But I can't stay here. So Naples it is.

It's not like I have other options. I gave up the miserable little studio in Miami before coming here. My savings are nearly gone and I need every dollar I've earned here to tide me over until I start working for Caroline. At least my parents will welcome me in with no questions asked. Dad will make my favorite tiramisu French toast and Mom will fuss over me and neither of them will push until I'm ready to talk, even if they'll be dying to know.

Because they love Ben.

The thought slows my hands. After only a few days, they love him like he's already family. Mom had hugged him like he belonged to her. Dad had called him *son.*

How am I supposed to explain this? They'll be heartbroken for me, I know that. But they'll also want to understand. And maybe that's what scares me most. Not that they'll take his side, exactly. But that they'll be gentle about it. Say things like *I'm sure he had reasons* and *you should hear him out* while I'm still bleeding from the wound.

Right now, all I can feel is that he chose keeping his secret over being honest with me. And that feels like I never really knew him at all.

I'm reaching for another handful of clothes when the knock comes.

Soft. Almost hesitant.

"Maddie."

His voice. Of course it's his voice.

I don't move. Don't answer. Maybe if I stay quiet long enough, he'll go away.

"I know you're in there." A pause. "I heard—I heard you crying. Maddie, I'm sorry. Please. Let me explain."

I keep packing. Throw in a shirt. Then another. My hands are shaking but at least they're doing something.

"I know how it looks. I know you think I—" He stops. Starts again. "I thought about what I'd say the whole drive over here. How I'd explain. And now I'm standing here and none of it—" He stops. "None of it is enough."

I don't answer. I can't. If I open my mouth, I'll either scream or sob, and I refuse to give him either.

"Maddie, please. I'm not asking you to forgive me. I'm just asking you to let me explain why I couldn't tell you."

Silence. I shove another blouse into the suitcase.

"There's a code. The letter writers follow a code to keep their responses confidential. That was Gramps's rule, and part of what made the program work was that Santa's identity stayed secret. That's what makes people trust it. It's what lets them say the thing they can't say anywhere else. If people knew who was reading, they'd stop writing. And some of them really need to write." A long pause. "You needed to write, Maddie. I heard it. And I couldn't be the reason you stopped."

My throat tightens. He *heard* it. He read my letters and heard exactly how much I needed someone to listen.

Instead of feeling seen, I feel stripped bare. Like he'd been watching me through a window I didn't know was there.

His voice catches. "I wanted to tell you. Every single day, I wanted to tell you. But I'd made a promise, and I thought..." I pause at my dresser, my hand on his sweater. The copper cable-knit. Still smelling faintly like him. I hear him take a shaky breath. "I was wrong. I should have found a way. I was trying to protect your freedom to say what you needed to say. To protect what we were growing into. And I know how stupid that sounds, because I ended up destroying both."

Protect me. He thinks he was *protecting* me? By reading my most vulnerable confessions and never saying a word? By watching me fall for him while he held every card?

I grab the sweater and yank the door open.

He looks terrible.

That's my first thought, and I hate myself for it. I hate that even now, even furious, some part of me catalogs the shadows under his eyes, the redness rimming them, the way his shoulders slump like he's bracing for a blow. He looks like someone whose world just fell apart.

He looks like I feel.

For one dangerous moment, I waver. The anger flickers, and underneath it is something softer—something that remembers how his arms felt around me, how safe I felt when he held me, how sure I was that this was the start of something real.

Then he opens his mouth.

"Maddie—"

"Protect me?" The softness vanishes. "You were protecting *yourself*. Protecting your secret. Don't you dare pretend this was about me."

"That's not—"

"Here." I shove the sweater at his chest. He catches it reflexively, and for a second our hands touch. I pull back like I've been stung. "Thanks for the loan. I won't be needing it anymore. I booked the first flight I could to Florida tonight and I am never looking back."

The lie tastes bitter on my tongue, but I don't care. Let him think I'm already gone.

His face crumples. "Maddie—"

"Don't call me that." I'm already stepping back, hand on the door. "You don't get to call me that anymore. You don't get to call me at all."

"Please." He holds up the sweater like he doesn't know what to do with it. Like giving it back is the worst thing I could have done. "Keep it. I want you to have it."

"I don't want anything from you."

The coat. The thought rises unbidden, and I glance at the burgundy wool draped over the chair behind me. I should give it back, too. Should throw it at his feet and be done with all of it—every gift, every gesture, every piece of him I let into my life.

But the thought of handing it over makes something twist painfully in my chest. The coat that fits like it was made for me. The coat he bought because he saw me shivering and thought of me.

Or maybe thought of what I'd written to Santa about being cold.

I can't tell anymore. I can't tell what was real and what was calculated, and that uncertainty is its own kind of torture.

I leave the coat where it is. I don't want to think about what that means.

"Maddie." His voice comes out raw. "I love you. That part will always be true."

I look at him—really look—and for a second I see it all.

The desperation. The grief. The way he's clutching that stupid sweater like it's tethering him to me.

And then I think about all those letters. All those intimate confessions he read and responded to while looking me in the eye the next day and pretending he didn't know my deepest fears.

"If you loved me," I say quietly, "you would have told me the truth."

I close the door in his face.

For a long moment, nothing. I stand with my hand pressed flat against the wood, breathing hard, waiting for his footsteps to retreat.

They don't.

"I learned his handwriting. I learned his voice."

The words come through the door, muffled but clear. I don't respond, but I don't move away either.

"After Gramps died, I couldn't—" His voice breaks. "The letters were his thing. I couldn't let it die with him. He'd been answering them for fifty years, and when he was gone, I just...I couldn't let them go unanswered. So I practiced. For weeks. I sat with drafts of his old letters and I practiced until I could write like him."

I close my eyes. I don't want to hear this. I don't want to feel anything but anger right now.

"I handle every letter in the Winterbloom box. Some days it's thirty letters. Thirty people pouring their hearts out to a stranger because they need someone to hear them. Sure, most of the time it's kids wanting toys, but sometimes it's kids asking for their parents to stop fighting. Widows writing to dead husbands. People hurting over things they've never told anyone." A shaky breath. "I answer every single one. Because it's all I have left of him, and because those people deserve a response from someone who cares."

I press my forehead against the door.

"When your first letter came through, I knew I should hand it off. Even though the Winterbloom letters are my responsibility, I knew I should give it to Heloise, maybe, or Dr. Sinclair. Anyone but me." He stops. "Because we worked together. Because I'd see you every day knowing what you'd written. I knew it wasn't fair to you."

I don't move.

"But I couldn't. Because even when you thought I was a lazy freeloader, even when you were uptight and driving me crazy, I could tell there was more going on with you. You were as hard on yourself as you were on me, and I recognized it because I do the same thing." Another break. "Your letter confirmed that you needed to be heard. Really heard. And I couldn't pass that off to someone else. Not you."

I think about that first letter. Wine-drunk and desperate, scribbling my fears onto paper because I had nowhere else to put them. I think about the response that came back—kind and wise and exactly what I needed.

I still don't speak. But I don't walk away.

"I told myself it was fine as long as I never used what you wrote to—" He exhales hard. "I never tried to say the right thing because I'd read your letters. I fell for you because you care about details that don't matter to anyone else and you called me out when you thought I didn't. Because you pretend you don't need anyone and then you show up for people anyway. Because you looked at my grandfather's fading legacy and saw what it could be again. Because when I'm with you, I feel like the version of myself I actually want to be."

Silence. I can hear him breathing hard through the door.

"But I should have told you. I know that. The code, the promise I made—none of it should have mattered more than being honest with you. I got so caught up in protecting the secret that I forgot I was keeping it from someone who deserved the truth."

I feel the tears starting again. I hate them. I hate that he's making me cry when I want to be furious.

"I'm not asking you to forgive me. I know I don't deserve that. But before you leave—" His voice splinters. "Before you go, read the letters again. The ones I wrote you. Please."

I don't answer.

"Just read them. And if you still think I was manipulating you, if you still think I used what you told me against you, then I'll understand. I won't try to contact you again. I'll let you go." He chokes on that last word, then clears his throat. "But read them first. Please, Maddie, that's all I'm asking."

I hear him stand. His hand touches the door—I can feel the slight pressure against the wood, or maybe I'm imagining it.

"I'm sorry," he says, so quietly I almost miss it. "I'm sorry I broke this."

Then his footsteps move down the hall. Slow and heavy. The stairs creak.

And then nothing.

He's gone.

I stand at the door for a long time after. My hand is still pressed against the wood, like I'm holding something in. Or holding something out. I don't know anymore. My forehead rests against the cool surface, and I breathe. In and out. In and out. Trying to find the edges of myself again.

The room is too quiet. The kind of quiet that presses in, that makes you aware of your own heartbeat.

I should finish packing. I should call the airline and book a flight and get out of here before I have to see him again. Before I have to walk past the hothouse or the market stalls or any of the hundred places where I started believing this was real.

Instead, I find myself moving toward the bed.

The letters are in my nightstand drawer. I've kept them all —every cream-colored envelope inscribed in gold, every response written in that elegant script I now know belongs to Ben. I told myself I was keeping them because they were beautiful. Because the words mattered. Because someone had taken the time to really see me, and that felt worth preserving.

Now I don't know what they are. Evidence? Manipulation? Some twisted game I didn't know I was playing?

Read them. That's all I'm asking.

Four envelopes. Four letters I've clung to, archived, treasured.

I don't want to read them again. Reading them means giving him a chance to be right, and I'm not ready to let go of my anger yet. Anger is easier. Anger is armor.

But his voice keeps echoing in my head. The way it cracked when he talked about his grandfather's handwriting. The desperation when he asked me to just *look*.

I pick up the first letter. The one that arrived after my breakdown at the mailbox.

> *When we've been hurt—really hurt, the kind that changes how we see the world—we protect ourselves however we can. We build walls. We wear armor. We assume the worst before the worst can surprise us. It's not a character flaw. It's survival.*
>
> *But survival mode isn't meant to last forever. And the fact that you're confiding these fears about who you're becoming? That tells me the person you're afraid you've lost*

is still in there. Still paying attention. She's just finding her way back.

I read it again. Then again.

He didn't tell me what to do. He didn't say *stay at Winterbloom* or *give Ben a chance* or anything about himself at all. He only listened. And reflected back something I needed to hear.

I pick up the second letter.

The failure isn't in the first impression. It's in refusing to update it when new information arrives.

You're clearly someone who pays attention. Who notices when reality doesn't match the story you've constructed. That's not a flaw—that's rare. Most people would rather be consistent than correct.

I set it down. Reach for the third—the one about my grandmother. The one I almost can't bear to look at now, knowing he read what I wrote about the letter.

You told me about your grandmother. The letter that stayed in the drawer. You've carried that weight for years—the knowledge that you waited too long, that fear led to a choice you've always regretted.

But carrying a lesson is not the same as learning it.

You already know what you're afraid of. You already know what you don't want to repeat. The question isn't whether you'll recognize the moment when it comes. It's whether you'll be brave enough to act differently this time.

My chest aches. I remember reading this for the first time

and feeling like someone had finally put words to the thing I'd been circling for years. I cried then, too. But they were different tears—relief, not grief.

The fourth letter. The last one. The one I found the night of the staff party, right before our first kiss.

> *Fear is a liar, and a clever one. It doesn't always arrive shaking and obvious. Sometimes it wears a sensible coat and speaks in practical tones. "This is the smart move," it says. "This is what makes sense." And we believe it, because wisdom sounds so much better than fear.*
>
> *Whatever you decide, make sure you're the one deciding. Not the version of you that's still protecting herself from things that might hurt.*
>
> *You've earned the right to trust yourself.*

I lay the letters out on the bed. All four of them. And I look at them—really look.

He never told me to stay.

He never told me to choose him.

But does that matter? He still knew. He still read every vulnerable word I wrote and kept it from me while I was falling for him. The letters being kind doesn't make the secret okay.

Does it?

I press the heels of my hands against my eyes. I'm so tired. Tired of crying, tired of thinking, tired of feeling like the ground keeps shifting under my feet.

I look at the clock on the nightstand. Nearly eleven. I've been sitting here for over an hour, lost in letters and memories and the wreckage of what I thought we were building.

Outside my window, the night is dark and still. Somewhere out there, Ben is—what? Back at his cabin? At the hospital with Gloria? Sitting alone with a sweater he didn't want back, wondering if I'll ever speak to him again?

The anger is quieter now. Still there, but muted. Underneath it is something else, something heavier. Loss, maybe. Or the beginning of understanding.

I gather the letters carefully and set them on the nightstand. I should sleep. I should book a flight. I should do something other than sit here replaying every moment of the last few weeks, trying to figure out which parts were real.

The knock makes me jump.

Not soft this time. Not hesitant. Three sharp raps, efficient and urgent.

"Madison?" Heloise's voice, muffled through the door. "I'm sorry to bother you so late, but we have a situation. We need your help."

Chapter 24

What (Brain)child *Is This?*

"Madison?" Heloise calls again. And here I am with mascara halfway down my face and a suitcase to pack.

I consider not answering. I consider pretending I'm asleep, or gone, or dead. But Heloise coordinates the Santa's Helpers program with the efficiency of a four-star general, and something tells me she'll just keep knocking.

I open the door.

She takes in my face—the blotchy skin, the swollen eyes—and doesn't comment. But she also doesn't back down. "Get your coat. I'll explain on the way."

"Heloise, I'm not really—"

"It's about the proposal."

"The Holloways said no."

"That was this morning. It's not morning anymore." She tilts her head, studying me with that knowing look I remember from my first visit to the community center.

I want to say no. I want to be anywhere but here, in this place that's tangled up with a man I thought I knew and a future I thought I was building and a betrayal I'm still trying to understand. I want to tell her that I don't care anymore, that I'm leaving, that whatever's happening has nothing to do with me.

But that last part isn't true. And we both know it.

"Give me two minutes."

She nods. "Bring your laptop."

I splash water on my face, drag a brush through my hair, and pull on the burgundy coat before I can think too hard about what that means. When I step into the hallway, Heloise is already heading for the stairs.

"When word spread through town that Gloria collapsed after the Holloways decided to sell to the developer, the Santa's Helpers called an emergency meeting to figure out how we could help. But while we were thinking, the town came up with its own plan. We've been fielding letters all season—you know how it works. But today, the letters changed."

"Changed how?"

"People stopped writing to Santa." She glances at me as we reach the lobby. "They started writing to the Holloways."

I don't understand. "The Holloways?"

"The Letters to Santa program has been vital to Snowdrop for fifty years. This town grew up with those letters. They learned to trust them. To believe that putting words on paper could make a difference."

"So when they heard about Ben's proposal falling through—"

"They did what Ford invited them to do. They wrote. Personal letters. Testimonials. Stories about what Winterbloom means to them, what Ford and Gloria built, why they don't want Ian Preston turning Snowdrop into another Vail." She glances at me. "By noon we had two hundred. By dinnertime, over a thousand. They're still coming."

Over a thousand letters. In one day.

My heart thumps. I think about Ben at his table, practicing his grandfather's elegant handwriting until he could make it his own. Answering thirty letters a day because he couldn't bear to let them go unanswered.

We're climbing into Heloise's car when she stops. "The mailbox. We should check it."

"Now?"

"There are still guests here. Couples. Families. People who came for tomorrow's wishing tree celebration on New Year's Eve. If they've heard about what's happening, some of them might have written, too." She's already changing course, heading for the little red mailbox in the center of the market.

The vendor stalls are shuttered for the night. We crunch across the snow toward the red mailbox near Santa's Workshop. The one where I dropped my first letter, tipsy and desperate, a lifetime ago.

Heloise pulls a key from her pocket and opens the little door at the back.

"Oh my," she says softly.

It's stuffed. Envelopes crammed in so tight she has to work them out carefully, a few at a time. There are the preprinted ones, some colorful Christmas cards, plain white security envelopes, and even a few on the chalet stationery. Dozens of them.

"Some of these are from children." She holds up a lumpy envelope with crayon handwriting. Something small and hard shifts inside, clinks. Coins. A child's contribution. She looks at me through tears.

My eyes ache from all the crying I've done, but just the

same, they fill, too. Especially when Heloise adds, "It's not only the children. It's everyone. People have been putting money in their envelopes all day. Cash, checks, whatever they had. All donating what they can to raise Ben's offer on Alpenglow."

"They're sending money?"

She nods as she passes me half the stack. "To save Ford Bennett's legacy and protect the character of the town he helped to shape."

We hurry back to her car, arms full of letters from people who loved this place enough to say so. People writing on behalf of Ben and Winterbloom.

I think about Ben standing outside my door, voice cracking as he explained why he couldn't tell me the truth. *Some of them really need to write.* Ford taught this town to believe in letters. And now they're writing to save everything he worked for. Everything Ben loves.

Something twists in my chest. I look out the window at the dark trees rushing past.

Heloise pulls into the community center parking lot. It's nearly midnight, but every window is blazing with light.

"What exactly am I walking into?"

"Come see for yourself," she says.

The community center is unrecognizable.

The converted church hall where I dropped off stationery weeks ago has become something else entirely. Every table is buried under envelopes, stacked in towers that threaten to topple. The Santa's Helpers team are there, along with Judy, Irwin, and Sienna—all opening envelopes, separating money from letters, and sorting everything into boxes.

"We needed more people on hand to get through everything, but we're trying to keep it quiet. No sense in getting Ben's hopes up if this doesn't work," Heloise tells me.

At the center of it all, Dr. Sinclair sits at a table covered in papers, reading glasses perched on her nose, calculator in hand. Beside her, a man wearing a fleece vest and the overwhelmed look of someone whose quiet night took a turn is gesturing at a laptop screen.

Sienna spots me from across the room. She's at my side in seconds and pulling me into a hug.

"You came. Thank God. I ran into Heloise after I dropped you off and she recruited me, but it's you we need." She pulls back, hands still on my shoulders. "This is incredible but also kind of a disaster and nobody knows how to structure a community investment fund."

"A what?"

"That's Marcus, from the credit union."

She points to the man in the fleece vest. The credit union. Ben had the idea of adding them to the proposal last week. I find myself feeling proud of him, then I remember our argument and the pride starts to sting.

"Marcus has this idea about letting people buy shares in Alpenglow—like, actual ownership stakes—so we can get closer to matching Ian Preston's offer," Sienna adds. "But we need someone to figure out the logistics."

I look at the letters and think of the people writing, still believing that words on paper can change things. At all of them who showed up for Ben and Gloria because they couldn't stand to watch Winterbloom and Alpenglow—and Snowdrop's charm—disappear.

And I think about Ben, alone somewhere, grieving and not knowing any of this is happening.

"Show me what you've got," I say.

Marcus stands when I approach, extending a hand. "You're Madison? Heloise said you put together the original proposal."

"With Ben." I shake his hand. "What are we working with?"

"Honestly? Enthusiasm and good intentions. The letters are powerful—they'll show the Holloways how much this community cares. But emotional appeal alone won't close the gap with Preston's offer."

"How big is the gap?"

"Big. Preston's got deep pockets, and Ben's proposal was already stretching what the Bennetts could manage." Marcus pulls up a spreadsheet on his laptop. "The donations coming in tonight—cash and checks in the envelopes—they help, but we're still hundreds of thousands short."

"Which is where the shares come in."

"That's the idea. If we could structure it so community members could buy ownership stakes in the property—real equity, not just donations—we might be able to close the gap. The credit union could manage the investment pool, handle the legal structure." He runs a hand over his hair. "Problem is, I've never actually set up anything like this. I know the theory. I don't know the execution."

"Neither have I." I pull out a chair and sit down across from him. "But walk me through what you're thinking. Let's see what we can figure out together."

For the next hour, Marcus and I hammer out the basics. Investment tiers—what's the minimum buy-in that makes this accessible to regular people, not only the wealthier business owners? Voting rights—do shareholders get a say in how Alpenglow is run, or is this purely financial? Return structure—how do investors get paid when the property becomes profitable?

Dr. Sinclair leans in from the next chair. "The framing matters. People need to feel like partners, not donors. There's a psychological difference between giving money away and investing in something you're part of."

Partners. I think about Ben and how much he'd love that—the community not just saving Alpenglow but owning a piece of it alongside him. Building it together, side by side. The way Ford and Gloria built Winterbloom.

"You're right," I say. "This can't feel like charity. It has to feel like opportunity."

"So we need tiers," Marcus says, warming to it now. "Different investment levels with different benefits. Higher tiers get priority booking at the lodge, maybe discounts—"

"No." The word comes out sharp. "Everyone gets benefits. If someone scrapes together a hundred dollars because they believe in this place, they shouldn't get less than someone who can easily write a five-thousand-dollar check."

Marcus pauses. "Then what's the incentive for larger investors?"

"Responsibility." I'm thinking out loud now, the shape of it coming together. "Everyone gets a voice. But higher tiers get the heavier votes—the financial decisions, the operational calls. That's not a perk—that's an obligation. You're not buying better treatment. You're buying more responsibility."

Dr. Sinclair nods slowly. "That works. It signals that every contribution matters equally. The hundred-dollar investor and the five-thousand-dollar investor are both owners. The difference is in governance, not privilege."

"So, a hundred dollars gets you a community supporter share. The same benefits as everyone else—dividends, discounts, recognition. Plus a vote on events, traditions, the things that make this place feel like home. Plus all the community supporters together elect one representative to the board.

One seat at the table for the people who believed when it was just a hundred bucks and a hope."

The people around me are nodding now, and this support helps me clarify the next points. I keep going.

"A thousand gets you limited voting rights on major decisions. Five thousand or more, you're a founding investor with full voting privileges." I look around for something to write on. The irony isn't lost on me—I'm surrounded by over a thousand envelopes and I can't find a single scrap of paper. Sienna slides me a napkin and I start sketching. "The message is: your hundred dollars matters exactly as much as someone else's five thousand. You're all owners now."

Dr. Sinclair smiles. "This is the way. Ben would approve."

Marcus nods slowly. "The credit union could administer it. We've got the infrastructure for member-owned accounts. It's not that different from how we handle share certificates now."

"What about the timeline?" I look up from my napkin. "When is Preston's offer going in?"

"Tomorrow afternoon." Judy has appeared at my elbow, coffee pot in hand. Of course she'd know—she's the one who had the intel about Preston in the first place. "His lawyers are drawing up the paperwork tonight."

"Then we need to reach the Holloways before that." I look at Marcus. "Can the credit union issue a letter of intent? Something that says you're prepared to structure and administer a community investment fund, contingent on shareholder commitments?"

"I'd need to call my board chair. But yes, I think so. If we frame it right."

"Frame it as an investment in Snowdrop's future. Not charity. Opportunity." I'm scribbling now, the old instincts kicking in despite everything. "The Holloways care about legacy. Their family built Alpenglow. They don't want to sell to Preston any more than Gloria wants to sell to him—they just don't see another option. We have to show them there is one."

Judy sets a cup of coffee in front of me without comment, but her hand squeezes my shoulder as she passes.

"How many shares do you think we could realistically sell?" Marcus asks.

"In this room tonight? Not enough. We need the businesses. The merchants' association. The people who've been here for decades and have actual capital to invest."

"Hank Morris," Heloise says, settling in beside Dr. Sinclair. "He'd go in big. The brewery's been good to him."

"The Fosters," Sienna adds. "They just celebrated forty years. They love this place."

"Dorothy from the thrift shop. The Chens. Mr. Park. Even Agnes," I say, thinking aloud.

"The Bergstroms," Irwin adds from two tables over. "Their kids learned to ski at Alpenglow."

"What about out-of-towners?" Sienna grabs a pen and a napkin of her own. "Longtime guests. The families who come back year after year, the couples who got engaged here, the people who've been making memories at Winterbloom for decades. Some of them have real money. And they'd want to be part of saving the place."

I stare at her. "Sienna. That's brilliant."

"I mean, we have the mailing list. We know who the regulars are." She shrugs, but she's smiling. "People get attached to places. They might not live here, but that doesn't mean they wouldn't invest."

Names start flying. I grab another napkin and start a list, rough estimates based on what people think each business or longtime guest might commit. It's guesswork, utterly—napkin math on an actual napkin—but the numbers start adding up.

"If we get commitments from even half of these," I say, "plus whatever comes in from the community shares, plus the donations already in the envelopes—"

"We're still short," Marcus says. "But we're close. Close enough that the Holloways might take us seriously."

Close enough. It's not a guarantee. It's not even a plan, really—it's a hope held together with a napkin and community spirit and the desperate belief that sometimes wanting something badly enough can make it real.

"Okay." I take a breath. "I need to revise the proposal. Add the community investment structure, update the financials, include the letter count and the donation totals." I look at Marcus. "Can you draft that letter of intent from the credit union?"

"Give me an hour."

"And someone needs to call the Holloways." I check the time. Ouch. Twelve-fifteen. "Tonight. Before Preston's lawyers get to them in the morning."

"Tonight?" Sienna's eyes go wide. "It's after midnight."

"So wake them up." Judy's voice is firm. "They're selling off a piece of this town's history. They can lose a little sleep."

Heloise is the one to make the call.

"I've known the Holloway children since they were in diapers," she says, reaching for her phone. "Paul, Margaret, and little Jamie—they spent their summers here, and I stayed with them at nights when their parents went out."

"Start with James," I say. "He had doubts about Preston. At the meeting."

Heloise's eyes sharpen with approval. She dials and steps into the hallway.

While she talks, I work. I pull out my laptop and open the proposal I built with Ben. The file was last saved yesterday. It feels like ages ago.

I scan through it, feeling proud of how good it is. Ben's vision was so solid—the sustainability initiatives, the integration plans, the community partnerships. What we need now is the financial structure to back it up.

I create a new section: Community Investment Fund. I outline the tier system, the voting rights, the credit union's role as administrator. I pull numbers from Marcus's spreadsheet and plug them into projections that are mostly optimistic guessing but look official enough to take seriously.

Judy refills my coffee. Irwin comes in stamping snow off his boots, another box of letters in his arms. "I drove around to check the other mailboxes in town," he says. "People have been stuffing them all day."

Marcus works beside me, drafting the letter of intent on a yellow legal pad Judy found in back, then typing it up on his own laptop. Longhand before digital; I recognize the need to think with a pen before committing words to a screen. He keeps asking questions—interest rates, payout schedules, liability structures—and half the time I don't know the answers, so we figure them out together. Dr. Sinclair weighs in on language. Sienna cross-references the guest database for out-of-town regulars, building a contact list of people who might invest from afar.

Twenty minutes later, Heloise comes back. She's smiling.

"Well?" Judy asks.

"Jamie is in." Heloise sits down, but there's energy in her now, not exhaustion. "He's been sick about selling to Preston. Said he couldn't sleep tonight anyway. He was lying awake trying to figure out if there was any other option."

"And now there is," Sienna breathes.

"He wants to see the revised proposal by seven a.m. He and his siblings are all staying in Denver, so he's going to talk to Paul and Margaret first thing in the morning, then they want to meet here at eleven. That gives them time to review everything before their two o'clock meeting with Preston's lawyers."

"What are our odds?" Marcus asks.

Heloise considers. "Jamie is with us. He thinks Margaret could follow—she's sentimental about the lodge because her wedding reception was there. But Paul..." She sighs. "Paul is practical. He sees the numbers Preston is offering as security for his family. Convincing him will be the real work."

I check the time. We have four and a half hours to finish the proposal, then four more to wait, and hope, and see if any of this was enough.

I think about all the times I've pulled all-nighters for events that didn't matter. Celebrity tantrums. Corporate egos. Last-minute keynote changes for people who'd forget my name the next morning. I'd lie awake reworking timelines for bridezillas who'd scream at me anyway, sweat over details for clients who never thanked me once.

All of that was just practice for this.

"Let's get to work," I say.

The hours blur together after that. I lose track of how many times I revise the investment section, how many questions Marcus and I debate, how many cups of coffee Judy silently refills. At some point the sky outside the stained-glass windows shifts from black to indigo to the pale gray of dawn.

Derek drops off more letters and a box of muffins no one has time to eat. At six a.m., Hank Morris from the brewery shows up with thermoses of hot cider and a check for ten thousand dollars.

"Ben's a good guy," he says, pressing the check into Heloise's hand. "His grandpa would be proud of what he's trying to do."

I keep my head down and keep working. But I hear everything.

I hear Judy telling someone that last year, the first Christmas after Ford died, Ben spent the whole season making sure Gloria didn't have to carry anything alone. I hear Dr. Sinclair mention that Ben answers every letter within two days because he can't stand the thought of anyone feeling forgotten. I hear Irwin say that Ben reminds him of Ford in ways that matter more than business plans and spreadsheets.

"He's got his granddad's heart," Irwin says. "That's worth more than any investor's money."

I don't look up. I don't say anything. But the knot inside me loosens, bit by bit.

By six-thirty, we have a proposal. It's rough in places, held together with optimistic projections and community spirit, but it's real. Marcus's letter of intent is signed and scanned. The donation tally from the envelopes—just over fifty-two thousand dollars—is documented and attached. The list of potential investors runs three pages long.

"It's good," Marcus says. He looks as exhausted as I feel. "It might actually work."

"It has to work," Sienna says.

Heloise reads through the final version one more time, her lips moving slightly as she scans. When she reaches the end, she nods.

"Send it. Jamie is waiting."

I hit send. The email disappears into the digital void, carrying everything we've built tonight toward three siblings in a Denver hotel who hold the future of Winterbloom in their hands.

The room exhales. People start gathering their things, murmuring about catching a few hours of sleep before the eleven o'clock meeting.

I should be exhausted. I am exhausted. But underneath the tiredness is something else. A clarity I didn't have when I walked through those doors a few hours ago.

I've spent the whole night listening to people talk about Ben. Not the Ben who lied to me—although that Ben is real, and I'm not ready to simply forget it. But they've brought into focus the Ben who writes meaningful letters to strangers because his grandfather taught him everyone deserves to be heard. The Ben who took care of Gloria when she was grieving. The Ben who built systems out of color-coded sticky notes because he refuses to let his brain be an excuse for letting people down.

The Ben who stood outside my door and told me he loved me. Who asked me to read the letters again. Who said he was sorry for breaking this.

I think about what he told me through that door. That he learned his grandfather's handwriting. That he couldn't let the letters go unanswered. That some people really need to write, and someone should be there to write back.

He wasn't using my secrets against me. He was helping me heal from them the only way he knew how.

It doesn't erase the lie. It doesn't make the betrayal okay. But sitting here in the gray morning light, surrounded by evidence of how much this community loves him, I can finally see it for what it was: a man caught between a promise to his grandfather and the truth he owed me. He chose wrong. But I don't think he chose maliciously.

And I think—maybe—I'm ready to tell him that.

"You okay?" Sienna appears at my elbow, her face soft with concern.

"Yeah." I close my laptop and stand, pulling on my burgundy coat. "I think I need to head back. Get some rest before the meeting."

She studies me for a moment. Whatever she sees makes her smile.

"Okay. I'll drive you."

"I think I want to walk. But come get me for the meeting at ten-thirty? Let's go together."

I step out into the cold morning air. The sun is starting to crest the mountains, turning the snow pink and gold. The walk back to Winterbloom takes fifteen minutes, and I spend every one of them thinking.

When I reach my room, I don't lie down. I couldn't sleep if I wanted to.

Instead, I sit at the little desk by the window overlooking the market beginning to stir, pull out a sheet of the pre-printed stationery I've been writing on for weeks, and pick up my pen.

I have one more letter to write.

Do You *Hear* What I Hear?

The door to the community center opens at just past eleven p.m.—twelve full hours after our first meeting that morning—and I've never been so relieved to see the three exhausted Holloway siblings in my life.

It's been a brutal day. The Holloways arrived at eleven this morning, listened to our pitch, then left for lunch and a "private family discussion." They pushed the follow-up to four. Then six. Then eight. Then ten. Every delay sent another wave of panic through our little group—Heloise pacing by the window, Marcus refreshing his email constantly, Sienna stress-eating Judy's cranberry-orange muffins.

We lost Sienna to Winterbloom's New Year's Eve wishing tree event, so it's a smaller group waiting to see this through: Heloise, Marcus, Dr. Sinclair. Judy, who refused to leave despite the last party of the season going on at the chalet. And me, wearing yet another power-sheath dress, running on fumes and sheer stubbornness.

We've pushed the tables together into something resembling a conference setup. The proposal sits in the center, printed and bound. The letter of intent. The donation tally. The investor commitment list, three pages long.

It looks official. It looks real.

I just don't know if it's enough.

The Holloways walk in. James first, looking tired but determined. Margaret behind him, clutching her purse like a lifeline. And Paul, bringing up the rear with the grim, annoyed expression of a man who would rather be signing Ian Preston's contract.

"Thank you for coming back," Heloise says, rising to greet them. "I know this has been a long day."

"That's one word for it," Paul mutters.

James shoots him a look, then turns to us. "We've been going back and forth for hours. Margaret and I are ready to sign. Paul has..." He pauses diplomatically. "Questions."

"Concerns," Paul corrects. "I have concerns. This is a significant financial decision and I'm not going to be rushed into it because of—" He gestures vaguely at the room. "Sentiment."

"No one's asking you to be sentimental," I say, keeping my voice even. "We're asking you to look at the numbers."

"I've looked at the numbers. Preston's offer is higher."

"Preston's offer is cash, which is important. But ours is community, which means something as well." I slide the investor list across the table. "Dozens of local businesses. Exposed to the risk, invested in the outcome. Plus longtime guests from across the country who want to be part of this. Plus the donations—over fifty thousand dollars from people who dropped cash into envelopes because they believe in what Winterbloom and Alpenglow represent."

Paul barely glances at it. "Belief doesn't put my kids

through college. Set them up with a nest egg that might actually help."

"No, but equity does. The credit union is structuring this as a real investment fund. Returns tied to performance. These aren't donations, Mr. Holloway. They're stakes."

Margaret leans forward. "Paul, these are people we grew up with. The Morrises, the Fosters—"

"I know who they are, Maggie. That's not the point."

"Then what is the point?" James's patience is visibly thinning. "You've been blocking this all day. Tell us what you need to hear."

Paul is quiet for a moment. Then: "I need to know this isn't going to fall apart in two years. That we're not going to sell our grandparents' legacy to a nice story that can't sustain itself. That Ben Bennett won't turn around and sell to Ian Preston and make the profit that could have gone to me." He glances at his siblings. "Us."

Margaret winces. James exhales slowly, like he's been hearing variations of this all day.

"That's fair," I say. "That's actually exactly the right question."

I walk him through the projections. The seasonal revenue from Winterbloom. The potential from Alpenglow once the ski operations resume. The cost savings from shared infrastructure, the marketing synergies, the community investment creating built-in customer loyalty.

Paul listens. He asks hard questions. I answer the ones I can and admit when I can't.

"The truth is, there are no guarantees," I finally say. "But there's a plan. A real one, built by someone who's been studying this property for years. Someone who knows every trail on that mountain and every family that used to ski it."

"Ben Bennett," Paul says flatly. "The guy who couldn't make his own business work in Boulder."

I feel my spine stiffen. "The man who's been managing Winterbloom while caring for his aging grandmother. The grandson who's kept Ford Bennett's legacy alive."

The room has gone quiet.

"I've worked with a lot of executives," I continue. "A lot of people who looked perfect on paper. Ben Bennett is the hardest-working, most dedicated person I've ever met. And if you think past failure disqualifies someone from future success, then I guess none of us deserve a second chance."

Paul holds my gaze for a long moment.

James clears his throat. "Paul, you changed your major six times. Took you seven years to graduate. Dad didn't write you off. He said you were finding your path."

"That's different."

"Is it?" Margaret's voice is gentle. "We've all had false starts. That doesn't mean we can't get it right eventually."

Paul's jaw clenches. He looks down at the proposal, then at his siblings, then back at me. I can see the calculation happening—the war between what makes financial sense and what feels right.

"I need a minute," he says.

He walks to the window, staring out at the dark street. No one speaks. The clock on the wall ticks. Heloise catches my eye—a silent question. I give a tiny shake of my head. *Wait.*

Finally, Paul turns back. "If I do this—"

Then the door bangs open.

"What exactly is going on here?"

I can only assume this is Ian Preston standing in the doorway. He's younger than I expected—mid-forties, expensive coat, the kind of tan you get from ski vacations instead of working outside. Behind him, a man in a suit who must be his lawyer hovers uncertainly.

"Ian." James stands. "This is a private meeting."

"A private meeting about the property I'm supposed to be closing on tomorrow?" Preston strides into the room like he already owns Alpenglow. "I got a call from my attorney saying you postponed our meeting. Then I hear you're over here entertaining some kind of feel-good fantasy this town cooked up overnight?"

"We're exploring our options," Margaret says quietly. "We have that right."

"Your options?" Preston laughs, but there's no warmth in it. "Your option is a guaranteed payout from a serious developer. Not—" He snatches the proposal off the table, flips through it dismissively. "What is this, a bake sale? You're going to save a ski resort with church fundraiser money?"

"That church fundraiser money represents real investment from real people," Marcus says. "Structured through the credit union with proper—"

"I don't care how it's structured. This is amateur hour." Preston tosses the proposal back on the table. "Paul, you're a smart man. You know what this property is worth. You know what I'm offering. Are you really going to throw millions away because of some event planner?" He glances at me, cruelty flickering in his expression. "Madison Lark. I looked you up. Saw that video with millions of views. What was it they called you, the ice-chicken girl? And now you're playing business consultant?" He laughs. "Paul, this is who you're trusting with your family's legacy?"

The words hit like a slap. My face goes hot. I open my mouth to respond—

But Paul beats me to it.

"Ian."

Preston turns, confident. "Yes?"

"You just walked into a private meeting uninvited. You insulted the people in this room. You threw their proposal on the table like it was garbage." Paul's voice is calm, but something has shifted in his expression. "Is that how you plan to treat the community once you own the property?"

Preston blinks. "I—this is business, Paul. I'm trying to protect your interests."

"No. You're trying to protect yours." Paul stands. "My grandfather built Alpenglow because he loved this valley. He made mistakes at the end, sure. He got too focused on competing with the big resorts and lost sight of what made this place special. But he never treated people like they were beneath him."

"Paul—"

"We're done here." Paul turns to James. "Where do I sign?"

Preston's face cycles through several emotions—confusion, anger, a hint of what might be panic. "You can't be serious. Over this? Over a tone issue?"

"It's not about tone, Ian." Paul picks up the pen Marcus offers him. "I don't want my grandparents' business falling into the hands of someone they would have seriously disliked."

He flashes Ian one more look, then bends over our contract. And signs.

Margaret signs after him, then James. Three signatures, dark ink on cream paper.

"This isn't over," Preston says, but his voice has lost its certainty. "My lawyers will—"

"Your lawyers will find everything in order," Marcus says. "The credit union has reviewed the structure. It's solid."

Preston looks around the room—at Heloise with her quiet

satisfaction, at Judy with her arms crossed, at me with what I hope is my neutral face...the one someone I'm really starting to miss once told me is smug.

Preston's nostrils flare. For a moment I think he might say something else—threaten us, demand a recount, flip the table. His hands clench at his sides.

Then he turns and walks out. The door swings shut behind him.

For a moment, no one moves.

Then I let out a sound that's half-laugh, half-sob, and suddenly everyone is talking at once. Heloise is hugging Margaret. James is shaking Marcus's hand. Judy is already on the phone, probably calling Irwin.

Paul catches my eye across the chaos.

"For the record," he says, "I want ten thousand in shares added to my contract. Founding investor tier."

"Voting rights and everything," I tell him with a smile.

"Someone in this family should have a seat at the table." The corner of his mouth lifts. "Might as well be the difficult one."

I almost laugh. "Welcome aboard, Mr. Holloway."

James appears at my elbow, grinning. "We need to tell Ben. Tonight."

I check my watch. Eleven-thirty.

"The New Year's Eve celebration," I say. "He'll be there. They all will."

"Then that's where we're going." James looks at his siblings. "What do you say? One more trip to Winterbloom?"

Margaret is already reaching for her coat. Even Paul nods.

Heloise touches my arm. "There's one more thing," she says quietly. "Someone should say a few words. At the announcement. Someone who put all this together."

My stomach flips. "Heloise—"

"Not for the deal. Marcus and I can handle that part." Her eyes are warm. "For Ben. Don't forget. I saw your eyes when I came to your door last night. You two have some unfinished business, don't you?"

The letter in my coat pocket feels suddenly heavy.

"Yes," I say. "We do."

"Then let's go. We've got a countdown to catch."

A CUP OF *Kindness*

THE CHALET GLOWS AGAINST THE DARK LIKE something out of a dream.

Through the windows, I can see the crowd inside—guests and vendors and local attendees, all dressed for celebration, champagne flutes catching the light. It's nearly midnight on New Year's Eve, and I'm standing in the snow outside, trying to remember how to breathe.

"Ready?" Heloise asks.

I'm not. But I nod anyway.

We go inside the back way, through the staff entrance, so no one sees us arrive. Heloise, Marcus, Dr. Sinclair. The three Holloway siblings—James in the lead, a sentimental Margaret, even Paul looking moved despite himself. We're a strange little procession, carrying the weight of what we're about to do.

The service hallway is quiet, our footsteps muffled by the celebration. I can hear music, jazzy and warm, and the murmur of conversation. But beneath the festive sounds, there's something else. The solemnity of people gathered to say goodbye to something they love.

We pause at the edge of the beautiful Timberline Ballroom, hidden from view. At the head of the room, facing a wall of windows looking out over the frozen lake and the sparkling grounds, is the glimmering wishing tree—Ford Bennett's New Year's tradition. Tall and packed with tiny white lights, its branches heavy with paper and ribbon. Wishes. Hundreds of them—scraps of cream and gold and silver, handwritten hopes for the year to come. Some are secrets, folded tight. Others hang open, their words visible: Peace. Love. Health. Home. Courage.

That last one snags in my gut. Courage. Something I'm going to need a lot of in the next few minutes.

Around the base, exactly as I'd planned, dozens of candles flicker in glass holders, casting dancing shadows on the hardwood floor. But what I didn't plan—what makes me gasp—are the winter-blooming flowers everywhere. Jasmine and hellebore and Christmas roses on the mantle, the windowsills, lining the stairs. Not cut arrangements but potted plants from Ben's hothouse, lush and fragrant and alive. He must have spent hours wrapping them against the cold, trucking them over and carrying them in. Carefully positioning each one for this: a last celebration at Winterbloom, framed by everything he's grown.

Ben, Gloria, and I had planned every detail of this night in between entertaining my parents and working on the proposal last week. I thought I would be here to help set up, to make sure every detail was perfect. Instead, Ben and Gloria think I've abandoned ship. Regardless, the décor team did a beautiful job. It looks exactly the way we planned it, only better. Ben's flowers give it a wild, almost primal edge that brings our plans to life.

I scan the crowd for Ben, but if he's in here, I can't find him—or any of the Bennett family. My heart is already pounding, and not seeing him kicks it into a higher gear. I touch the letter tucked into my coat pocket and try to steady myself.

Near the tree, I spot a familiar figure. Evie, Mike's daughter, in a red velvet dress and her signature hot pink glasses, looking deliriously tired but determined. She's clutching a stuffed elephant to her chest—gray and soft and clearly well-loved—and tugging on her father's hand.

"But Daddy, Louise needs to make a wish, too," she's saying, loud enough that I can hear her from here.

Mike crouches down to her level and says more consecutive words than I've ever heard him utter. "Sweetheart, it's almost time. We're about to count down to midnight."

"But Louise didn't get to make her wish. She was napping."

I watch as Mike glances at the tree, then at his exhausted daughter, then guides her toward the little table I'd instructed the décor team to set up—cream paper cut into strips, cups of pens in gold and silver, ribbon for hanging. Everything a wish-maker might need.

"Okay. One wish. For Louise. Then we watch the countdown."

Evie's face lights up. She scribbles something with intense concentration, folds the paper carefully, and reaches up on tiptoe to hang it on a branch. Louise the elephant gets a kiss before being tucked back under her arm.

"There," she says, satisfied. "Now Louise won't miss the new year."

Something tugs loose inside me. I think about wishes and

letters and all the things we write down because saying them out loud feels too big. I think about the letter in my coat pocket, the one I wrote this morning at the little desk by my window.

I think about the man I'm about to give it to.

A hand touches my arm, and I turn to find Sienna. She's watching Evie and Mike with a soft expression—something wistful that she blinks away when she catches me looking.

"Maddie," she says, pulling her gaze away. She loops her arm through mine. "Here we go."

I look toward the front of the room. And now I can see them—the Bennett family, making their way through a side door to a podium near the tree. Trip and Trish, formal and polished. Frances behind them, steady as always and looking more like herself in dressy jeans and an Aztec-print sweater. Gloria's at her side, walking slowly but upright, one hand on Frances's arm. She's pale and overtly tired, but it's clear that she insisted on being here. This is her legacy, too.

And Ben.

He's wearing a sage green sweater that I know without looking is the same shade as his eyes, fitted in a way that makes my fingers want to touch it, that makes my brain forget how to think. His jaw is tight. His shoulders, squared. There's a carefulness to his steps that I've never seen, like he's carrying something he can't set down. He makes sure Gloria is comfortable in a chair at the front, then turns to face the room.

He clears his throat. The crowd goes still.

"Thank you all for being here tonight." His voice is steady. Warm. "New Year's Eve at Winterbloom has always been about gratitude. My grandfather, Ford Bennett, started the wishing tree tradition thirty-five years ago. He believed that, at the turn of the year, we should look back at the people who made it meaningful and look forward to fulfilling the dreams we're finding the courage to make real."

He pauses, scanning the crowd. I shrink back slightly, keeping to the shadows.

"This year, I have more to be grateful for than I can say. For the vendors who fill this market with creativity and heart. For the staff who work harder than anyone knows. For the guests who come back year after year and make Winterbloom feel like home." His gaze finds Gloria. "For my grandmother, who poured her love for my grandfather into building this place. Who shared my drive to keep it alive when he couldn't anymore."

Gloria's chin lifts. Even from here, I can see her eyes shining.

"Many of you know that Gran and I were planning something big for Winterbloom in the new year. We wanted to bring our neighboring ski lodge, Alpenglow, back to life. To build something that would combine my grandparents' legacy with the Holloway family's and carry both into the future." Ben's voice doesn't waver, but I see his hand tighten on the note cards he's holding. "Those plans didn't work out the way we hoped."

A murmur ripples through the crowd. Ben swallows hard, composing himself, then takes a breath and continues.

"So tonight, instead of announcing the launch of that endeavor, I want to say thank you. To everyone who believed in what we were trying to do. To everyone who reminded us why this place matters." He looks down at his notes, then sets them aside. Whatever he says next, he's saying from memory. From the heart.

All at once, I'm absolutely deluged with pride. He's steady. He's strong. He's confident.

He's the leader his grandfather knew he would be.

"Gramps always said Winterbloom was more than a business. He said it was a promise, that it would always be somewhere people could come to remember what matters. Family. Connection. The magic of believing in something bigger than yourself." He swallows. The next part comes out rough. "I hope whoever takes over next will honor that promise. I hope they'll see what he built and understand why it's worth protecting."

The room is silent. Agnes has her hand pressed to her mouth. Derek is staring at the floor. Lacey Powell is dabbing at tears. Even Bree has stopped filming.

And Trip—Trip is watching his son with an expression I've never seen on his face. Not pride, exactly. But close. Recognition, maybe. The dawning awareness that he's been wrong about something important.

"So thank you," Ben says. "For sixty years of holiday seasons. For trusting us with your traditions. For making Winterbloom what it is." He lifts the glass in his left hand. "To Ford and Gloria Bennett. And to all of you. Whatever comes next, I'm grateful for every moment we've had."

He steps back. The applause that follows is warm but muted, the sound of people clapping for something they're mourning.

I watch him cross to Gloria, crouch beside her chair, take her hand. She cups his face in both hands and says something I can't hear. He nods, and I see him blink hard.

He thinks this is the end. He thinks he's failed.

My heart hurts for him. But not for long. He doesn't know what this town has been building while he was working up to saying goodbye.

Heloise touches my elbow, then nods to the rest of our group. “Now,” she whispers.

I watch as she steps forward, the Holloway siblings and Marcus and Dr. Sinclair following. I stay where I am, half-hidden behind a pillar, my heart hammering against my ribs.

Ben’s head snaps up at the movement. Confusion crosses his face, then recognition as he sees the Holloways. His brow furrows.

“I’m sorry to interrupt,” Heloise says, the microphone Ben just left behind carrying her voice across the room. “But we have an announcement of our own.”

Gloria sits up straighter. Frances puts a hand on her mother’s shoulder. Trip looks like he’s about to object, but something in Heloise’s expression stops him.

“Yesterday morning, Gloria Bennett collapsed,” Heloise continues. “Many of you heard. What you may not know is that it happened right after a meeting where the Holloway family turned down the Bennetts’ proposal to purchase Alpenglow.”

A murmur runs through the crowd, but I notice it’s different among the locals. Some of them are exchanging knowing glances. Suppressed smiles. They know what’s coming. They helped build it.

Ben, though, has gone completely still.

“When word got out, something extraordinary happened. Something I’ve never seen in my long years of living in this town.” Heloise pauses, letting the silence build. “People started writing letters.”

She gestures, and Irwin steps forward carrying one of the boxes I saw at the community center. He sets it on a table near the front, and even from here I can see it’s overflowing—

envelopes of every size, some addressed in careful cursive, others in crayon.

"Thanks to Ford Bennett, Snowdrop is a community that knows how to write letters. But these weren't Letters to Santa. They were letters to the Holloway family," Heloise says. "Asking them to reconsider. Telling them what Winterbloom means to this community. What Alpenglow meant to their parents and grandparents." Her voice softens. "Some of them included money. Five dollars from a child's piggy bank. Fifty from a retired teacher. Whatever people could spare."

Ben's face has drained of color. Gloria presses her hand to her heart.

"By morning, we had over a thousand letters," Heloise continues. "And just over fifty-two thousand dollars in donations."

The gasp that moves through the room is audible. Ben takes a step forward, then stops, like he doesn't trust his legs.

Marcus steps up beside Heloise. "The donations were a start, but they weren't enough to close the gap with Ian Preston's offer. So a few of us got together at the community center to come up with another idea." He pulls a folder from under his arm. "A community investment fund. Local residents and businesses buying ownership stakes in the property. Real equity, not charity. Real partners, not donors."

Gloria reaches for Ben's hand. He takes it without looking, his eyes wide and still fixed on Marcus.

"Business owners dug deep," Marcus continues. "But so did retired couples. Young families. People who've never owned a share of anything in their lives." His voice warms. "They wanted in. Not because they expect a return, but because they believe in what Winterbloom and Alpenglow mean to this town. They believe in Ben's ability to see it through."

"We also reached out to longtime guests," Dr. Sinclair adds. "Families who've been coming to Winterbloom for decades. People who got engaged here, celebrated anniversaries here, brought their children and grandchildren here. They wanted to be part of keeping this place in the family, too."

Ben's face has gone blank with disbelief. I understand—I'm not sure I believe it yet, either, and I was in the room when the deal was done.

James Holloway steps forward. He's tall and thin, mid-forties and gray at the temples. Old enough to remember what Alpenglow was before his grandfather started chasing Vail. Old enough to possess the quiet authority that comes from knowing he's following his heart.

"My grandfather built Alpenglow because he loved this valley," James says. "He loved the mountains. He loved the town. He loved skiing and what it represents—families and making memories and learning to fall down and get back up." He glances at his siblings. "Somewhere along the way, he got bitter about the corporate competition. He wanted to be bigger, better, more. But beneath all that, he wanted it to be personal. He built it for Snowdrop, and for the people—near and far—who felt like it was home."

He turns to Ben.

"When you presented your proposal, I saw something I recognized." James's voice trembles. "A grandson trying to honor what both our families built. Trying to protect something that matters more than money."

Margaret is crying openly now. Even Paul is blinking back tears.

"Ian Preston would have paid us more," James continues. "And then he would have built his condos and his chain restaurants all over the mountain. He would have put our grandparents' names on a memorial plaque and paved over everything Alpenglow really was." He shakes his head. "That's not legacy. That's betrayal dressed up in cheap fake gold."

He extends his hand to Ben.

"My brother and sister and I talked it over. We're not selling to Ian Preston." A smile breaks across his face. "We're selling to you. Alpenglow is yours. And we'll be investing in those community shares, too."

The room erupts.

I can't see Ben's face because people are surging forward—Judy and Irwin, Agnes and Harriet, vendors I recognize and guests I don't, everyone wanting to shake his hand or clap his shoulder or simply be near the center of this miraculous, impossible, beautiful thing.

But I see Gloria. I see her rise from her chair, Frances steadying her elbow, and make her way to her grandson. I see her pull him into an embrace that lasts and lasts. I see Ben's shoulders shake, once, before he collects himself.

And I see Trip.

He's standing apart from the crowd, watching his son, something cracked open behind the careful composure. When Ben finally looks up and their eyes meet across the chaos, Trip nods. Just once. And then—so brief I almost miss it—the corner of his mouth lifts.

A small thing. But Ben sees it. And something in his face changes, too.

The noise is starting to settle when Heloise raises her hand.

"One more thing," she says, and the room quiets. "There's someone else who needs to say a few words. Someone who spent all night helping us put this together. Someone who put her whole heart into making sure this deal came through."

My breath catches, not from fear but from the weight of

what I'm about to do. Standing in front of everyone in this room. Standing so close to Ben. Saying out loud what I've only let myself write.

Heloise turns toward the pillar where I'm standing. Her eyes find mine.

"Maddie," she says. "Come on up."

Maddie. Not Madison. After everything we built together last night, the familiar name feels right. And if I stay—when I stay—maybe I'll be Maddie to this whole town.

I slip the letter out of my pocket and hand my coat to Sienna. The crowd parts as I make my way to the front. My legs are shaking in my Florida ankle boots, but I keep moving. I can feel everyone watching—Judy with her hands clasped under her chin, Sienna with tears already streaming down her face, Gloria with that knowing look she's had since the day I arrived.

And Ben. My Ben, who's staring at me like he can't quite believe I'm real. Like he's afraid to blink.

I take Heloise's place behind the microphone, a few feet away from him.

My voice comes out steadier than I expected when I say, "I wrote you something. I was going to leave it in the mailbox. Let Santa find it." A small smile. "But some words are too important to hide in mailboxes. Or desk drawers." I turn to glance at the crowd. "I should probably do this in private. Pieces of it won't really make sense to anyone but us. But I've learned the hard way what happens when you wait for the perfect moment. So you're all my witnesses tonight."

I turn back to Ben. He's completely still, barely breathing, like any movement might break whatever spell is letting this happen.

"Someone wise once told me that letters are sometimes more for the person holding the pen than the person meant to receive them. A way of saying things we can't say out loud." I take a breath. "But some things need to be said out loud. So that the person you love knows exactly how much you mean them."

I unfold the letter. The paper trembles in my hands.

And I read.

"Dear Ben,

"Twelve years ago, I wrote a letter I was too scared to send. When the person I wrote it to died before reading it, I felt like a failure. And I locked the part of myself that loved without limits in the same desk drawer where I'd kept that letter. For twelve years, I locked away the part of myself that loved without fear.

"Then I came to Winterbloom. And I met a man I didn't expect. A man who drove me crazy at first, and then made me laugh, and who kept showing up for me in ways I didn't know I needed. A man who coaxes flowers to life in the dead of winter because he believes beautiful things are worth fighting for. A man who writes letters to strangers because his grandfather taught him that everyone deserves to be heard.

"I fell in love with you twice, Ben Bennett. Once when I didn't know you were Santa. And once again after I did.

"I love that you learned your grandfather's handwriting so the magic of the letters would feel the same. I love that you answer every letter within two days because you can't stand the thought of anyone feeling forgotten. I love that when you made a promise to your grandfather, you kept it—even when keeping it meant risking everything with me. You chose wrong, but you chose wrong for the right reasons. And that matters."

I have to stop. Breathe. Ben's eyes haven't left my face. The weight of his attention is almost too much. But I don't look away. Not this time.

"Because of who you are, you never told me to stay. You never told me to choose you. You listened. And then you asked me questions that helped me listen to myself. You helped me see that the letter I never sent to my grandmother wasn't a failure. It was practice. Practice for learning to say the things that matter before it's too late.

"So this is me saying what matters, to you. I'm not hiding anymore. I'm not keeping letters in desk drawers or waiting for the perfect moment that never comes.

"I'm choosing to stay. I'm choosing Winterbloom. I'm choosing you.

"Not because you're the safe option, but because you're worth the risk, every day.

"Love, Maddie."

I fold the letter. The room is so quiet I can hear the wicks of the candles snapping near the wishing tree.

Ben hasn't moved. His eyes are bright. He opens his mouth, closes it. Tries again.

"Maddie," he finally manages. His voice cracks on my name.

"I'm sorry I gave back the sweater," I whisper to him. "But I'm keeping the coat."

He laughs—a wet, broken sound—and then he's crossing the space between us in two steps and his hands are on my face and he's kissing me like the whole room isn't watching, like the only thing that exists is this moment, this choice, this new beginning.

The room erupts for the second time tonight. Cheering, applause, someone whistling—Derek, I think. I hear Sienna's sob-laugh somewhere to my left. I hear Judy say "Finally!" to no one in particular.

When we break apart, Ben keeps his forehead pressed to mine.

"I thought I'd lost you. I thought you were gone."

"Let's just say it's a good thing this town writes a lot of letters. It gave me time to cool down and think."

"You're really going to stay?" he whispers. "Oh, Maddie. Please stay."

"That's what I just said I was doing, Ben Bennett. Keep up."

He laughs again, and this time it's pure joy.

He pulls me into his arms properly then and lifts me right off my feet. Over his shoulder, I catch Gloria's eye. She's still seated, Frances beside her, but she's smiling.

"I knew," she says as Ben sets me down. "I knew you were exactly what this place needed."

I remember those words. From my first day. From a woman who saw something in me I couldn't see in myself back then.

"Thank you," I say, crossing to her chair to take her hand. "For giving me a chance."

"Thank you for taking it," she says, patting my arm.

The crowd is starting to move again, people checking the time, realizing midnight is moments away. Someone starts a countdown—ten, nine, eight—and Ben pulls me close.

"Welcome home, Maddie."

"Thanks. There's nowhere else I'd rather be."

Seven. Six. Five.

"So what happens now?" I ask.

Four. Three.

"Now?" He grins. "Now we build something spectacular. Together."

Two. One.

The room explodes with cheers and noise and the first

notes of "Auld Lang Syne." Ben kisses me again as the clock strikes midnight, and I kiss him back, tasting champagne and promise and the sweet impossible fact of this moment.

When the chaos finally settles, when all the champagne has been poured and all the toasts have been made and Sienna has hugged me approximately fourteen times, Ben takes my hand.

"Come with me," he says. "There's something I want to show you."

We slip out the back, through the service hallway, into the cold night air. Snow is falling—soft, lazy flakes that catch the light from the windows. I pull my coat tighter, and Ben notices.

"Miami girl. Since you're staying, I'll give you back the sweater, too."

"Good. We both know I'll need it." I shiver for emphasis, and he laughs, pulling me closer.

He leads me around the back of the chalet to the door of the hothouse.

Inside, it's warm. Warm like Florida, like summer, like a promise kept against all odds. The winter-blooming flowers are sparse now—so many of them carried into the celebration—but what remains is still beautiful. Jasmine climbing the walls. Hellebore nodding in ceramic pots. Roses and orchids, pale and perfect in the low light.

"I spent all day taking flowers into the chalet, thinking it was my last chance to let people see what this place could grow." He turns to me. "I didn't know you were out there saving everything."

"Well, it was mostly the town. I didn't do it alone." I slip my coat off my shoulders and lay it carefully over his workbench. "Turns out I have some competition. A lot of people love you, Ben Bennett."

"But you're the one who matters most." He takes my hands. "Thank you for coming back."

I look around at the hothouse, at the evidence of everything he's nurtured and protected. "Some things are worth coming back for. This place. These flowers. You. Especially you."

He lets himself answer by kissing me. Slower this time. Without an audience. Without a countdown. Only the two of us, surrounded by growing things, at the start of our new beginning.

When we finally pull apart, I lean into him, my head against his chest, listening to his heartbeat.

"You know what I love about this place?" I say, looking around at the flowers.

"Tell me."

"Your grandpa and you built something that shouldn't exist. Winter-blooming flowers in the Colorado mountains. It should be impossible." I turn back to him. "But you did it anyway. Because you believed it was worth the effort." I step closer, take his hand and hold it against my heart. "I want to be someone who believes things are worth the effort. I want to build impossible things with you."

He's quiet. Then he pulls back just enough to look at me—really look, like he's memorizing this moment.

"You know what I saw the first time you walked into my grandmother's office?"

"A disaster in an inadequate coat?"

"A woman who was going to change everything." His voice drops to almost a whisper. "I didn't know how right I was."

"Ben—"

"I love you, Maddie. I loved you when I was writing those letters and couldn't tell you. I loved you when you were furious with me and I thought I'd ruined everything. I'm going to love you when you're cold and grumpy and homesick for Florida sunshine." He cups my face in his hands. "I'm going to love you for as long as you'll let me. Longer, probably. I'm stubborn that way."

"Must be a Bennett trait."

"Definitely a Bennett trait."

"Didn't you say you wanted to show me something?"

He grins. "I did. But it was more that I had something I wanted to see."

"And?"

"And I'm looking at it." His eyes don't leave my face. "You, in my hothouse. Staying with me."

Outside, the snow keeps falling. Inside, the flowers keep blooming.

And for the first time in twelve years, I'm not afraid of what comes next.

SWEET

Silver Bells

LATE MARCH IN COLORADO SMELLS LIKE possibility.

That's what I told myself as I shuffled through the snow from the chalet to Ben's cabin this morning. The Winterbloom crew keeps warning me that spring doesn't really arrive here until May, but I swear there's something different in the air this morning. A hint of something green and hopeful under the snow.

But I'm relieved when I slip inside and Ben ensconces me in blankets on his couch beneath the big front window. He's got the fireplace roaring while he makes us breakfast. My Miami Dolphins mug sits on the counter next to his WORLD'S OKAYEST GRANDSON mug. The massive fern above his bed is still thriving. The plants that were seedlings when I first came here are curling over the tops of their pots. Ben Bennett could coax a cactus to bloom in a blizzard.

He is less adept in the kitchen, however.

"You're burning the eggs," I observe.

"I'm caramelizing them."

"That's not a thing."

"It's absolutely a thing." He pokes at the pan with a spatula, frowning in concentration. "I saw it on a cooking show."

"You saw someone burn eggs on a cooking show and decided it was a technique?"

"I saw someone cook eggs in cream until the edges crisped to create what he called 'textural contrast.'" He slides a plate onto the coffee table in front of me with a flourish. The eggs are, objectively, slightly charred. "Trust the process."

I take a bite. They're actually not bad—buttery and, with the green chili sauce he's layered on top, weirdly good. "Huh." I take another bite. "Okay, these are awesome. I stand corrected."

"High praise from the woman who ate ice cream soup for three months."

"That was a dark time. Let's not speak of my ice cream soup era."

He grins and drops onto the couch beside me, balancing his own plate on his knee. Outside, snow is flurrying past the window. Inside, the fire crackles. Books are still stacked everywhere: gardening manuals, business strategy, that dog-eared copy of *When Attention Wanders* that I've seen him highlight more than once. There's a new one on the nightstand, too —*Respectful Renovations for Mid-Century Modern*. He's thrown himself into the Alpenglow project full force.

"So," Ben says between bites. "Big day. Gran's checkup at ten, then the meeting with James Holloway at two. Do you still want to work on the farmers market proposal before we head over to Alpenglow?"

"Done. I revised it twice last night." I pull up the document on my phone and show him. "I added the vendor rotation schedule and the parking logistics. Oh, and I talked to Chef Raúl about the food demo station—he's in, and he wants to do a preview tasting for Gloria first. I think he just likes feeding her."

Ben takes my phone, scanning the notes. "This is good. Really good."

I steal a piece of toast from his plate. "Thanks. You did good convincing the Bergstroms to anchor the produce section. That was the hard part."

"They just needed someone to listen to their concerns."

"You listened for two hours."

"They had a lot of concerns."

This is how we work now. Him with the relationships, the vision, the ability to make people feel heard. Me with the systems, the logistics, the spreadsheets that turn dreams into deliverables. Three months into my official role as Winterbloom's Director of Operations and Events, I'm still getting used to the idea that this is my job now. My real job. Not a temporary escape from Miami, but an actual career.

An actual life.

"What time is Gloria's appointment?"

"Ten. I'm picking her up at nine-thirty." He pauses, something soft crossing his face. "She's doing better. She's actually listening to the doctors now. Delegating. Taking days off." He shakes his head, marveling. "Frances threatened to fly in and physically remove her from the office if she didn't start resting. Apparently that was motivating."

"Frances is terrifying. I respect her immensely."

"She respects you, too. She told me you're the best thing that's happened to Winterbloom's operations in twenty years."

"She said that?"

"Direct quote. Also, she said if I mess this up, she'll make me shovel her entire ranch by hand." He grins and starts pulling on his coat. "I should check the seedlings before we leave. I want to make sure the baby lettuces are getting enough light."

"I'll come find you in a few minutes. I want to add something to your wall."

He pauses in the middle of zipping his coat. "Yeah?"

"I made you a note. For the system."

Something warm flickers across his face—that particular look he gets when I speak his language. The sticky note language. The language of a man whose brain works in colors and categories and carefully arranged tasks.

He kisses my temple—casual, natural, like he's been doing it for years—and opens the door. Sienna is on the other side.

"Hey, Ben," she says, stepping back to let him leave before shaking the snow from her hair. She stomps her boots on the mat like she's trying to murder it. "Mads. I need help."

She fills Ben's backup mug—one with a cartoon cactus that says *Don't Be a Prick*—and starts pacing. In this cabin, that means approximately four steps in each direction before she has to turn around.

"Did you know Mike is the lead vendor for strategizing year-round operations?"

"Yes. I asked him to do it."

"And you also want me consulting on marketing and aesthetic design for all the new offerings?"

"Of course. You'll be perfect for—"

"That means I have to meet with him. Regularly. For months." Sienna stops pacing. "He texted me this morning to confirm our first planning session. Texted, Maddie. He barely talks to anyone, and he texted me a full three sentences about seasonal pizza concepts."

"That sounds...productive?"

"It sounds like torture. Months of sitting across from him while he talks about wood-fired ovens and I try not to stare at his forearms." She groans, dropping onto the couch and nearly disappearing into the pile of blankets. "Evie drew me a picture yesterday. Of me. With purple reindeer. She said her dad helped her pick the colors."

"That's adorable," I say carefully.

"It's confusing. Does he talk about me to his daughter? Does he just think I like purple? Does he even know I exist as a person and not just the marketing lady who keeps buying pizza?"

"You do buy a lot of pizza."

Sienna throws a pillow at me.

"And then," she continues, "Evie told me last week that her dad said I was 'nice.' I've been analyzing the word nice for six days. Nice like friendly? Nice like boring? Nice like he wants to ask me out but doesn't know how because his whole personality is awkward silence and pizza dough?"

"Sienna."

"What?"

"Breathe."

She tips her head back, staring at the fern above Ben's bed. For a moment she looks very small—her five-two frame swallowed up by flannel and fleece. "This is going to be a disaster. I moved to Colorado to get away from a guy, and now I'm stuck working with one who makes me forget how words work."

"Um, you moved to Colorado *with* a guy," I remind her.

"A guy who left. Mike has a kid. He's not going anywhere. Which means I'll keep on liking him and he'll keep on not noticing I'm alive."

"Or," I say, "you'll spend months working with him and getting to know him better."

"I know him fine. I know he makes the best pizza I've ever had and his daughter draws me pictures and he looked at me once during the Christmas party like—" She stops. Groans. "Never mind how he looked at me. It was once, and he's barely made eye contact since. This is a professional collaboration. I'm going to be professional."

"You're going to be great. So great that he'll realize you're brilliant and funny and exactly what he's been missing, and Evie will get a stepmom who buys her art supplies and teaches her about color theory."

Sienna stares at me. "That's...weirdly specific."

"I'm manifesting."

"You don't believe in manifesting."

"I believe in you."

Her face softens. She sits up, finally taking in her surroundings properly—the Dolphins mug in my hand, me in Ben's copper cable-knit sweater with BRB embroidered on the cuff.

"Look at you," she says quietly. "All settled in here in Snowdrop."

"Getting there."

"No. You're there." She smiles—her real smile, the one that cemented us as friends years ago in that terrible marketing class. "I knew it the minute he gave you that coat. You were staying. You just hadn't figured it out yet."

I can't argue with that.

Sienna leaves with a promise to report back after her first Mike meeting and a threat to call at midnight if she spirals. The cabin feels quieter after she's gone. Warmer, but that could be because I'm starting to feel at home in this little space. I rinse our mugs and leave them in the dish rack—a domestic detail that would've felt foreign six months ago and now feels like the most natural thing in the world. Then I slip on my burgundy coat.

The cold hits immediately, sharp and bright, but I barely notice. I'm too focused on the two sticky notes in my pocket. On what I'm about to do.

The heavy hothouse door gives way, and the front section hits me with its wall of warmth and color—crimson poinsettias, pink amaryllis stretching toward the glass ceiling, jasmine climbing its wooden trellis. The plants from New Year's Eve are all back in their places, recovered from their trip to the chalet, green and fragrant and thriving.

I push through the second set of glass doors, into the back section where the air goes earthy and humid. Wet soil and green leaves and the soft bubbling of the fountain. Seedlings under grow lights. Herbs in neat rows. Winter lettuces in their raised beds.

Ben is at his workbench, transplanting something delicate into a little green pot. He looks up when I approach, and his whole expression shifts—the focused crease between his brows smoothing out, his shoulders dropping an inch. Like I'm the thing that finally lets him relax.

I come to stand beside him, looking at the wall. The sticky notes are still there. Hundreds of them, arranged in columns and clusters, arrows connecting tasks across categories. Green for hothouse. Yellow for events. Orange for time-sensitive. But there's a new section—a cluster in the corner I haven't noticed until now.

Pink notes. I step closer.

MADDIE'S BIRTHDAY – APRIL 14

- PLAN SOMETHING SPECTACULAR

LARKS VISITING – LATE FEBRUARY
- RESERVE YURT?

ANNIVERSARY OF FIRST FIGHT
- BRING FLOWERS AND AN INVOICE FOR $7,920
(SHE'LL THINK IT'S FUNNY)

"You started a section for me."

"You're part of the system now."

At that, I lean over and kiss his cheek. He sets down the seedling and wipes his hands on a rag, watching me study the notes.

"Since I'm part of the system now," I say, "I think I should contribute."

I pull the first sticky note from my pocket.

Maddie's parents visiting for Christmas.

Ben's face brightens. "Good! They should visit all the time." He takes it from me and presses it to the wall himself.

The second sticky note is still in my hand. I turn it over, looking at the words I wrote this morning in my own handwriting. Then I take a deep breath and press it to the wall. Yellow. For events.

Ben and Maddie's wedding
- Christmas Eve.

For a long moment, neither of us moves. The fountain

burbles. The grow lights hum. The humid air presses close, full of green and growing things.

"Maddie." His voice catches.

"You don't have to answer right now." My heart is pounding, and my words start tumbling out in a panic. "I know it's fast. I know you might want more time—"

"Yes."

"—and Christmas Eve is just a thought—"

"Maddie." He turns me to face him. His eyes are bright. "Yes."

"Oh." I blink. "Oh. Good. That was easy."

"Easiest decision I've ever made." He's smiling now. The smile that makes him look like the person he's always been underneath all the chaos and self-doubt.

And then he's kissing me—or trying to. We're both smiling too hard to do it properly. His mouth finds mine and we last maybe two seconds before I laugh against his lips, and he pulls back grinning, and then we try again, and it's still a mess because I can't stop looking at him, at the joy in his eyes playing out on his face.

"We're bad at this today," I manage.

"No. We're perfect at this," he says, and kisses me again. This time it lands. His hand slides into my hair and the laughter fades into something quieter, deeper. It's a kiss that says *I found you* and *I'm keeping you* and *this is just the beginning.* When we finally pull apart, his eyes are bright.

"Wait," he says. "Don't move."

He reaches behind the workbench and pulls out a book. *The Groom's Guide to Wedding Planning*—and it's absolutely bristling with sticky note flags. Teal ones, which I don't think I've seen in his system before.

"New category," he says, a little sheepish. "I needed a color that was just for this."

I take the book. The flags mark sections on venues, vows, first dances. One marks a page on How to Write a Meaningful Toast. He's been doing research. He's been *planning*.

"I didn't expect you to beat me to the proposal," he says, flipping the book open to reveal a sticky note on the inside cover, in his own familiar handwriting:

PROPOSE TO MADDIE
- HER BIRTHDAY
- DON'T CHICKEN OUT

I laugh, but it comes out wobbly. "You had a sticky note."

"I always have a sticky note."

"For proposing to me."

"It was a high-stakes task. I didn't want to forget the ring."

"The—"

He's already reaching into the workbench drawer—one that is usually full of seed packets and twist ties—and pulling out a small velvet box. When he opens it, the ring inside catches the grow lights: a simple band, a glittering oval diamond, surrounded by tiny diamonds that sparkle like sun on snow.

"I saw it and thought of you," he says—the exact words he spoke when he gave me the coat. "Bright. Classic. With a sparkle that catches people off guard."

I can't speak. My throat is too tight. This was not something I expected today.

He lifts my hand, his thumb brushing my knuckles. "I had a plan. A speech. But then you proposed with a sticky note, so—"

"It's your love language."

"It is." He slides the ring onto my finger. "So are you."

After a few minutes of kissing that starts out celebratory and turns into something that would scandalize the baby lettuces, we finally break apart, breathless and giddy. I pull back to look at him properly.

"For what it's worth, all those sticky note flags in the book are adorable. In my vast professional experience planning weddings, the best ones are when the groom cares as much as the bride." I look down at the ring, then back at him. "It's rare. But I expected nothing less from you."

"I wanted to be ready." He looks at me and I see someone who's learned to trust himself, and who trusts me to see him clearly. "I like this better than what I had planned. Us getting engaged in front of this wall, where we had our first real conversation."

"Where I first got to know the real you." I reach up and touch his face—the stubble he ignored, the strong line of his jaw. "You know, you started falling in love with me through letters. And letters ended up saving this place. So it seems fitting we'd get engaged in front of a wall full of notes."

He pulls me close. Outside the glass walls, snow is still falling. Inside, surrounded by green and growing things, we stay wrapped around each other.

"Christmas Eve," he says. "We could do it at Alpenglow. It should be ready. Our wedding will be the first."

"We'll invite the whole town."

"And use the vendors for food and décor."

"And Agnes will bless our energy."

"And Sienna will cry alongside a blubbering Linda Lark."

"And my grandmother will pretend she orchestrated the whole thing."

"She probably did." I smile against his shoulder. "Some

things are worth the wait, she'd say. And then she'd take full credit."

"She'd be right." He tilts my chin up, his eyes finding mine. "You were worth the wait. You were worth everything."

I think about the woman who showed up here in November—unemployed, heartbroken, and undernourished from binging ice cream soup in a freak Thanksgiving heatwave. The woman who thought she'd lost herself somewhere between the hysterical ice chickens and a mentor who made her doubt everything she knew to be true.

She didn't know that losing everything would lead her here. To this hothouse in the mountains. To this man who writes letters and grows impossible flowers and believed in her before she believed in herself.

To this place that became home when she wasn't looking.

The sticky note glows yellow on the wall behind us.

Ben and Maddie's wedding
- Christmas Eve.

The best addition to his system yet.

A NOTE FROM Sarah Wright Reed

Thank you for reading *Merry Little Letters*. Exploring Maddie and Ben's love story was one of the most fun experiences I've had writing, and I'm thrilled to share their story with you. If you enjoyed the book, would you consider leaving a review? Even a line or two can make a huge difference in an author's career. Thank you!

Want to keep up with my author news? Please join my **mailing list** at *sarahwrightreed.com/subscribe*. I'll send the inside scoop on life, new releases, and works in progress. If you want exclusive content in an inclusive space, please join *my Facebook reader group*. We'll share encouraging words with each other and you'll even get the chance to review advance copies.

Thank you again for reading *Merry Little Letters!* It means more to me than I can say.

xo,

Sarah Wright Reed

WITH *Gratitude*

A special thank you to my mom, who is always my first reader and who enthusiastically embraced Ben and Maddie and the Winterbloom setting. An extra-special thanks for her helping me realize that the paper lantern ceremony I originally wrote might burn down the whole forest...the luminaries are a much safer option!

Deanna Matzen is the best alpha reader of all time, and I hope I never have to write another book without help from your sharp instincts and eagle eye. I'm here to return the favor anytime you need me!

Thanks also to my wonderful writing group members, Danyelle Ferguson, Allison Gygi, and Judy Mendenhall (and her husband Irwin ~ shout out to you both for letting me use your names in the book)! You are the most encouraging, supportive friends a writer could have, and I will never stop being thankful for you.

Emily Chun and Erin Moser put up with me talking way

too much about Ben and Maddie during our coffee dates. Thanks, girls! I love our friendship, and our weekly meetups!

My husband and kids put up with the whirlwind of me writing this story throughout our Christmas season. Thanks for your patience and support. I'm the luckiest to have you!

And many thanks to you, dear reader. Sharing a story that came straight from my brain and my heart is a mildly terrifying privilege, but your support makes it so worthwhile.

xo,

Sarah Wright Reed

Sarah Wright Reed writes contemporary women's fiction that blends humor and heart with a hefty dose of romance. Her characters are learning to own their journeys and embrace love: for their families, their communities, their partners, and themselves. When not writing, she's wrangling her twin kiddos and too many pets alongside her husband at their home in Colorado. Join her monthly mailing list at sarahwrightreed.com and be the first to hear about book releases and special promotions. Encouragement and inspiration included in each issue, just to make you smile.